MY FATHER'S WORLD

MICHAEL PHILLIPS
JUDITH PELLA

BETHANY HOUSE PUBLISHERS

MINNEAPOLIS, MINNESOTA 55438

Cover illustration by Dan Thornberg,
Bethany House Publishers staff artist.

Copyright © 1990
Michael Phillips/Judith Pella
All Rights Reserved

Published by Bethany House Publishers
A Ministry of Bethany Fellowship, Inc.
6820 Auto Club Road, Minneapolis, Minnesota 55438

Printed in the United States of America

Library of Congress Cataloging-in-Publication Data

Phillips, Michael R., 1946–
    My father's world / Michael Phillips, Judith Pella.
        p. cm. — (The Journals of Corrie Belle : v. 1)

    1. Overland journeys to the Pacific—Fiction.
I. Pella, Judith. II. Title.
III. Series: Phillips, Michael R., 1946–   Journals of Corrie Bell : v. 1.
PS3566.H492M9   1990
813'.54—dc20   89–78391
ISBN 1–55661–104–8   CIP

To

Patrick Jeremy Phillips

The Journals of Corrie Belle Hollister

My Father's World
A Daughter of Grace

The Stonewycke Trilogy

The Heather Hills of Stonewycke
Flight from Stonewycke
Lady of Stonewycke

The Stonewycke Legacy

Stranger at Stonewycke
Shadows over Stonewycke
Treasure of Stonewycke

The Highland Collection

Jamie MacLeod: Highland Lass
Robbie Taggart: Highland Sailor

The Authors

The PHILLIPS/PELLA writing team had its beginning in the longstanding friendship of Michael and Judy Phillips with Judith Pella. Michael Phillips, with a number of nonfiction books to his credit, had been writing for several years. During a Bible study at Pella's home he chanced upon a half-completed sheet of paper sticking out of a typewriter. His author's instincts aroused, he inspected it more closely, and asked their friend, "Do you write?" A discussion followed, common interests were explored, and it was not long before the Phillips invited Pella to their home for dinner to discuss collaboration on a proposed series of novels. Thus, the best-selling "Stonewycke" books were born, which led in turn to "The Highland Collection."

Judith Pella holds a nursing degree and B.A. in Social Sciences. Her background as a writer stems from her avid reading and researching in historical, adventure, and geographical venues. Pella, with her two sons, resides in Eureka, California. Michael Phillips, who holds a degree from Humboldt State University and continues his post-graduate studies in history, owns and operates Christian bookstores on the West Coast. He is the editor of the best-selling George MacDonald Classic Reprint Series and is also MacDonald's biographer. The Phillips also live in Eureka with their three sons.

CONTENTS

10

PROLOGUE

A few months back, Uncle Nick said to me, "You oughta make that diary of yours into a book."

"Who would read it?" I said. "No one cares what a little girl wrote when she first came West."

"You ain't a little girl now, Corrie Belle Hollister," he answered, looking me over from head to foot. "No, siree. You done a mite lot of fillin' out since you came to California ten years ago. Why, I remember that day I walked into ol' Drum's place and saw you standin' there—"

He paused for a minute with a smile on his face.

"Besides," he went on, "I think a whole lot of folks back East would read anything you wrote, now that you're a famous reporter from one of the Union's newest states."

"Aw shucks, Uncle Nick," I said. "I'm not famous, and you know it!"

"That ain't what Drum says."

"He doesn't count," I said back. "He's prejudiced!"

"Your name's in all the big papers in Chicago and St. Louis and New York. If that don't make a body famous, then I reckon there's no gold in them hills, neither."

"There really is about none left, Uncle Nick," I said.

"Well, the gold may be gone, but they're still readin' what you're tellin' 'em, and that's a fact, Corrie."

"Nobody cares about a reporter's name," I told him. "They only read the story, that's all."

11

"Your ma taught you not to lie, Cornelia." His voice was stern, but that little twinkle in his eye said he was just teasing me. "Lord knows our pa taught us both better'n that, though your ma kept to it a mite straighter than I did. But, Cornelia," he said again, "You know people are interested in *you*, not just what you write. A young lady reporter, sendin' stories all 'round the country from the rough and wild gold fields and minin' towns of California's mother lode— why to them city folks, somebody like you makes the wild West a romantic and interesting place. I reckon you're just about one of California's most famous young women."

"It ain't so," I argued, and I tried to make my voice stern, but he saw right through my act. He always does. He's still kid enough himself to understand me, even though he's seventeen or eighteen years older than me. He's just like my ma. She was always a step ahead of me, and Uncle Nick's got that same Belle blood and quick eye.

I wouldn't talk any more about it to him right then. But he kept badgering me about the idea, and pretty soon I found myself getting used to it. I still couldn't see why anybody would want to read my diary. But seeing a book with my name on it was a thought I couldn't get rid of.

I asked my editor at the *Alta* about the notion of a book.

"That's the most fool idea I've ever heard," Mr. Kemble said. "You're a reporter, Corrie . . . a hack. You're no book author."

"And you reported in 1848 that there was no gold in California," I said quietly.

"What's that got to do with it?" he shouted, not liking to be reminded of his infamous story in the *California Star*.

"Maybe your prediction about me'll be the same way," I said timidly.

"Come on, Corrie, we've got real news to cover! Here the country's in the middle of a war with itself. People pouring into California by the thousands. Folks back East are interested in what kind of place this is out here. They don't want to read the reminiscences of some runny-nosed kid."

I guess Kemble's words riled me some. Pretty soon I found myself taking Uncle Nick's side on the idea of a book.

By that time, though, I suppose I should have known my editor better than I did. He may have put up a blustery front, but he wasn't one to turn his nose up at an idea that might be good. The day after our talk he fired off a letter to a friend of his who worked for a publisher in Chicago.

Then two months ago the friend wrote back and said that his company wanted to make a book based on my diary. Mr. Kemble brought up the subject again, and told me what he'd done.

"The narrative portion of the story will be edited, of course," said his friend in the letter that came addressed to both of us. "But we want you to retain the colorful phrasing and homespun flavor of the language in the dialogue. We feel it will add realism and authenticity to what you say."

I was so happy I threw my arms around Mr. Kemble and hugged him.

We got right to work on it. I was only fifteen when I came to Miracle Springs, and my writing was pretty rough. But we worked on the sentences, trying to correct the grammar without losing any of the "homespun flavor," as Mr. Kemble's friend Mr. MacPherson put it. He did say, after all, that he didn't want me to try to make every single word into high-sounding book English.

But until then, here's what happened, every so often in just the words I used in my diary, with a few things added here and there so you can make some sense out of it.

Uncle Nick says you will like reading it. Mr. Kemble still says he think's the whole notion's foolhardy, though down inside I think he's just as excited about it as I am.

I don't quite know which one to believe. I reckon you'll have to make up your own mind.

Corrie Belle Hollister
Miracle Springs, California
1862

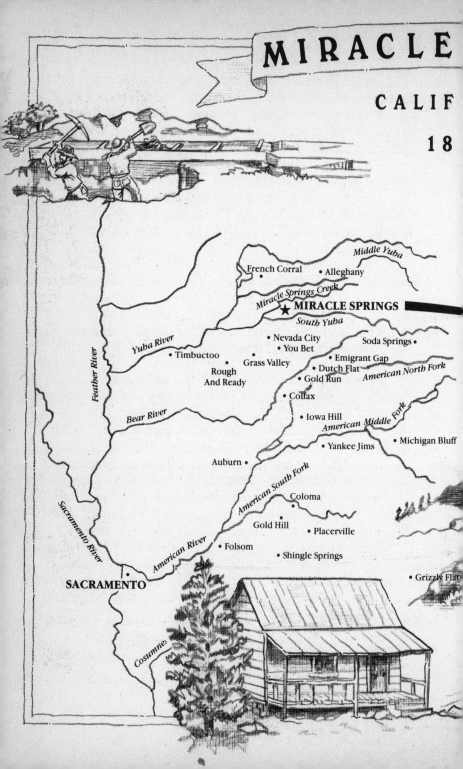

MIRACLE

CALIF

18

Middle Yuba

French Corral • Alleghany

Miracle Springs Creek

★ **MIRACLE SPRINGS**

South Yuba

Yuba River

• Nevada City
• You Bet   Soda Springs •

• Timbuctoo   Grass Valley   • Emigrant Gap
Rough   • Dutch Flat
And Ready   • Gold Run   American North Fork

• Colfax

Bear River

• Iowa Hill
American Middle Fork

• Yankee Jims   • Michigan Bluff

Auburn •

American South Fork

Coloma

Gold Hill   • Placerville

Folsom •

• Shingle Springs

• Grizzly Flat

SACRAMENTO

Cosumnes

CHAPTER 1

GETTING TO CALIFORNIA
IN 1852

Ma always told me I should keep a diary.

"Corrie," she'd say, "when a young woman's not of the marryin' sort, she needs to think of somethin' besides a man to get her through life."

I think she was making a roundabout comment about my looks, though she never came right out and said I wasn't comely enough to snag a husband. I guess she figured a diary would be a good idea, too, since I had my nose in a book all the time, and I ought to get some practical use from all that reading.

"It sure ain't gonna get you no feller though," she'd say, "any more'n that nose full of freckles!"

"What's keepin' a diary got to do with marryin'?" I asked her.

"No man wants a wife that's smarter'n him—" She paused, then added with a sly wink, "Leastways, not so's it's obvious!"

Then she took my chin in her rough, work-worn hand, and smiled down on me with that loving look that was almost as good as a hug, and said—as if to make up for saying I wasn't a marrying kind of girl—"I reckon you'll do okay though, Corrie."

I was just a kid then, probably not more than ten, though

I can't exactly remember. I didn't know what all the fuss was about. The last thing I wanted back then was to marry some ornery, dirty-faced boy. So what she said didn't bother me. I was perfectly content with my books.

"You could be a teacher, Corrie," Ma said more than once. Then she'd go on to speculate, "Teachin's a right respectable way for a spinster to get by in this world."

She talked a lot about women getting on in the world alone, probably on account of Pa's leaving like he did. It was hard on Ma, being left with the farm to tend, and four kids and another on the way. I suspect more than once she wished she'd been a spinster herself!

Back then, when I remember her first talking to me about what I ought to do, I didn't have the faintest notion what a spinster was, and I was hardly of a mind to start preparing for my future. But whatever spinster meant, I did know what a teacher was, because I liked our Miss Boyd. As for teaching myself, I'd have to wait and see.

"If you're going to know book learnin' and all that, Corrie," Ma said, "you gotta do more'n just read. You gotta learn how to write good, too. And I figure there ain't much better a way than to keep a diary."

Well, maybe Ma was right. Though I never did much about her advice after that.

Until I got to be fifteen, that is. By then I knew what a spinster was, and I knew about plain-looking girls. And I knew why the two always went together. So I began to see what it might be like to be alone in the world, and to figure maybe Ma's idea about me teachin' was a good one, though I was still a mite young to be going to a teacher's school or college to learn how. Besides, Miracle Springs doesn't even have a school for kids, much less a college.

Once Ma was gone, I knew I had to get thinkin' mighty fast about something. She was right about that. The kids were looking to me for tending, right out there in the middle of nowhere. And it sure wasn't likely to be any different once we got to where we were going. Even if we found Uncle Nick, they were still going to be looking to me to be a kind of ma to them—and a teacher, too. Even if it was only little Tad, and Becky, Emily, and Zack, I was bound to be teaching them a thing or two since Ma couldn't.

So I figured it was time I started that diary.

Of course I didn't know how. I knew how to write, and that was about it. So I just started to put down what happened, though it didn't seem there was much exciting in it.

I sure did miss Ma. She'd have told me what a diary was supposed to be like. I wish I'd started back when she first told me to do it. Or even last spring when we left our little patch of ground in upstate New York to come out West. Then I would have written about the wagon crossing after leaving St. Louis, about the plains of Kansas, the grand herds of buffalo, the scare with the Sioux near Ft. Laramie, the day Emily and I almost got left behind picking berries, and the snow that was still on the mountains in Utah in July. Most of all, I wish Ma could have been there to show me how to do it right.

But even if I had started back then, I probably wouldn't have written about the desert and what happened to Ma. I never want to remember that, though I'll never forget it.

So by the time I got started writing things down, we were in California, and the long trip was mostly behind us, just like Ma wanted. But she'd never get to see it.

"We gotta get over them mountains before the snows come," she kept saying, telling the wagon-master every day to hurry us along.

He always just smiled and said, "Not to worry, Mrs. Hollister. We'll be past them Sierras by the first weeks of October. You'll be relaxin' in front of your brother's warm stove long before the snow ever comes."

Ma couldn't help worrying. She had some terrible foreboding about the winter. It didn't help that folks were still talking about the Donners, who had so much trouble crossing the mountains seven years before. All through the summer, hot as it was, she kept thinking about the snows getting ready, someplace up by the North Pole, I reckon, to sweep down and kill us all at the California border. I wish we'd had a few handfuls of that snow when Ma took her fever. Captain Dixon called that awful stretch of desert the Humboldt Sink. I thought the ground was hot till I laid my hand on Ma's flaming cheek. I wanted to cry, but Ma was always so strong, and I decided it would help her to think that maybe I was learning to be strong, too.

So I didn't cry. I didn't pray either, though I tried once or twice. But no words would come. It felt like trying to coax water from that horrible dry sand. I wish I'd tried a mite harder. Sometimes I wonder if God would have let her live if I just could've gotten those words out.

We finally did get to California. Captain Dixon was right. He got us over the Sierras before the snows. But the mountains were getting cold, and I was glad when we reached the Feather River and Captain Dixon said it would only be a few more days before we'd be able to see the Sacramento Valley. He said when we got there, it would feel like summer by comparison.

Not long after that, we neared Sacramento City. Several of the wagons took off on their own, but Captain Dixon stuck with those few of us that were still together, because he said he was paid to go all the way to Sacramento and there he would go. I don't know how we'd have made it without him and some of the other men helping us drive the wagon and tend the team. I figured he was just about as fine a man as there could be.

As good as it felt to get to California, I don't mind confessing I was beginning to feel a little scared, too. The wagon train had become kind of a family, especially after Ma died. Everyone was so kind to us. Suddenly I realized that in just a few days Captain Dixon would leave, and my brothers and sisters and I would be all alone.

I knew we'd be with our uncle on his ranch, but seeing him for the first time was going to be a fearful moment. I was hardly more than a baby when he struck out on his own, and his visits were rare enough after that. All I knew about him is what Ma had told us.

I supposed we'd know soon enough. When we left Independence, the Captain said it would be the middle of October when we arrived, and he wasn't far off. Back then we thought Ma would be there to find Uncle Nick. But now we were on our own.

"Don't you worry none, Corrie," the Captain told me. "If we don't find your uncle right off, I'll take care of you and the young'uns. There's a nice boarding house, and there'll be room for all of you, and a place for your wagon and horses, until I locate your uncle and tell him how things are."

That Mr. Dixon was a nice man.

CHAPTER 2

WHY WE CAME WEST

The hills were the color of autumn as we descended from the mountains—pretty enough, but not quite so bright with orange and red as back home.

As I looked around, I thought that even if they hadn't discovered gold here four years ago, I would have liked to come. Of course, it never was the gold that made Ma start talking about the West. After Pa left, she struggled to make a go of the tiny farm. It wasn't much good before that, but Pa must have had a way of keeping it going when most men would've given up. Ma never talked much about Pa.

For a few years pure stubbornness kept Ma going. She said she wasn't going to give anyone a chance to say, "I told you so." I think she mostly meant her own pa. But more than that, she was determined to keep the farm going for Pa's return. Then word came to us that Pa was dead, and it seemed to take the vigor right out of her tired body.

After that, she couldn't keep it up so well, what with the five of us kids to tend besides. Her pa, my Grandpa Belle, offered to help, but she would have none of it. They weren't on the best of terms. But when he died last year she took it hard—we all did, because we loved him and he was a good man even though he could be mighty stern sometimes.

Not long after Grandpa died, Ma had a visit from a neighbor who had just returned from California. He had gone to try his hand at gold mining, but apparently it didn't work out because he didn't stay long. He must have seen Uncle Nick, Ma's brother, because she started talking about going out West to see him. She had no family in New York, unless you counted a couple of cousins she hardly knew. She said it was family that mattered and she didn't care what Uncle Nick had done—I didn't know at the time what she meant. But he was family, she said, and they ought to be together.

Uncle Nick left home a year before Pa did. Though he came back two or three times, he was almost a stranger to me. I could hardly remember what my own pa looked like. I'd never be able to recognize Uncle Nick.

Ma said he used to bounce me on his knees. "He'd croak out a lullaby too, now and then, Corrie," Ma said, "when he figured no one was lookin'. You know what plumb fools men are about lettin' a body see their feelin's. He always tried to be the tough one, but I knowed him better."

After Pa left, we never saw hide nor hair of Uncle Nick, either—not until that fellow come to see us after Grandpa Belle died. I don't know all he said to Ma, but he did say he'd seen her brother and heard that he owned a ranch near a place called Miracle Springs, California. Ma figured he must have struck gold in the mines because there couldn't have been any other way for our uncle to afford a spread of land.

When Grandpa Belle's "estate," as Ma called it, was settled, she came into a little sum of money. It was only a few hundred dollars, but more than we'd ever see again in once place, Ma said. Most folks told her to put it into the land, but by then she had no heart left for it. She said it was time for us to pull up stakes and strike out for something new. She always said she was more like her brother Nick than was good for her.

All the folks at home thought she'd taken leave of her senses. "Why, what are you thinking, Agatha Hollister?" I overheard one lady tell her. "It's a fool's errand if you ask me, a woman traveling west alone, and with five young'uns to boot!"

But Ma was a determined woman, and she said no one ever accused her of being faint-hearted. Besides, my thirteen-year-old brother Zachary was old enough to handle a wagon and team right well.

She said she reckoned I could take a fair load on my shoulders too. "You're the oldest, Corrie. And I figure you're just about as grown-up as a girl of fifteen ought to be—with gumption to match."

I still start to cry when I hear Ma's voice coming back to my mind like that. But sometimes her words make me proud.

It probably *was* crazy. Ma said so herself ten times a day those first months on the trail—especially since she had no way to notify our uncle that we were coming. But when Ma set her mind to something, that was that!

"Too much of that Belle blood, I tell you, Corrie!" she said. "It'll be the death of me yet! You just make sure when you get older you keep your own Belle blood in check."

Oh, Ma! It makes me so sad when I think that you're not here to tell me things anymore!

But I know what she'd say. "Come on, Corrie. This is a time to pull in your chin, wipe away them tears, and be strong. Don't betray that Belle blood in your veins, Corrie."

The farther west we got, the more I could tell Ma wanted to lay eyes on that "land of promise" they called California. She would have made it, too, if she hadn't slipped and broken her ankle and then gotten that infection. The Humboldt Sink is practically in California. She was so close.

Even now, when I close my eyes and let my mind wander back to that day Ma died, I can see it all as clear as if I was going through it all again. I was in the wagon sponging down her burning skin with the precious few spoonfuls of water Captain Dixon thought could be spared. It hardly made any difference, because the cloth in my hand turned hot in seconds. But at least I felt I was doing something useful.

"Corrie," Ma had said to me, her voice weak and as brittle as the parched earth outside, "fetch me something from that trunk. It's a book wrapped in a lace handkerchief. You'll see it right on top."

I found it easily enough. I remember her packing it when we left home, but I had never really looked at it before. I held it out to her but she was too weak to take it.

"You go ahead and look at it, Corrie," she said.

It was a small Bible, just a little bigger than my hand. It had a pure white leather cover and gold edges on the pages. I had never seen anything so fine and beautiful.

"Your pa gave that to me on our wedding day, Corrie." The corners of her lips strained at a smile. "It was his way of tellin' me he was ready to settle down and be a family man. I'll admit that before we was married, he was kind of a wild one. But I reckon he had good reason. He was orphaned young, left to be raised by his no-account older brother, who was killed before your pa was old enough to take care of himself. His brother's crowd was a bad influence, and he just never had a chance to learn decent ways. But I saw his heart, Corrie. I knew it was good, and I loved him for that." She sighed and had to stop talking for a minute to rest.

I gave her a sip of water. Maybe I shouldn't have let her go on, but Ma was determined, and I probably couldn't have stopped her, anyway.

"Your Grandpa Belle opposed our marriage," she went on. "By then, my brother and your pa had started runnin' together, and I guess my own pa thought Nick had been led astray. I knew better—Nick had his own wild streak. He was just a kid, and by then your pa wanted to change his ways, Corrie. And he did, too, after we was married. He worked hard on that farm and he was a good husband and father—I couldn't have asked for better.

"Everything that happened afterward . . . well, it just

happened. I don't blame him none. And I don't want you to either, Corrie. Sometimes a man can't shake his past no matter how hard he tries. I'm gonna be seein' your pa mighty soon, and I'll finally have the chance to say all these things to him."

"Ma, don't—"

Even if she hadn't stopped me, I couldn't have finished anyway. My throat was getting choked up listening to her.

"Corrie, I have to tell you all this! You're a big girl. You gotta face the fact that I'm gonna die soon. I only wish I hadn't dragged you all out here in the middle of nowhere. But you gotta be brave, honey. Won't help none to do nothin' else."

"Ma," I said through my tears, "you oughta rest." It was a stupid thing to say, I reckon, but I think I just didn't want to hear anymore about her dying.

"I got all the years of eternity to rest, Corrie dear. And I gotta tell you about your Uncle Nick, too," she went on, ignoring my plea. "I never said nothing before, 'cause I didn't want to put no one in a bad light. But now I have to tell you that your uncle was in some bad trouble. That's why he came out West. I thought he died with your pa, but when I heard he was still alive and was out here, I knew I had to come find him.

"Nick's all you got now. I figured when we got to that camp where his ranch is, I'd be able to find him easily enough. Now you're gonna have to do it alone. Captain Dixon said he'd help, but he's got his own responsibilities too, so you gotta look out for yourself. Just remember what I always told you—a woman's gotta be strong, she's got to be able to make her way alone if she has to. Ain't no weak-kneed woman gonna make it out here, Corrie. You hear me? You gotta be as tough and strong as a man—maybe tougher, 'cause they won't make it easy for you."

I nodded that I understood, though my mind was racing with the thoughts that Ma was about to die. I tried to be brave, but I just couldn't stand it!

Then she reached up from where she lay and took my chin feebly in her fingers like she used to do. They were so hot, I was afraid they would burn right into my chin.

She smiled. "What I said a long time ago, Corrie," she whispered, gazing at my face with a peaceful, contented smile, "about you not being of a marryin' sort. Well, I was wrong, Corrie. You've turned out to be a right decent lookin' girl. You're gonna get along just fine without me, Corrie. I know you'll make me and your pa proud!"

"Oh, Ma!" I cried, burying my face in the folds of her dress.

"Come now, we'll have none of that!" she said, though her voice was too soft to carry much of a threat. But I wiped my eyes and pulled myself up and tried to look cheery.

"Now there's more I need to tell you about your uncle," she said. "He's usin' a different name—not Belle. The fellow that told me he was there said he's going by Nick Matthews. Don't ask me why, but that's who you got to be lookin' for. Don't even mention the name Belle, just in case he's in trouble. Can you do that, Corrie? I know it's an awful load to put on a young girl, but there ain't nothin' else for it."

"I'll try, Ma." I took her hot limp hand in mine.

"That's a good girl, honey. And you keep that Bible. It's yours now, to remember me by. And to remember your pa, too. He was a good man."

Then she added—the last words she ever spoke—"It's by the mercy of God we got this close. Find your uncle, Corrie. You'll need him now more'n ever."

CHAPTER 3

SACRAMENTO

Sacramento was bigger than I'd imagined.

It hardly seemed possible that such a bustling place could be just three or four years old. But that's what Mr. Dixon said. When you took a closer look, you could see its newness in the dirt streets and the clean look of the timber in the simple, single-level buildings, and the freshly-painted store signs.

There was activity everywhere—people on foot or horseback, wagons of every shape, size and kind rumbling up and down the streets, people calling to one another. Here and there in the din I heard shouts of "gold" and "new strike." As we rode by a saloon I heard one man saying to another, "Did you hear 'bout them varmints what jumped ol' man Ward's claim over yonder by Grass Valley?" But we were out of earshot before I heard what the other man said in reply.

I was glad Uncle Nick didn't live in this town. I'd never lived in a big city before, and I didn't have a hankering to start now.

I was sitting up front next to Zack, who was driving the wagon. I could tell he was trying hard to act like a man. Some of the other kids in the train had jumped from their wagons and were whooping and running about excitedly. But Zack sat still and straight, reins slack in his hands, eyes steady on the team, a serious look on his face.

Poor Zack. He had to grow up awful fast, especially since we left the East. Along with that resolute look in his eyes, I could see the pain, too—a different kind of pain than just from the hard work his calloused hands showed he'd done the many months on the trail. But he held the team steady, gripping the leather straps, eyeing the new town, with just a hint left of my little brother. I could see it in the way his lips were parted a crack in wonder. He was almost a man, but still a boy at the same time.

I suppose Ma might have said something similar about me. I turned around and poked my head inside the wagon.

"Hey, kids," I called. "Come on up here with me and Zack. The three of you gotta see all this!"

Eleven-year-old Emily's curly blonde head peeked out first. She was the pretty one in the family, all delicate like a China doll I once saw in a store window. She sure wouldn't have to worry about being a spinster or a teacher. I gave her my hand and she wiggled onto the seat next to Zack. After her, with a little help, scrambled seven-year-old Tad. He was small for his age, and as the baby of the family, had been petted and pampered. Now he plopped into my lap.

"Is this Sacramento?" he asked.

"Yes," I answered him.

"Can I drive?" he asked, reaching for the reins.

"You're too little," responded Zack in his most grown-up voice.

After Tad, nine-year-old Becky bounded out of the wagon and up to the front, squeezing her chubby little body in between me and Emily. Becky always made me think of one of those bubbly springs we saw on the trail. Ma used to say she was plumb "full of vim and vinegar!" If she had her druthers I suspect she'd have jumped right down onto the street with the other kids and been off out of sight like a shot. She wasn't afraid of anything, nor did she have the good sense that goes along with a healthy dose of fear. I put my arm around her shoulder to steady her a bit. I wanted us all to make a good impression on Uncle Nick.

Gradually, after the first awe of seeing the long-anticipated town wore off, I found myself concentrating on the faces I saw. I began to examine every one we passed, wondering if one of these folks might turn out to be Uncle Nick. How would I know, anyway? I didn't know what he looked like. Somehow I guess I thought I'd see some resemblance to Ma.

"Shucks, Corrie," I could hear Ma say as we bounced along, "there ain't no way you can tell a man from some female kin o' his."

Still, I couldn't help thinking about all her talk of the Belle blood, and I thought that maybe I'd be able to tell.

There were all kinds of folks in Sacramento. I suppose it wasn't much different than I imagined it would be after listening to Captain Dixon talk to all the grown-ups around the campfire at night. There were lots of rough-looking, grizzled prospectors. They looked just like some pictures Ma had shown us. One or two were leading mules all loaded down with gear. But there were men dressed in nice city clothes too—probably the ones who had found lots of gold. And there were plenty who looked like the men in the Midwest too, with their high, leather boots, buckskin coats, and wide-brimmed hats. All around, horses and wagons moved in every direction.

There weren't too many women. Ma said there wouldn't be. She figured she might even find us a new pa once we got here. The few women I did see were all dressed up in fancy silk or calico. I didn't suppose they did much prospecting, judging from their get-ups.

Captain Dixon rode up on horseback next to our wagon. "Well, you young Hollisters," he called out cheerfully, "here we are! What do you all think?"

A raucous chorus of shouts flew back at him from around me. He laughed, unable to distinguish between the high-pitched voices.

"I'll take you kids on down to Miz Baxter's boarding house. Then I'll see what I can find out about your uncle."

He paused and rubbed the whiskers on his chin thoughtfully. "Someone with the name of Nick Hollister oughtn't be too hard to locate," he added.

"His name ain't Hollister," I said quickly.

"That's right. I do recall your Ma sayin' he was *her* brother. Never thought about the man's last name. What is it then? You don't want me chasin' round for the wrong man."

"Matthews," I said, "Nick Matthews." I felt my cheeks flame, 'cause I know better than to tell lies. But this was different—it was Ma's wish. And she did say it was the name he went by. Zack threw me a surprised look, and I was just glad he didn't say anything.

Captain Dixon must not have noticed it; he just nodded and rode off on his palomino with us following in the wagon.

Miss Baxter's Boarding House was located in a quieter part of town, down a side street from the main road. It was a frame house painted white and was the most civilized building in town—at least it was the most civilized one we had yet seen. There was a white board fence around the front yard, and a row of geraniums planted along the front of the house were still in bloom, though it was the middle of October. Inside, the house was furnished plainly. Miss Baxter said she was waiting for a shipment to arrive from the East. But what was there was nice; I hadn't seen a parlor or a kitchen or even a real floor in months.

Two hours after Captain Dixon deposited us with Miss Baxter, and she'd fixed us a fine supper of chicken and dumplings, the captain walked into the front room where we were sitting by the fire waiting. I thought he looked more sober than usual.

"Seems your uncle ain't nowhere in town," he said. "He's most likely up in Miracle."

"What'll we do now?" asked Zack, sounding more than

ever like the little boy he was struggling not to be.

Captain Dixon scratched his head thoughtfully.

No one said anything for a long time. I suppose we were all too shy to ask what was really on our minds. But someone had to ask, and since I was the oldest, it was my job to do it.

"Captain," I said, my voice sounding small in my ears. After all, Captain Dixon only signed on to take the wagon train to Sacramento, not to traipse all over tarnation with a passel of kids. "Do you think maybe we could go up there after him?"

Captain Dixon didn't say anything for a while, then he kind of mumbled, "Well, lemme see. Yep, that's an idea all right—" As his words trailed away half-finished, he went off to the other room and talked with Miss Baxter. They kept their voices low so I couldn't tell what they were saying. In a minute or two he returned.

"Miz Baxter says you can all stay here tonight. We'll git an early start come daybreak. It's a three-day ride to Miracle."

CHAPTER 4

MIRACLE SPRINGS

I can hardly remember anything about the next three days except their being long.

When Captain Dixon said he'd take us to Miracle, we were five happy kids. The thought of waiting around in that unfamiliar city, not sure if Uncle Nick would ever turn up, was none too appealing a thought. Especially if we had been left alone, having to scour through the crowded, rough streets searching for our uncle on our own. So we all joyfully hugged Captain Dixon—all except Zack, that is. He just shook his hand like a grown-up man.

But the long drive took some of the fire out of our enthusiasm. There's nothing worse than thinking you're all done with something, only to have to start all over again. After all those months on the trail, another three days should have been nothing. But they were the longest of all.

Anyway, we finally got there about mid-afternoon of the third day. Miracle was nothing like Sacramento, except that it was new. But I suppose everything around California was practically new, because of the gold rush.

Captain Dixon told us that the people who started this town all came two years ago, after a rich strike was discovered on a little tributary of the Yuba River that came to be called Miracle Springs. The town just naturally got named after the springs. There weren't more than two streets and

33

a few buildings in the whole town, and five of the buildings were saloons. Most of the population was housed in a ramshackle conglomeration of tents of all different sizes and shapes.

Captain Dixon said that the people of Miracle hadn't decided if their town was a mining camp, a for-real town that was going to grow like Sacramento, or if it was already becoming a ghost town. The two-year old strike was gradually playing out, and only the serious miners were still scratching a few dollars out of the mines and streams. But quite a few families, and here and there a farmer or two, had come to the area hanging onto their hopes for the future.

"Ranchers like Uncle Nick?" I said.

"I suppose so," replied the Captain vaguely.

For such a little town, a lot of people were milling around the streets. It was Saturday, the Captain reminded me—the day everyone comes to town. As we pulled the wagon up to a stop in front of one of the biggest of the buildings, the town's only General Store, Captain Dixon told us to stay close to him.

We trailed inside behind him like a brood of little ducklings following their mama. For the first time in months, I felt at home. The store was filled almost to bursting with everything imaginable, and reminded me of the Mercantile in Bridgeville, the little town near our farm in New York. The smells of leather, licorice, pickles, feed, peppermint, and burlap all mingled together in a wonderful, homey way. But I wish I hadn't picked up a bar of lemon verbena soap. The strong aroma immediately brought tears to my eyes; Ma used to use it all the time, and it reminded me so much of her. I had to fight back tears the rest of the day because the smell lingered on my hands.

It was easy to guess the proprietor by his appearance, dressed in a white shirt and string tie, with a leather visor stuck on his forehead over dark, brilliantined hair. I suppose the proprietors of stores like these all looked the same. At least he was dressed just like kind old Mr. Johnson back in Bridgeville. This gentleman stood behind a coarse wooden counter, absorbed in sorting through a stack of important-looking papers. He stopped when the door closed behind Becky, looked up, and his thick eyebrows raised right up to his visor as he watched us approach. He had the biggest, bushiest eyebrows I'd ever seen. He said nothing, but his eyes shone with both question and surprise as Captain Dixon walked up to the counter with his little batch of silent ducklings in tow. Maybe folks weren't used to children here in Miracle. I didn't know what to expect. But when he opened his mouth, his voice was friendly.

"Afternoon. Can I help you folks?"

"We're looking for someone," said Captain Dixon.

"I see—" His voice trailed off as his eye followed Tad, who had wiggled his hand from mine and was going for a bright red ball he'd spied.

"Perhaps your children would like a sweet treat?" the storekeeper continued, stopping Tad, as I supposed he intended, in his tracks.

"Uh—they ain't my kids," replied Captain Dixon. "I'm just looking after them until I can get them to their kin."

"And might that be who you're looking for?" asked the storekeeper as he began passing around a glass jar of hard candy.

I was kept busy trying to listen with one ear and contain the squeals of delight from the others at the same time.

"That's right," said the captain. "I'm Jim Dixon, and I'm looking for a Nick Matthews."

The man stopped suddenly, the jar just out of Tad's reach. All at once he seemed oblivious to us kids, and didn't even notice Tad's heroic attempts to wrap his dirty little fingers around a piece of candy. Finally I took out a piece and gave it to Tad. But the storekeeper continued to stare at Captain Dixon.

"That so?" he finally said in a questioning voice. "The young'uns' father?"

"Their uncle."

"You certain of that?"

"Sure as I can be, never havin' met the man. But I knew their ma."

"Hmmm—"

"You know him then, Mister?"

"In a manner of speaking."

"Know where we can find him?"

"Not exactly," replied the storekeeper. "Though he's got a claim hereabouts, but I never—"

"I know who Nick is!" chimed in a voice from the back of the store where a display of saddles was piled.

We all glanced around eagerly in the direction of the new voice. A man came toward us slowly, older and more weathered than anyone I'd ever seen, even more 'n my old Grandpa Belle. His face was covered with a matted gray beard which continued up the sides of his cheeks, around his ears, and up over the top of his head—one big clump of hair, with only his two eyes and a red nose peeking out from it. Toward the back of his head he wore a battered old slouch hat, but his hair seemed too unruly to be contained and spread out in all directions from underneath it. His clothes Ma would have long since tossed out as rags, and around his neck was tied what looked to be a blue bandanna, though it was so covered with grime you could hardly tell the blue from the brownish-gray of his beard. As he approached, two half-sets of teeth made their appearance out of the mass which covered his face—neither the most complete nor the whitest teeth I had ever laid eyes on, but at least the smile surrounding them seemed friendly.

"What's that you say, Alkali?" said the storekeeper.

"Ya heard me well enough," answered the old prospector, his grin widening.

"This here's Alkali Jones," said the storekeeper by way of introduction. "Knows everything and everyone in Miracle, and been here longer than all of us put together, I don't doubt."

"Hee, hee! I reckon yer right 'bout that," said Jones.

"Pleased to make your acquaintance," said Captain Dixon. The two men shook hands. Mr. Jones' hands were as brown and tough as an Indian's.

"What can you tell me about Matthews?" asked the captain.

"Mayhap the young'uns oughta step outside," said Alkali Jones. I thought I detected a slight wink in the Captain's direction as he spoke, but I could tell it wasn't meant for me. "These all be Nick's kin?" he squeaked. "Hee, hee!" His high-pitched voice sounded like gravel scraping over glass.

"That's right, they're his kin. So I figure what you've got to say you can say to us all."

We moved a few steps away, but were too curious to take the old miner's suggestion and go outside.

"Have it yer way, stranger. Don't say I didn't warn ya." He paused, and then, still half-trying to keep his words from us, said in a low voice, "He's done skipped."

"Skipped? What do you mean?" asked Captain Dixon.

"Skipped town, that's what! What else could I mean? Hee, hee!"

"Why?"

"The sheriff's after him, that's why! Ya must be a tinhorn, stranger—why else would a man like Nick pull up and leave his claim?"

"How long ago?"

"I dunno. Last week some time, weren't it, Bosely?" The storekeeper half nodded, half shrugged.

"What did he do?"

"Some say he shot a man, Mister," said the storekeeper seriously. "Others say he was framed."

"Whichever it be, he ain't been seen in Miracle since," added Mr. Jones.

"Well, isn't there anybody in town who can tell me anything about it, or where he might possibly be?" asked the captain.

"The sheriff sure doesn't know," said the storekeeper. "I heard he's been clear down to Placerville looking for him."

"Them that knows ain't sayin', I can tell ya that! Hee, hee!"

"And who might that be, Mr. Jones?"

"Friends o' his."

"Where might I find these friends?"

"Likely over t' the Gold Nugget. Ya passed it on the way in t' town."

"I see," said the captain thoughtfully. "Well then, I'll just leave the kids here while I go have a talk with these gentlemen."

"I wouldn't be doin' that!" said Mr. Jones, wiping his grimy shirtsleeve across his nose. "Ya don't want t' be disturbin' them now . . . no, siree!"

"These kids here have been on the trail for months," exclaimed Captain Dixon. "Their poor ma took sick and died when we were almost here, and now they're orphans except for this Matthews fellow. So whatever's going on ain't more important than this!"

I wanted to cheer for the captain, standing up for us like he did, but I just stood there and kept quiet.

"That's up t' you, of course," said Mr. Jones. "All's I knows is there's been a mighty se-erious game o' poker since last night. An' 'bout two hours ago Nick's partner put their claim on the table, an' then lost it square."

"Don't matter. I'm gonna see him," insisted Captain Dixon.

"Have it yer own way, stranger. I'm jist tellin' ya he said he'd shoot anyone who interrupted the game afore he'd had a fair chance o' winnin' back the land."

"Drum's no hothead," put in the shopkeeper. "I don't think he would—" but he was cut off in mid-sentence.

"Ya know as well as I do, Bosely, that this fracas with Nick's got him a mite riled."

"How much longer do you suppose the game'll last?" asked Captain Dixon.

"No tellin'."

Captain Dixon sighed, thought for a minute, then bustled us kids outside. He went back into the store, I guessed to ask directions, then took us to a boarding house. This one was run by an old Italian woman named Mrs. Gianni. She took us to her kitchen and set about fixing us something to eat. The Captain told us to wait there while he went to see what he could find out.

CHAPTER 5

IN FRONT OF THE GOLD NUGGET

We sat in Mrs. Gianini's boarding house around a rough table covered with a red-checkered cloth. Slabs of apple pie were on the table in front of us. It was nearly the best pie I ever tasted—almost as good as Ma's. But I couldn't eat much. Zack ate his and finally began to work on mine.

We'd been waiting so long that a little bit more oughtn't have mattered much. But after an hour I could hardly stand it any more. I began to wonder if that nice Captain Dixon hadn't just given up and gone back to Sacramento.

Then I remembered that old miner's words. Could someone have shot the captain? Surely Ma's brother couldn't have friends like that. I told myself those were just wild tales like the ones we heard about Kit Carson and Davy Crockett.

Finally the waiting became too much to bear. The other kids had finished their pie, Tad was getting cranky, and Becky was wiggling around. I didn't want to wait another minute.

"Look here," I said, trying to sound firm like Ma, "I'm going to find out what's going on."

"But Captain Dixon said to stay put," said Emily in her dainty way.

"Well, supposing something's happened to him?"

Zack's head shot up with a worried look as he caught the meaning in my words.

"I'm goin'," I said firmly, rising up off the chair.

"Well if you go, we all go," put in Zack. "We gotta all stick together."

I didn't argue. I didn't feel quite so brave as my words sounded, and I was glad for the company, even if it was just a passel of young'uns.

Mrs. Gianini told us to stay where we were, but we all bounded out of her place, leaving her with her hands in the air. The little ones held each others' hands and followed on mine and Zack's heels as if we were the ma and pa of the bunch. But inside my stomach was a knot. I was worried and scared, and I missed Ma terribly.

The sun was setting as we marched down the street, and the shadows made the town look all the more threatening. I noticed the brawling noise now, too. Laughter and shouts and catcalls poured out from the saloons. I could hear several gruff men's voices trying their best at "Oh, Susanna," but they sounded off-key, even to my tin ear. They were probably drunk. An even more off-key piano was being played along with them. It might have been comical if I hadn't been so anxious inside.

We found the Gold Nugget Saloon. It was noisy, with lots of men hanging around outside. I didn't relish the thought of walking up to the place, much less going inside, but I didn't know what else to do.

There was a place like the Gold Nugget in Bridgeville, but Ma didn't let us go near it. "Decent folk don't go into drinkin' houses," Ma had said. What little I knew about California told me that a drinking house way out here must be even worse than the ones in the East. I told myself that we had a mighty good reason to be there, but it didn't make it any easier to step up onto the wooden steps and go inside. I looked at my brothers and sisters, but they just looked back at me with big, wide eyes. They were looking to me to decide what we ought to do. My stomach was still all knotted up. Surely one of those rough-looking men standing around the place was going to start making fun of us. But finally I took in a breath, turned around, and started toward the swinging doors.

All of a sudden a female voice spoke up behind us. "Do you children need some help?"

I stopped dead in my tracks and turned around. I was more than a little relieved to be stopped from going inside that place, even if just for a minute.

There stood a woman, about Ma's age, or maybe a few years younger. She was tall and trim, but sturdily built. Even dressed as she was in a blue calico and matching bonnet, I could tell she wasn't afraid of work. She was pretty, but in a rough, earthy sort of way, and her tanned skin looked as if she spent a lot of time out in the sun.

"My name is Almeda Parrish," she went on to say to our blank faces. "I run the Parrish Mine and Freight Company. My office is across the way and I happened to notice you children. Do your mother and father know where you are?"

"Our ma and pa are dead, ma'am," I answered, trying to sound respectful.

"Oh, I'm terribly sorry." And I truly thought she was. "But this is hardly the kind of place for children. Do you want someone inside?"

"Well, Ma'am," I answered, "we just came from New York, and Captain Dixon, that's our wagon boss, he went to find out about our Uncle Nick. But he left over an hour ago, and we got kind of worried waiting on him. We've been—"

Without warning, tears welled up in my eyes, and I bit my lip to keep them back. I felt like such a baby.

"And this—Captain Dixon? You say he's your wagon boss?"

"He brung us all the way from the East, Ma'am," put in Zack, coming to my rescue.

Mrs. Parrish didn't seem to mind a girl crying. She stepped right up to me and put her arm around me. Then she said, "There, there, child. Don't you worry, we'll get all this straightened around."

When I had gotten all my tears out, she went on to say in a thoughtful tone, "Nick. . . ? Nick who?"

"Nick Matthews," spoke up Zack again.

She pursed her lips and nodded slightly, but said nothing. I didn't like the look that came over everyone's faces around here when Uncle Nick's name came up.

At that moment, a man walked out of the saloon doors.

"Sir," said Mrs. Parrish with authority in her voice. The man stopped and paid attention. "There is a man by the name of Dixon, a Captain Dixon, in this establishment," she said. "Would you go back inside and tell him to come out immediately? There are some children here very anxious to see him."

"That might not be sich a good idee right at the moment, Ma'am," he returned. "Ya see, the game's downright tense, an' any disturbance—"

"Well!" exclaimed Mrs. Parrish, "Of all the nerve! To think a game of poker is more important than this. I'll just have to go in after him myself!"

She hitched up her calico dress with both hands, and marched right inside as if she were Daniel walking into the lion's den. I peered over the top of the two swinging doors and could tell that the men inside were just as surprised as me at seeing a fine, well-bred lady suddenly intrude upon their private world. There were other women inside, but they were dressed a whole lot differently than Mrs. Parrish.

"Why, Mrs. Parrish, this is indeed an honor—" the man standing behind the bar began to say. But she paid no attention and marched right on past him.

She disappeared into another room at the back of the saloon. I could hear voices from inside through the open door, but I couldn't make out what anyone was saying. From the loud female voice it was plain that Mrs. Parrish was giving the men gathered there a piece of her mind.

In about two minutes Mrs. Parrish came out again, followed almost immediately by Captain Dixon. Several others straggled along behind them. Some of the men looked pretty mean and all wore guns on their hips.

"I'm sorry, kids," said Captain Dixon walking right up to us. "I'm afraid I wasn't too successful at finding out much about your uncle. None of the men were too talkative while their game was going on. About all I know for sure is what we heard before—that he's not here."

Just then, another man walked through the swinging doors, and the eyes of several of the onlookers swung around and glared at him. Unconsciously, I backed up several steps along the wooden sidewalk, and the younger kids clung close to me. Mrs. Parrish eyed the man intently, while all the other men who had wandered out of the saloon crowded around by the doors, some with grins on their faces, chuckling among themselves, looking ready for a good show.

The fellow was awfully tall. He had dark circles under his red eyes, and wore a full beard. A big hat was pulled down clear to his ears. I'd have guessed him to be thirty-eight or forty years old, but it was hard to tell. He'd probably been at the card table all night, like the man at the store said. His shoulders were broad; he could have hoisted both Becky and Tad up on them and hardly felt it. He wasn't unpleasant looking, but kind of fearsome all the same. He was dressed shabbily, his dusty old trousers held up with faded suspenders over a patched flannel shirt.

"Well, Mr. Drum," said Mrs. Parrish in a stern voice, "as you can see, the situation is as serious as I tried to tell you inside. Now, are you going to tell us where we can find Mr. Matthews, or not?"

"You ain't told me nothin' yet." He glanced at us kids with deep creases forming between his thick brown eyebrows. "What's this all about?"

"As I tried to tell you, these children are looking for your partner."

"Who are they?" asked Mr. Drum.

"It seems they more or less belong to Nick Matthews," said Mrs. Parrish.

Mr. Drum rubbed a coarse hand over his mouth. "Well, I've known Nick a long time and I know for certain he ain't got no young'uns."

"These are his nieces and nephews—he's their uncle!"

The lines on Mr. Drum's forehead and around his eyes got deeper. A look of real shock passed over his face, and he didn't say anything for a long time. When he finally did speak, his voice sounded as if he had just had the wind knocked out of him.

"Nick's nowhere to be found," he said.

"Are you expecting me to believe he'd just pull up and leave, without telling his partner—"

She was interrupted by the laughter of the men standing around.

"Ya must not know Nick Matthews too well!" shouted one of the men. "Why, he's a lightin' off fer somewhere new ev'ry month!"

"And he don't tell me his every move," added the big man called Drum. As he spoke, he kept throwing quick glances in our direction. "This sure ain't no place fer a bunch of kids. Where's their ma, anyway? Why'd she send 'em all by themselves after Nick?"

"I thought you understood, Mr. Drum," said Mrs. Parrish, her firm tone softening. "Their mother died en route to California."

Mr. Drum fell silent once more, his face like a stone wall.

"Hee, hee, hee!" came the rasp of Alkali Jones from among the onlookers. "I guess since Nick's gone, them's yore young'uns now, Drum! Hee, hee, hee!"

He spun around and glared at the old miner, then turned back and looked each of us over one at a time, his ruddy California color getting paler as he took in each of our faces.

When he came to me, I detected something that took away the fear I was feeling. His face still wore a scowl, but his eyes seemed to say that in spite of the bluster he might put on in front of all the tough-looking men in the saloon, down inside he was the kind that could feel sorry for a brood of homeless orphans. But the next moment, I began to think I'd read his eyes all wrong.

The exchange of looks and thoughts took only a few seconds. Then Mrs. Parrish spoke again.

"Well, Mr. Drum, what do you have to say for yourself?"

He shot her a glaring look that seemed to say, *Mind your own business, you busybody female*! But what came out of his mouth was, "I got nothin' to say for myself, 'cept that this is . . . some surprise. And I don't rightly see why you think it's got something to do with me."

"You are Matthews' partner."

"And Nick's gone!" he shot back. "How many times I gotta tell you that, lady?" He seemed more nervous than angry.

"You're closer to their kin than any of us," persisted Mrs. Parrish. "Mr. Dixon here has to be getting back to Sacramento—"

Captain Dixon nodded as she spoke.

"—And I only met these children ten minutes ago," she went on. "So I think it's high time you either told us where to find Mr. Matthews, or got on your horse and went to find him yourself."

"Even if I knew where he was—" he persisted, "which I don't—I wouldn't just ride off so the sheriff could follow me and haul Nick in for somethin' he didn't do!"

I figured by now it was my turn to speak.

"We're real glad to make your acquaintance, Mr. Drum," I said, trying to smile cheerfully. "My name's Corrie. I'm the oldest."

I curtsied like Ma taught me.

The man looked at me again. A strange expression came over his face, but it only lasted for a moment. Then he glanced around at the others.

He wiped his hands across his eyes as if he hoped that might make us all disappear. But we were still there. I told him the kids' names. A pitiful looking lot we were, having spent months on the trail with nary a bath in a month of Sundays.

"There sure are a heap of you," he said softly, scratching his whiskers. "And all such big, grown-up kids, too."

"There's a heap of you, too!" said Tad in a soft voice with wide-eyed awe.

That got a laugh from everyone, especially the men in the saloon, and a few others who had wandered up from the street to see what this strange little gathering was all about. But the fellow in front of us didn't laugh. He still seemed a little apprehensive about the sight of us all.

"Hey, Drum," called out one of the men, "seems to me you're cut out right well for nurse-maidin'!"

He pretended not to hear, but I know he did.

"So, Mr. Drum, what might your intentions be now?" asked Mrs. Parrish, still sounding very stern.

"Well, Mrs. Parrish," he answered after a moment's thought, "I'm meanin' no disrespect, but I reckon it ain't none of your dad-blamed business."

Then he turned back toward the gawking faces at the saloon door. "And it ain't none of yours, neither!" he snapped. "So git!"

No one waited to be told twice. They scattered like birds at a turkey shoot. Apparently his was a voice people listened to in Miracle Springs.

Mrs. Parrish wasn't as easily spooked. Even Captain Dixon took a step back, but Mrs. Parrish settled her hands on her hips and didn't budge.

"As one of the few voices of *decent* civilized society in this town," she said, "I think it *is* my business. Anyway, I am making it mine. These children came here looking for a home, and now it seems you are the only link there is to that home."

"A home!" From the expression on his face I don't think the thought had yet occurred to him. "You can't expect—! Even *you* can see, Mrs. Parrish, that Nick and I ain't fit to be taking care of no kids." He glanced a look at me as if to say, *I'm sorry.*

"We'd be able to help out on Uncle Nick's ranch," I offered, not wanting to sound too eager, but hardly able to keep quiet any longer. "I'm a fair cook, and Zack's a good hand with a plow and animals. As for the young'uns, they can learn. We won't get in your way. Then you can go find Uncle Nick and tell him we're here."

"Ranch? What ranch?" Mr. Drum said.

"The ranch a fellow from California told us Uncle Nick had."

"Since when do you and Nick Matthews own a ranch, Mr. Drum?" said Mrs. Parrish. I couldn't tell if her voice sounded angry or smug.

A reddish color started to come into Drum's face. I don't think he liked being questioned by a woman in front of all his friends from the saloon, several of whom had wandered back toward the door.

"Now, look here!" he said suddenly, a sharp, cross look coming over his face. "Not that it's any of your business, but Nick and I did have a ranch once—won it in a poker game and lost it the next night. How was we to know someone'd go spreading it around that we was ranchers, or that Nick's . . . sister . . . would take it in her blame fool head to come out West after . . . him."

"Listen here, Drum," spoke up Captain Dixon. "Don't you go speakin' so of the dead, 'specially in front of her own children. Mrs. Hollister was a fine, brave woman."

Mr. Drum looked ready to knock us all down and bolt. He opened his mouth as if he were going to say something, but nothing came out.

"Indeed, Mr. Drum," added Mrs. Parrish, and now her voice *was* angry, "you ought to be ashamed of yourself to speak so!"

Mr. Drum looked as if he was about to suffocate.

"And as far as the question of your and Mr. Matthews' reputations go," Mrs. Parrish went on as if she didn't see what distress he was in, "I must agree to some extent. Yet it appears *you* are all these children have. Technically, if Mr. Matthews doesn't return, then I would think these children would inherit his half of your property. You might as well face it, Mr. Drum—these youngsters may be your new partners."

"Look here, Mrs. Parrish, who knows when Nick'll be back? Why, I ain't even got a decent place for them to bunk down." He was looking more and more like a trapped polecat with all the eyes of the town on him. "What about you?"

"I'm not their kin," she answered matter-of-factly. "I have no connection to their uncle, or to any property to which they might have a legitimate claim. You do. And practically speaking, my business takes me too frequently away from home." She glanced at me apologetically.

"So does mine!" exclaimed Drum. "And I ain't got no intention of havin' no woman tell me my responsibility to-ward—my—my partner's kids!"

He was looking at Mrs. Parrish, but I thought I saw him throw just a momentary glance at me as he spoke. Something in his eyes seemed to want to say, *I'm sorry . . . I'd take you in if I could. But not now, not like this . . . not with the whole town staring at me!*

He spun around and bounded down the steps, striding across the dirt street to where his horse, a pretty bay mare, was tied at a hitching rail. Somehow all the fears I had over the past several weeks never included standing in the middle of a strange town with everyone turning us away.

But there went our only hope of locating our uncle, gal-loping off down the road, leaving only a cloud of dust and five pairs of disappointed, staring eyes behind him.

CHAPTER 6

THE TOWN BUSINESS WOMAN

Even though Mrs. Parrish was a kind lady, the menfolk in town seemed almost afraid of her. As we walked away from the saloon, I wondered about her being the only real lady in a town full of rough, gold-mining men. But they depended on her business for their livelihood, and so maybe they had to watch their step around her.

She almost reminded me of a stern schoolteacher who one just couldn't help liking, even for all her sober looks and strict words. I liked her anyway. Ma would have liked her, too. Now, *she* was a woman who could get on in the world by herself. She sure didn't look like she needed a man around!

She took us right to her house. Captain Dixon had to be on his way, but he took our wagon to Mrs. Parrish's and unhitched the team. She ran one of the town's livery stables there as part of her business, so they made arrangements with the man there for our two horses. I heard her tell him that she'd see to our care " . . . until that Drum comes to his senses, or until Nick Matthews gets back in town."

We all gave the captain big hugs. How we hated to see him go! He'd been about the only familiar face we'd known for quite a while now, and was just about the closest we'd gotten to having a father. Mrs. Parrish was nice, but we'd only just met her, and seeing Captain Dixon go off down the street brought a fearsome loneliness into me all over again.

He promised that he'd come to see us before he left for the East to guide another wagon train to California. I wondered if we might be going back with him. But with both Ma and Grandpa gone, we had no one to go home to back in New York. That little wagon was the only home we had left. We wouldn't be any better off in the East than we were here in Miracle. And I'd rather be orphaned and alone in California, than to face that trip across the country again with a batch of young'uns to watch after. I was practically just a kid myself!

It was late by the time the captain left and we all got settled in. Mrs. Parrish had a nice frame house—there were only two or three other houses in town, but hers was the nicest. I suppose most of the men lived in one of the two boarding houses, in the collection of tents at the end of town, or out on their claims in the hills someplace. It sure was nice being in such a pretty place. It was all done up fancy-like with beautiful carved furniture, chairs with needlepoint seats, chintz curtains, and fine china in the prettiest cherrywood hutch I ever saw. Mrs. Parrish said her husband had it all brought from the East, from their home in Boston. It came around Cape Horn, she said, in 1849, when she and her husband came to California.

She was a widow now. She didn't talk much about her husband except for that, and I didn't want to be impolite and ask too many questions.

She had two extra beds with feather mattresses. I could hardly believe how soft they felt after all those months sleeping in our wagon. Tad and Zack were asleep in seconds. Emily and Becky squirmed and giggled until I could get them settled down. But I couldn't sleep. With all the change, and everything that had happened, my mind was just too full.

Finally I got up and went to a little desk where Mrs.

Parrish had left a small lamp burning for us. I got out the old school notebook I was keeping my diary in, and wrote about the day—how we had come to Miracle Springs and about meeting Mr. Drum at the saloon. I tried to draw a picture of the front of the saloon. Lots of times I'd make drawings along with what I wrote, to help me remember. I couldn't help shedding a few tears. After all this time of anticipation, Uncle Nick was gone. And Mr. Drum left us here without even wanting to help us find him. I remembered that peculiar look in his eyes, as if he might have wanted to help if everyone wasn't watching. I felt so alone. I don't think I ever felt so lonely—even right after Ma died— as that moment standing there on the dusty street of Miracle Springs, watching that bay mare fade away from sight, and knowing nobody wanted us.

It helped to write it down that night. I was glad Ma got me thinking about keeping a diary, because it made the next few weeks easier to bear. I needed to be able to talk to somebody, even if it was only to myself. Most of what I wrote nobody'd ever lay eyes on. But just saying it made me feel better, like having a silent friend I could tell things to. And if I hadn't been keeping a journal, I wouldn't be able to remember a lot of what it was like when we first came to Miracle Springs.

I wrote late into the night by the dim light of Mrs. Parrish's lamp. It must have been past midnight when I finally crawled back into bed between Emily and Becky. But as tired as I was, I kept waking up all night, thinking that at any minute Uncle Nick would come to the door and take us to his ranch.

CHAPTER 7

MRS. PARRISH TALKS TO US

I woke up the following morning to a steady rainfall.

Emily and Becky were still sleeping soundly, and Becky had an arm wrapped around my neck. I gently loosened her arm and slipped out of bed. The sun was barely up, but the clouds made it even darker outside. The black sky reminded me that it was almost the end of October. Even in California, winter must be coming soon.

Mrs. Parrish fixed us all a fine breakfast of pancakes and sausages. The men in the mining camps called them flapjacks, she said, and prided themselves on tossing them way up in the air to flip them over. Then she had to leave for her office down the street.

Before she left, she showed us her bathtub in a little room all its own, showed us where to get the water, and told us to help ourselves to baths and anything else we needed. That was her polite way of saying we looked, and probably smelled, like a bunch of mountaineers. She told us where to find the pantry if we got hungry, and then invited us to come by the office later. She didn't say a word about Uncle Nick. I wasn't sure if that was good or bad, but I didn't want to ask.

After she left, I got the young'uns into the bath. All three of them could fit in that big tub of hers at the same time! I figured it'd be okay for me and Zack, since we were older, to have our own separate baths. While the kids were splashing around, I went to the kitchen to wash up the breakfast dishes; I'd asked Mrs. Parrish to leave them for me to do.

After a while Zack came in with that grown-up look on his face. "Corrie," he said, "I been doing some thinking."

He sat down in a chair by the table and took a leftover pancake from a plate. No matter how much might have been on Zack's mind, he could always eat.

"What about?" I asked, scrubbing away at the grease on the skillet.

"You know all them stories we heard about kids not that much older'n us who came out West by theirselves?"

I nodded. Half of them I never believed. "We ain't heard *that* many stories," I said.

"Well," Zack went on, paying my comment no heed, "there ain't no reason we couldn't do the same."

"I don't think I heard any stories about kids as young as us doing it," I added.

"Aw, come on, Corrie! We don't need Uncle Nick or nobody else. Pa left us and we all made out fine. Now Ma's gone, but we're older, too. We could get by."

"I ain't so sure," I said.

I didn't like the tone of Zack's voice. He sounded angry. It never occurred to me to be angry with Uncle Nick. It wasn't as if he had known we were coming and just skipped out on us, like Pa had done.

"I could get a job. Maybe even do some mining."

"Zack, you're only thirteen."

"That's old enough!" he shot back at me. "I might even strike it rich."

He bit into a piece of hotcake as if he was taking his frustration out on it. I decided I'd better not say anything more.

"Anyway," he went on in a minute, "I bet I could make us a living, just like Pa did, while you take care of the kids. Then when Emily gets big enough, she could take care of

Becky and Tad and you could get work, maybe taking in laundry or such like. Lots of women do that kind of thing."

"But that's just it, Zack," I replied, "I'm not a woman. I don't know enough about things—you know, about life, and all that—to take care of all of us. Especially way out here where there's hardly any civilization. And what about school? Ma always wanted us to have a good education. Seems to me we ought to go back to New York."

"And do what?"

"We got friends who'd likely help us."

"Ma would never want us to live off charity."

I was silent. Zack had me there. Ma was a proud woman all right. It was one thing to ask family for help, but quite another to go to complete strangers. Mrs. Parrish was nice, but we couldn't stay with her forever.

Maybe Zack was right. If we were young like Tad and Becky or even Emily, it would be different. Maybe then folks would feel as if they ought to take care of us. But Zack and I were old enough—at least, almost old enough—to take care of ourselves. But I didn't feel that way most of the time. Since Ma'd died, it hadn't been very comfortable being the one everybody looked to for decision-making. And I couldn't help thinking about what Ma had said about Pa when he was young, how hard it had been on him being all alone. I sure didn't want that to happen to any of us.

I was more than a little confused. I just didn't know what we ought to do.

Later in the day, all spruced up and fresh, we left the house and walked over to the Parrish Mine and Freight Company. On the way, I kept craning my head this way and that, looking for somebody that might be Uncle Nick, or some sign of Mr. Drum's bay mare. But neither was anywhere in sight.

The Mine and Freight Company was a hodgepodge of activities. Our eyes were wide open with curiosity when we walked in. Mrs. Parrish gave us a friendly greeting, and then took us on a little tour and told us about the company. They still operated a gold mine in the foothills several miles from town, and did some assaying of what the mines brought in. They even ran a bank, she told us, until Miracle got a real bank a year ago. Mostly the company was a freight outfit. They ran wagons—and pack mules, when necessary—between San Francisco and the Sierras.

"My husband," she said, her voice proud, "believed that the money to be made in the gold rush was not in the mines at all, but rather in supplies."

He was most likely right too, cause Mrs. Parrish lived better than any prospector I had yet seen.

The office itself was an orderly room with several file cabinets, and a big, thick oak counter across the front. Behind it sat two nice, oak desks, and next to them cabinets full of cubbyholes which had papers and files sticking out of them. One of the desks had Mrs. Parrish's name on it. At the other one sat a man she introduced as Mr. Ashton, her clerk.

Mr. Ashton looked like a city fellow. He didn't fit my image of Miracle Springs. He was dressed better than any man I'd seen in town, but he was balding and scrawny. He was nervous, too, and seemed to try hard to ignore us. When Mrs. Parrish presented us to him, his lips twitched up into what I guess was supposed to be a smile, then he went right back to work.

Behind the office was the huge livery stable where the company's stock and wagons were cared for between deliveries. Marcus Weber, a burly, free Negro, presided here as blacksmith, Mrs. Parrish said. He was more friendly than the clerk, and even helped Tad and Becky climb up on a couple of mules. His teeth were pure white, and he put them to good use when he smiled.

Our horses, Snowball and Jinx, looked very contented munching on hay and swishing flies away with their tails. I thanked Mr. Weber for taking such good care of them.

"Miz Parrish, she dun tol' me t' treat 'em like they was my own," said Mr. Weber, grinning.

"Not that he doesn't treat everyone's animals that way," Mrs. Parrish added with a laugh.

I thanked her, and tried to offer her money, but she wouldn't hear of it. I couldn't help wondering where all of this was going to lead. The youngsters were real taken with the office and the livery, but I couldn't keep from thinking, *What is to become of us? What should we do? And where will we live if we stay here and do what Zack suggested, trying to make it on our own?* I wasn't so sure I liked the idea of trying to be a ma to four children when I was barely more than a girl myself.

Mrs. Parrish must have been thinking of this, too, because as soon as we'd seen all around her place, she sent Mr. Ashton home for his lunch, and told us kids to sit down in some spare chairs around her desk.

"Children, I have been giving your situation much thought and prayer," she said, folding her hands together in a very ladylike way on the top of her desk and giving us a sweet look. "The younger children will not be able to understand all that is happening, but you, Corrie and Zachary, are old enough. And I think it is important for you to clearly grasp all the aspects of the situation facing you so that you will see why I must do what I have decided to do."

She stopped and cleared her throat daintily. "Do you have any questions?"

We all shook our heads.

"It is not my intent to speak ill of anyone," she went on, "but I think you should know, if you have not already guessed, just what kind of man your uncle is."

She stopped again and looked intently at Zack's face, then mine, for a long spell. Then, seeming satisfied, went on.

"This land here in the West is very wild and uncivilized. In many places, law is non-existent. Men have had to make their own law and have often resorted to methods that, in the East, would be found unthinkable. Survival has become the most important pursuit—along with getting rich—and the weak do not survive. At least that is how many of these westerners feel. I do not hold that opinion entirely myself, although I do see how it can come to be such in a frontier like this. Surely the weak do perish in the West, but survival should never take precedence over morality."

She paused again, took a deep breath, looked us over and probably saw the dumfounded looks on our faces, which told her we didn't understand what she was talking about. But she plunged ahead anyway, and what she said next, I think we understood well enough.

"Now, your uncle came here when the land was raw and wild. You can hardly imagine the difference five years can make. The population has multiplied many, many times over, just since 1847. And that first year or two after the first strike was a wild and reckless time. Some say it's not much better now, but at least it's begun to settle down some. I have never known your uncle well, and I'll not presume to make excuses for him. But the fact is, your uncle has lived a rather wild life here in the West. I am afraid this is not the first instance of his crossing paths with the sheriff, and as often as not I believe the trouble starts around a poker table. He is not, I believe, a lawless sort. I have heard that he and Mr. Drum have even helped the law out in some cases. But his is not a settled life, perhaps not even a safe one. Do you understand what I am saying?"

By now I had the gist of what she was trying to tell us.

"Mr. Drum doesn't seem like an outlaw," I said.

"And neither is your uncle," replied Mrs. Parrish. "Actually, Mr. Drum has seemed to be a steadying influence on Mr. Matthews. They've worked a claim together since before my husband and I were here, and some say they have done pretty well by it. Mr. Drum's always kept mostly to himself, only now and then pulling your uncle out of a scrape. Your uncle's a talkative sort of man, but no one knows much about his partner. In any case, with your uncle now gone and in fresh trouble, I'm just not so sure how advisable it is—"

"Are you meaning," I asked, even before she'd finished the sentence, "that it wouldn't be good for us to live with Uncle Nick? Or that maybe it's just as well he left town?"

I stopped, looking over at Mrs. Parrish to see if I could tell what she was thinking.

"Because, if you are," I continued, "—well I don't mean to disagree, Ma'am, especially since you probably know what you're talking about. But he's still our uncle, and—"

I took a deep breath. It was hard to speak out like that. Ma always taught us kids to be quiet around adults. But this was such a confusing situation, and I hardly knew whether I was supposed to think like a child or a grown-up. I was sure Mrs. Parrish had every right to box my ears, but I kept going.

"—And, well . . . after what you just said, maybe he even needs us a little, just like we do him."

She didn't box my ears. In fact, Mrs. Parrish just sat there and smiled at me. "You're a very perceptive girl, Corrie," she finally said. "You have put into words exactly what I have been thinking and praying about. I think perhaps this is God's further confirmation of my decision. I realize you hardly know me, and perhaps in normal circumstances it would not be my place to make decisions about—"

"Mrs. Parrish," I interrupted, feeling uncomfortable doing it, but knowing I had to speak, "my brothers and sisters and I are just kids. And we're real confused about what to do."

"You're hardly a child anymore, Corrie," she said, smiling sweetly at me. "Why, you're practically a lady."

"Thank you, Ma'am," I replied, feeling my cheeks getting hot. "But I'm still confused. I don't know much about God, but it seems maybe bringing you across our path might just be something like He'd do. Anyway, we're right obliged for the interest you're taking in us, because you and Captain

Dixon are the only adults we got left, at least maybe the only ones left with half-sensible heads. And now that the Captain is gone . . . well, we'd be right glad to hear whatever you want to say to us."

"Thank you for your confidence, Corrie. I hope I shall prove worthy of it."

She spread her hands out on her desk and looked down at them, and I even thought I saw a bit of flush creep up in her cheeks. But she went on in a brisk businesslike manner. "Now," she said, "here are my thoughts. I believe you should be with your uncle if at all possible. Not only because he is family, but because perhaps you can be good for him. As you said, Corrie, maybe you do need each other. Of course this is ultimately a decision the five of you have to make together, and certainly much depends on whether he is located and what is the outcome of this present fracas."

"Mr. Drum said he didn't do anything wrong," I put in optimistically.

Mrs. Parrish smiled. "Another thing you must understand about the West is that no one *ever* thinks he's done anything wrong, as long as he had a reason. And partners *always* stick up for each other. But time will tell, and we'll hope your uncle is cleared."

"What should we do now?" I asked.

"My counsel is that you do not try to go back where you came from immediately, but stay here in Miracle Springs and try to make a life for yourselves—at least through the winter. I will help you adjust, as I know others will also. And we'll pray really hard that your uncle will either be found or will return soon, and that this whole thing will get cleared up. Though you do have to realize that your Uncle Nick is not . . . well, let's just say he's not accustomed to family life. Even if this trouble with the sheriff blows over, the adjustment will no doubt be very difficult for him."

"What if he never shows up at all?" asked Zack, still sulking.

"Hmmm . . . yes, that is a problem." She folded her hands together and tapped her finger against her pursed lips. "But we must just hope that will work out somehow. And we certainly need to pray about it."

"Ma'am," I said shyly, "I believe in prayer, and Ma put a lot of stock in it. But I don't think I've quite got the hang of it, because it doesn't seem to work too well for me lately."

"Let's pray right now," she said.

"Here?" I always thought the most important praying had to be done in church. I didn't know what to make of the notion of praying right in some business office. What if someone came in and saw us?

"Here and now. Let's all join hands."

I didn't say anything more, and we all obeyed her.

"All right," Mrs. Parrish continued. "I'll do the talking, if you'd like. You can listen and learn. It only takes a bit of practice, and some faith too."

So she bowed her head, right there in that Mine and Freight Company office, and we did the same, and she prayed. Her words were simple, not much like the preacher's in Bridgeville, which were flowery and hard to follow. Mostly she prayed for Uncle Nick, that God would be with him right now no matter where he was, and work to soften his heart. I found myself wondering if God'd be with him even if he was in the Gold Nugget Saloon, but I didn't say it. She also prayed for us, using our names as if God knew and cared about each one of us.

It was an interesting prayer to listen to, and I thought it was the nicest I'd ever heard. I felt good after she was done, thinking that the minute we lifted our heads Uncle Nick would walk right through that door and take us home.

But he didn't.

CHAPTER 8

PICNIC IN THE WILDERNESS

The next day Mrs. Parrish took us on a picnic. It was a day I wasn't likely to forget.

I awoke early in the morning. The rain, which had been coming on and off, had stopped. The first thing I noticed, however, was that Emily was not in bed beside me.

I glanced around, and she was gone from the room. Thinking she'd gotten up and wandered to some other part of the house, I got out of bed as quietly as I could, dressed, and went to look for her. But she was nowhere in the house at all.

Finally, I went outside. I found her standing still, looking at the closed stable door.

"Emily," I said, walking to her, "is something the matter? You're up so early."

She turned and looked at me with a smile. "Oh, I'm just going to feed Snowball," she said.

"I'll go with you," I said. "It might still be a little dark inside the stable."

"No, thank you, Corrie," said Emily a little shyly. "But I'd rather go alone."

Still thinking she might be afraid in the stable by herself in the semi-dark, I started to object. But then I stopped. I could understand how she might want to be alone with her horse, even in a dark, strange stable. Snowball was the special friend Emily talked to when she was sad. We each had our own ways of trying to cope with missing Ma, and I knew Snowball helped Emily. So finally I reasoned that I just better leave the two of them alone for a spell.

I smiled, then helped her open the big stable door. Then I walked back toward the house. But at the last minute, I stopped and turned back to watch Emily disappear inside.

I couldn't help myself. Instead of going into the house, I softly crept toward the stable, then stopped and peeked through a crack in the door. I could see Emily with her horse.

In her hand Emily held the apple Mrs. Parrish had given her the night before at supper. She had saved it for her friend. She held it up to Snowball, whose big, white fleshy lips opened and took it from her, eating it in a single, quick bite.

"You know," I could hear Emily saying softly, "you look just like a big white snowball that came down from heaven one day in a cold snowstorm. I don't think Ma could have given you a more perfectly fittin' name, 'cause it's just like you."

She paused for a moment, then added, "I miss Ma, Snowball."

Her voice was sad, and thinking of Ma made her start to cry. But with only Snowball to see, she didn't seem to care about a few tears falling to the ground.

Snowball put her white chin on Emily's shoulder, as if she could sense the tender girl's feelings. Emily patted the wet nose lovingly.

"But you understand how I feel, don't you, Snowball?"

Snowball seemed to sway gently, as if she were saying, "Yes, I understand." I moved quickly away from the crack in the door. Suddenly it didn't seem right to intrude upon this special time between Emily and Snowball. Besides, if I watched any longer, I would start crying myself!

The sun came out gloriously a little while later. The sky was clear and blue, reminding me of an Indian summer back home.

At breakfast, Mrs. Parrish said the day was so fine she thought we ought to go on a picnic. She got no argument from us!

She had to go to her office for a while but I volunteered to fix lunch. By eleven o'clock, after the sun had a good chance to warm up everything, we all climbed into her wagon, a buckboard drawn by two of the finest-looking mules I'd ever seen.

"Could we take Snowball?" asked Emily as she got in. "She could pull your wagon real fine."

Mrs. Parrish laughed.

"I'm not so sure your Snowball would get along with either of my mules."

"We could take both Snowball and Jinx," persisted Emily.

"We'll do that next time, I promise," smiled Mrs. Parrish. "I wouldn't want to try out a new team I wasn't used to, and that wasn't used to me, especially with five children in the buckboard with me. Accidents do happen, you know."

Emily's disappointment was visible all over her face. "You really love your Snowball, don't you, dear?" said Mrs. Parrish.

"She eats apples right out of my hand, Ma'am," answered Emily, brightening.

"That's lovely. Maybe you could show me when we get back. There are some nice apples in the pantry."

Satisfied, Emily's spirits rose. Mrs. Parrish snapped the reins crisply and clicked her tongue in her cheek, and we were off.

We took a different road than the one into Miracle from Sacramento City. The terrain got more rugged and hilly, but Mrs. Parrish handled the team well. I could see that her mules were a better choice than our horses would have been.

We drove for about an hour. The country was so beautiful it made me tingle inside. We'd seen many grand sights in the last few months, but there was something about this land of California that made all the rest pale in my memory. Everything seemed bigger and richer and more alive. I could just imagine what it must be like in spring and summer.

Finally, Mrs. Parrish pulled the rig off the trail we'd been following. There was nothing that could rightly be called a *road* up there. In another minute we stopped, and we all bounded excitedly from the wagon, scattering in different directions trying to find the perfect place to settle. There was a small grove of old oak trees, a sparkling stream, and a clearing of soft grass where the afternoon warmth of the sun made me forget it had just rained the day before. We lugged a blanket or two and Mrs. Parrish's big basket over to the clearing. I helped Mrs. Parrish spread out the biggest blanket, though Becky kept bouncing all over it so we had to keep rearranging it.

"Becky," said Mrs. Parrish, smiling at her antics, "why don't you take this bucket and fetch us some water from the stream?"

Becky grabbed the bucket and flew down the little rise to the water. The rest of us then spread out the lunch.

We wanted to explore right away, especially the two boys and Becky. But we were hungry, too, so Mrs. Parrish suggested we eat a little first and then go exploring around the area, and then maybe finish our lunch afterward. So as soon as Becky got back with the bucket, which was only about half full, we sat down on the blanket. Mrs. Parrish said a blessing and then took to serving us out of the basket.

Something about eating outdoors made everything taste wonderful. It wasn't like eating on the dusty trail like we had hundreds of times in the last months. This was an official picnic, with a blanket and everything. I wish Ma could have been with us. She would have liked Mrs. Parrish.

By the time I'd finished my apple, the urge to wander and run about had disappeared. The warm sun felt so good on my face, and the fragrant earth, still moist and warming up from the sun, was sending out so many delicious, grassy smells that I thought this must be what heaven was like. Maybe Ma was up there right now, having a picnic of her own and watching us with a smile on her face.

Ma was on my mind a lot. Sometimes I'd come to myself and realize I'd been thinking a long while about something she'd said or something we'd done together. That happened on this day as we sat there and I was looking around at the woods and grass and trees and blue sky and clouds. Ma wasn't really one to talk about God all that much, not like Mrs. Parrish did. But every once in a while something would kinda burst right out of her, and now that she was gone, every once in a while I'd remember something like that she said.

It was so quiet and peaceful sitting there, I realled a time Ma and I were out walking alone together back home. It was a day just like this one—warm, with nice smells, the grass springy under our feet. It was just the two of us, and Ma had her arm around me, and we weren't really saying much.

Then all at once Ma exclaimed, "It's a beautiful place, airn't it, Corrie—this world God made!"

"It sure is, Ma," I said.

"An' don't you ever forget, Corrie, that God's your father too. And you don't need to worry none about not havin' an earthly pa. 'Cause God'll watch over you all the better for that."

"Yes, Ma," I said, though it's only now, with her gone, that I'm starting to realize what she meant.

"This great big beautiful place, it's your Father's world, Corrie, and you're *His* daughter too, not just mine. And this world's your home wherever you go in it. Always remember that, Corrie, 'cause you won't always have me."

Her words hardly stuck in my mind then, but they turned out to happen sooner than she figured. And now as we sat there with Mrs. Parrish it all came back clear as if it'd happened yesterday. And I looked around again and thought about what Ma'd said, *"It's your Father's world, Corrie, and you're His daughter . . ."* And the memory made me feel a little more at home in this strange place, just like Ma said I should.

I suppose the others were thinking thoughts of their own too, 'cause we all just kept lying there relaxed and cozy in the sun, listening to Mrs. Parrish tell us so many interesting things. She told us what it had been like right after the gold rush broke out, and we were full of questions. It's a wonder she didn't get sick of us! After a while, I saw even Zack starting to warm up to her and smile a time or two. She and Captain Dixon were like a ma and pa to us for a spell, at a time when we really needed them. I'll never forget what they did for us. People can be mean and selfish, I don't doubt. But then people can be nice sometimes, too, and when they are, it sure makes the world a better place. I just hope when I grow up, I can be that way to somebody who needs it— kind and understanding like Mrs. Parrish was to us.

She must have answered a thousand questions, then gradually we began asking about her. She and her husband got here early in 1849, almost with the first group of immigrants from the East. She said her husband had been having itchy feet for a new adventure for some time, and that the minute news of the gold strike broke in the East he was talking about the opportunities to be had.

"Why, I was practically packing up our things the next week!" she said with a laugh. "I knew from the very start that he'd have to go. It was in his blood from the first instant," she added, and a faraway look came into her eyes, as if she was having to fight away some tears that the memory brought. I knew the feeling, because I had it almost every night when I was alone and awake after the young'uns were asleep. I'd think of Ma, and it would come over me again that she was really gone and wasn't ever coming back. I knew the kind of pain Mrs. Parrish felt and so I asked no more questions about her husband.

"Men are that way, you know," she said after a little pause, looking at Zack and Tad with a different kind of smile. "Sometimes there are things they just have to do, and there's no use trying to stop them. Conquering something new . . . bold . . . adventurous—it's part of the way God made men."

She took a deep breath, and glanced away, probably trying to push back the memory, and then looked back with a fresh smile on her face, just as Tad asked:

"Did you and your pa come on a wagon too, Miz Parrish?"

She laughed. "No, honey, we came in a ship around Cape Horn. But I came with my husband, not my pa. Do you know where Cape Horn is?"

Tad shook his head. I didn't know exactly where it was either, but Ma always said it was a way only the rich could afford.

"Cape Horn is at the very bottom of South America," Mrs. Parrish went on. "We got on a ship in New York and sailed all the way down the coast of the United States, through the Caribbean, down past Brazil and Argentina and the rest of South America, around the Cape, and then up the other side, past Peru and Panama, then Mexico, and finally here to California and San Francisco."

"Wow!" exclaimed Tad. "That musta taken years!"

She laughed pleasantly again. "No, Tad, but several months."

Mrs. Parrish never said much about her life in Boston, but she must have been rich. The only thing she said was that she was one of only a handful of women in California in 1849, and that she had to forget her genteel Boston ways mighty quickly.

"Mining was hard work back then," she said. "It still is, of course, but methods were so primitive at first. That's why we wanted to bring in newer and better equipment for the men to use."

"Did you mine for gold, Mrs. Parrish?" asked Emily.

"I didn't much myself," she answered, "though I tried my hand at the pan a few times and helped my husband with the sluice box. We were mostly here to set up the business, but Mr. Parrish couldn't keep from trying his hand at anything that struck his fancy. We made a pretty good strike, too, that first spring after we were here. But then he came down with tuberculosis the next winter and couldn't keep up with the work. That's when we decided to get into the freight business to go along with selling supplies. 'If we can't get it out of the ground, Almeda,' I remember him saying to me, 'then we'll haul it over the ground for those that do. We'll sell them the equipment to mine with, let them do all the hard work, then transport it once they're done. It's an ingenious scheme!' And it was, too. I've made a good living these three years. I'm only sorry my husband couldn't have lived to see his scheme, as he called it, materialize.''

Again that faraway look came over her face, and she looked away.

After a few more questions we started talking about the town. She told us that two years ago Miracle had a population of over two thousand.

"It was mostly men, and almost every one of them a miner with a dream of getting rich in a month or two. Most of them didn't live right in town, of course, but on their claims in the surrounding foothills, in shacks and cabins and whatever they could throw together. They weren't concerned with their living quarters, only their search for gold. But after a winter or two, with most of the men working eighteen- and twenty-hour days, and not finding the riches they dreamed of, a good many left. There's probably only a thousand or so left around Miracle now. There's still gold here, and the town's still one of the active ones in the foothills, but only a few really find much.''

We'd been so absorbed in everything Mrs. Parrish was saying that we didn't even notice when Becky wandered away. Mrs. Parrish had been telling of a fellow who had come from the East with a box of "California Gold Grease," expecting to rub it all over his body and roll down a golden hill while a fortune stuck to his skin. Zack laughed and was about to tell Becky, who was always getting into a pile of dirt, that that kind of gold mining would suit her, when we suddenly realized she wasn't there.

We looked around nearby, but she was nowhere in sight and none of us had any idea when she'd slipped away. Usually Becky's presence was plainly noticed by everyone. But I recalled Ma saying more than once that when Becky got quiet, trouble was brewing. We called and yelled, but all our shrieks brought no response.

Mrs. Parrish told me to stay with Tad and Emily while she and Zack went to go search in the woods. The little clearing, surrounded by trees and that wonderful stream, had seemed so inviting an hour earlier. Now all of a sudden it appeared dim and dangerous. This country was not like the little wood at the edge of our farm near Bridgeville. This was the frontier, the wild West, vast and unexplored.

Then my mind started thinking about Indians. The Indians around here were supposed to be friendly, but my imagination immediately conjured up images of the Sioux, Comanche and Apache we'd heard so many awful stories about coming across the plains.

But I wasn't as worried about Indians as I was about cliffs and gulleys and rock slides and deep pools in the streams. Becky might get herself into any kind of danger, even as tough and brave as she was, in this rough, foothills country.

In the distance, the calls of my brother and Mrs. Parrish floated through the air unanswered. Growing afraid, sensitive Emily wrapped her arms tight around me and Tad snuggled close.

About half an hour passed, and Zack and Mrs. Parrish's beckoning voices grew dimmer and dimmer as they went farther from the clearing. I wanted to get up and go help them, but I knew I had to stay with the youngsters. Just when I thought I could stand the uncertainty no longer, off in the distance I saw a man on a horse approaching.

I hardly had time to know whether to be glad or afraid, because when the rider got a little closer, I saw that it was none other than Uncle Nick's partner, Mr. Drum.

He rode into the clearing, sitting proud in the saddle, so sure of himself.

"What's going on here?" he asked in a gruff tone that made me tremble a little inside.

"We came for a picnic with Mrs. Parrish," I answered timidly, just staring up at him. He looked about ten feet tall from where the three of us still sat on the ground. "But Becky's gone and got lost."

"A picnic . . . in these parts?" he half-exclaimed, shaking his head grimly. "Blasted woman! Where are they lookin'?"

I pointed to where I had last seen Zack and Mrs. Parrish. Without another word, he wheeled his bay mare off in the opposite direction. I couldn't tell from the look of annoyance on his face if he was going to join the search or was fed up with the lot of us and had taken off again—this time for good.

More time passed. Pretty soon, as the quiet around us seemed to get deeper and more eerie, I started to think maybe Zack and Mrs. Parrish had gotten lost, too. I had no such worry about Mr. Drum. Finally Zack came trudging out of the brush all covered with dirt, followed in another minute or two by Mrs. Parrish, who looked especially dismal. She knew better than any of us what getting lost in this country could mean.

I told them Mr. Drum had come, but neither of them seemed too excited. Maybe they had no hope he would take up the search. But I tried to keep faith. And when I saw the bay mare nose its way through the bushes, I couldn't help grinning real big. There was Becky perched up on the saddle in front of Mr. Drum, his strong arm around her chubby frame.

"This who you're lookin' for?" he said, reining in his

horse. He then lifted Becky out of the saddle as if she weighed no more than a feather and set her down. He was looking very stern, his mood made all the worse by the delighted look on Becky's face. She didn't seem the least remorseful for all the stir she had caused.

"We were at our wits' end, Mr. Drum," said Mrs. Parrish in a more helpless tone than I had yet heard from her. "It is providential that you came by when you did."

"Providential's what you call it, is it?" he replied in a tone full of meaning that went far beyond my years.

Mrs. Parrish just looked at him and wrinkled her brow, as if she didn't have any notion of what he was talking about. "What do you mean?"

"You're sayin' it's just pure coincidence that you came up this way?"

"I assure you, we were just out for a picnic."

"And you didn't know me and Nick's claim was up here?"

"I have no idea where your claim is."

"Is that so, Mrs. Parrish?" he said suspiciously. "Why, I'm real surprised that a woman of your moral and religious reputation would stoop to lies, especially in front of children."

He might have been riled, but I also thought maybe he enjoyed putting Mrs. Parrish on the spot. The two of them didn't seem to like each other much.

She looked down at the ground, pink flushing her cheeks. I couldn't tell at first if she was angry, and about to shout something back at Mr. Drum about his nerve at making such an accusation, or if maybe she was embarrassed at what he'd said. I guess I would never really know. At least she didn't yell at him.

"Well," she said after a moment, "I don't know *exactly* where your claim is."

He continued to nod skeptically.

"And even if perhaps I did hope to encounter you or that missing partner of yours," she added, the heat rising in her voice, "it was a precious small hope that I would discover any help for these poor children from that quarter!"

Mr. Drum opened his mouth to reply—a response which was bound not to be too nice, because what she said made him mad. But before he could, their conversation was interrupted by Tad's voice.

"Did Uncle Nick come home yet?" he asked, "Are you here to take us to his house?" It was an awfully bold question from such a high-pitched voice. I wish I could have taken it back for him.

"Now look, I ain't—" Mr. Drum began. Then he stopped and got down off his horse. Slowly he walked toward Tad, then knelt down beside him on one knee. Tad's eyes were huge as he watched the man approach.

"Look, boy," he said softly. "I'm doing everything I can to find your uncle. I rode clean out to Soda Springs yesterday, but he wasn't there. Tomorrow, I'm going to get up before sunrise and ride down to Gold Run, Yankee Jim's, Coloma, Shingle Springs, and Placerville. And if I still ain't found him, I may go out to Grizzly Flats. Them's all places he sometimes gets a hankering to see. But until I can find him, there just ain't much more—"

Mrs. Parrish's voice interrupted him before he could go any further. "I have to leave morning after next myself," she said, first to him and then with an apologetic glance at me. "I was trying to find the right time to tell you."

She paused, then looked back at Mr. Drum. "These children need a guardian, Mr. Drum. Today's near mishap is further evidence of that."

He rose and walked back toward his horse.

"Wouldn't have happened at all if you hadn't got the fool idea of bringing them out into this wilderness!" he retorted.

"Be that as it may, the fact remains that in another place, in New York where they came from, they might possibly have been able to fend for themselves. But such cannot be expected of them in this land. And I'm afraid their claim to an interest in the stake you and your partner, their uncle, share, binds their fate inextricably to yours—whether you find Mr. Matthews or not."

"You just don't understand, Mrs. Parrish." He was not arguing now. In fact his voice sounded almost contrite, pleading. The large, tough-looking man seemed to be struggling with some feeling inside which he wanted to keep from showing anyone.

"I do not know you well, Mr. Drum," said Mrs. Parrish. "You have been an enigma in these parts ever since you and Matthews came, so folks tell me. But one fact has always come through as part of what people say about you—your reputation, as I believe men call it. And that fact is that you are a man of honor. I simply cannot believe that you would be so derelict in your duty as not to step in if their uncle cannot be found. These children must not be left unprotected."

"It won't do them no good to have a man—especially one like me—carin' for them."

"I disagree," said Mrs. Parrish firmly. "In this country, I might even go so far as to say they need the care of a man *more* than a woman."

"I'm sorry, Ma'am; I just don't see it your way. They need a ma right now, and since they ain't got one—" His voice seemed to quiver momentarily. "Then I figure they need a woman, and you seem to be *it*. If you ask me, Ma'am, it's you who's hidin' from your duty to the kids. And besides, like I said before, you don't understand nothin' about me, and I'll thank you to keep your nose outta tryin'."

He turned and swiftly mounted his horse, and that was the end of their talk. I almost felt like the man was hiding something, and that if he kept talking one minute more he might . . . but that's plumb silly! Grown-ups, tough men like him, don't cry.

He glanced around at each one of us kids, with a look that said he hoped we might understand, even if she didn't, then dug his heels into the bay's flanks and was off.

CHAPTER 9

A SURPRISE FOR US ALL

Two days after the picnic, we got more than one surprise. The first came when Mrs. Parrish called us for breakfast.

I honestly couldn't tell if she was the same lady—except for her feminine figure, I might have even thought she was a man. She had on well-worn buckskin breeches, and a tan leather jacket with long fringe on the bottom and sleeves. On her feet she wore a pair of high leather boots. And when breakfast was over, she grabbed a dusty, wide-brimmed hat, a pair of heavy gloves, and led us outside.

We walked with her down to the freight office, and waited while she brought one of the empty wagons around. She had already gone over everything with us at her house, what we were to do while she was gone. Now we just waited to say goodbye.

When she came around the corner of the building, driving that team of mules with the reins in her hands, something inside me swelled up—pleasure, maybe, at something so rugged and western. Maybe it was just that she was a woman, like I might be someday. I don't know. But it made me feel proud to see her perched up there on the seat of that wagon, calling out orders to them mules and swinging them into line, looking just as natural as she did behind one of her fine Chippendale tables or at her desk in the freight office. She was a fine-looking, strong woman, who seemed able to do most anything.

75

She jumped down off the wagon and gathered us children around her. "You know," she said gently and apologetically, "I wouldn't go today if I didn't have to. But this is the last big supply run before winter sets in, and I must take all three wagons." She was back to talking in her soft Boston voice, and coming from a buckskin-dressed woman, looking fit for riding on the range, it did seem a mite unusual.

"I will be gone at least two weeks, maybe more. But as I said, I want you to make yourselves at home in my house. Mrs. Gianini will look in on you from time to time. I wish I didn't have to leave you, but—"

Before she could finish her sentence, the sound of approaching hoofbeats made us all abruptly turn our heads. Mr. Drum, on his bay mare, half-skidded to a stop right there in front of the freight office, followed by a big cloud of dust from the street.

He jumped off his horse and strode up to us. He looked around quickly, then stared right at me for a second. His eyes seemed to be swimming in tears. As I returned his gaze, suddenly something inside my brain seemed to dawn, and all at once I realized I *knew* those eyes staring at mine! In an instant, all the funny little questions that had been nagging me the last couple of days started to fit together. At the same time, I told myself it couldn't possibly be!

There wasn't time to reflect on it, however. Just as quickly, he looked away from me, placed his hands on his hips, and spoke in a voice that was resolved, even if he had difficulty saying what he intended.

"I've come for the kids," he said.

"Did you find Uncle Nick?" asked Tad excitedly, having no idea what was happening.

"No, boy, I didn't find your uncle," he replied. "But I don't figure that matters none now."

"What do you mean, Mr. Drum?" asked Mrs. Parrish, surprised as any of us.

"Just that, Ma'am," he said. "You see . . . my name ain't Drum—well, not exactly, that is."

"I'm afraid I don't understand," she answered. "Nor do I see what this has to do with the children."

"Perhaps if I could just have a word in private with you, Ma'am," he said.

She nodded, saying nothing, and he followed her into the office. The four younger children watched with bewildered eyes. But I knew what he was telling her. I should have known from the first. My heart was beating wildly now!

When they came back a minute or two later, Mrs. Parrish had a handkerchief in her hand, which she used to dab at her eyes every so often. She was the first one to speak.

"I have some very wonderful news to tell you all," she began. Her voice was soft and husky. Then she turned to Drum and said, "But I think you should be the one to tell them your real name."

The man stepped forward, cleared his throat awkwardly, then stumbling over the words, began, "You see, kids, when I came here, I was in a heap of trouble, like your uncle is now. So I didn't want folks to know who I really was. I changed my name a little, and let the rumor get out that I was dead, so the men looking for me would stop trying to hunt me down. But like I told Mrs. Parrish, Drum's not my name—well, not my last name, anyway. More like a nickname, you might say, which I let folks *think* was my last name. Really it's my first name—Drummond. . . ."

Even before the word was out of his mouth I found myself moving toward him, tears blurring my eyes. I reached his side and slowly put my arm around his great big waist, hardly hearing the rest of what he said to the other kids.

"Drummond, that's my name . . . Drummond Hollister. You see, kids, I'm your pa, and I ain't dead at all."

CHAPTER 10

ANOTHER WAGON RIDE

The ride out to the claim was almost eerily quiet. Nobody said a word till we were over halfway there, and Pa seemed content to let it be that way, looking straight ahead and holding the reins in his hands.

He and Marcus Weber had hitched up Snowball and Jinx to our wagon, and before we knew it we were sitting there again, as we had for most of the last six months, riding out of Miracle Springs with none other than our own pa sitting on the bench driving, his bay mare following along behind. It was sure some sudden change.

I knew Becky, Emily, and Tad were probably more bewildered than anything. They'd all been too young even to remember Pa. After all, he left even before Tad was born. But I figured Zack remembered him. He'd have been around four or five, and I knew his silence wasn't just from the bewilderment of the sudden turn of events. Even though Ma had never bad-mouthed Pa, the harshness of her life—all our lives—after he left spoke for itself. Zack and I were old enough to feel hurt and even angry sometimes.

It didn't help that Grandpa Belle never had a good word to say about Pa, and even at times seemed to go out of his way to speak ill of Pa in our hearing. Zack thought a lot of Grandpa—a boy needs a man around, and Grandpa was all Zack had. So I had a feeling some of Grandpa's words were going around in Zack's mind. I could tell he was struggling with just how he was supposed to feel about this man who was his pa, but who had left him when he needed him most, like Grandpa used to tell him. Maybe some of the same things were going through Pa's mind too.

As for me, now that we were all there in the wagon together and I had a chance to think, I could hardly believe I didn't recognize Pa right away. The beard changed his looks considerably, of course, and the hat. But you'd have thought I'd have known the eyes and voice right off.

Funny, though, how the mind plays tricks on you. Maybe some part of me, way deep down inside someplace, *did* remember the voice. And I noticed his eyes the first time he walked out of that saloon. But another part of the mind can block out the memory altogether. The feeling of pain comes back, the hurt of the loss, and wipes out the memory. "It's God's mercy you kids is young," Ma used to say, "You'll forget your pa soon enough, and his being gone will be easier on you."

But Ma never could forget Pa, and I don't doubt her pain was awful. She hardly ever said anything against Pa and even tried to hush Grandpa when he'd get started. There were times when she did flare up about Pa though, like when Tad was a baby—colicky and crying, and chores needed to be done, and us older kids were bickering or whining over some little thing. Or when some snooty neighbor would make some careless remark about us being abandoned. Then she'd come close to blaming him for everything, but I think it was just her way of hiding the shame and hurt she felt at being left alone. With all that, I know she never stopped loving him. Her words on the day she died seemed to prove that, though I guess I never heard her say it too often.

We all sat there quietly, bouncing along the dirt road, Pa encouraging the horses along every now and then with a slap of the reins. Zack and I sat on each side of him, staring straight ahead, and the three little ones dozed in the bed of the wagon. Here we were—orphaned less than two months ago, left alone on the streets of Miracle Springs with no one wanting to take us in, handed around from one place and one person to the next—from Captain Dixon to Miss Baxter, to Mrs. Gianini, to Mrs. Parrish, and now all of a sudden here we were sitting in our *own* wagon again with our very own pa! You'd have thought we'd have all been shouting and laughing with joy. But we all sat silent and somber. I guess it didn't feel so much different than if he had been a stranger sitting there. There would probably have been more talking if it *had* been Captain Dixon. We certainly knew him better than this strange man called Drummond Hollister. All we knew about him was what Ma had told us—which was very little—and what Grandpa Belle had said, which was more than we wanted to hear.

"I'm real sorry about your ma," Pa said, breaking the silence abruptly.

An awkward moment or two followed. No one said anything.

"How'd it happen?" he asked, still staring out over the horses' heads.

"Fever," I said, "out in the desert."

"She broke her ankle, Mr. Drum," piped up Becky from behind.

He started to answer her, thought better of it, and kept it in. I didn't know whether to correct her or not, but I kept quiet too. Zack was stone-faced. He didn't seem to like Pa at all.

We rode on for another ten minutes or so. Then all at once, without even planning it, I heard my own voice: "Why didn't you tell us who you were right off, sir?" I blurted out. "Why'd you say you didn't want us?"

The words sounded bold in my own ears. Probably the way they really came out was soft and sheepish. And even though Pa just kept staring straight ahead, I could tell he'd heard me and was thinking hard.

"Well . . . Cornelia," he hesitated at my name. I think it was uncomfortable for him to say it for the first time, but I liked hearing him say it.

" . . . is that still what they call you?" he asked after a pause.

"Folks started calling me Corrie, sir," I answered. "I guess it was after you . . . left."

I thought I saw Pa wince, but with the beard it was hard to tell.

"Well . . . Corrie," he said, "when Dixon came into the Gold Nugget sayin' something about a bunch of kids looking for a fellow named Matthews, I didn't pay much heed. For all I knew, he mighta been one of the sheriff's men tryin' to get an angle on Nick. An the game was mighty hot, so the boys shut him up real quick. But then that Parrish woman barged in like she did, upsettin' everything, and insistin' I come out and do something about them—you kids, that is, . . . well, it kinda caught me off guard."

He stopped and a questioning look came over his face.

"How'd your ma ever find out about Nick?" he asked.

"A fellow from Bridgeville came back from California and told her he'd seen Uncle Nick and that he was using a different name."

Pa shook his head. "Nick never said nothin' to me—the blamed fool! He's determined to get the both of us strung up yet!"

"But," I said—maybe I was being forward, but I still had my questions—"after you came out and saw it was us, why didn't you say anything right then?"

" 'Cause it was a shock to see you standin' there," he said matter-of-factly. "And besides, hearin' about your ma's dying, just then—well, it sort of—"

He stopped again.

"You must know what I mean," he half-blurted out after a moment. "She was my wife, you know . . . mother to my kids. It weren't none too pleasant to hear out of the blue that she was dead."

I couldn't help wondering why it took him all this time to start having feelings of affection for Ma and the rest of us. It didn't seem to me that he'd have cared one way or the other about her dying. Maybe I was being too hard on him. But maybe I had more hurt in me than I realized, too. I couldn't see how Ma could have been so forgiving of him. It just didn't make much sense to me what he was saying.

"You still could have told us who you were," I said.

"It just ain't that simple," he said. "I had lots of things on my mind."

"Things more important than us?"

"Things kids can't understand. I had to have some time to think."

"But we had no place to go, and you said you wouldn't take us!" I was afraid I was going to start crying any minute. I should have stopped, and I knew he had every right to box me if I went on, but I just couldn't stop the words from pouring out. As I remembered all he'd said outside the saloon just three days ago, I felt more and more hurt by what he'd done.

"I know . . . and I'm sorry about that," he said, his voice *sounding* earnest enough. "But I had to try to find Nick and see what he knew about all this; I had to look out for him—the blasted idiot! Don't you see? I had to talk to him before I could say anythin' out in public."

I guess I *didn't* see, but I kept my mouth shut. Even though part of me was wanting to break out and give Pa a bunch of hugs and kisses, another part of me—maybe the part of Grandpa in me—was riled and hurt. And I just couldn't get the two parts to agree on what to do.

"The men were all listenin' . . . and they all think I'm Drum. And I gotta keep it that way! For your good as well as my own . . . and Nick's."

"Did you find Uncle Nick?" I asked softly, after another minute.

Pa sighed. "No, he ain't nowhere anybody's seen him,"

he said. "On top of everything, now he's gone and got himself in trouble with the sheriff *here*, as if we didn't have trouble enough already! And now with the five of you showin' up outta nowhere, and with someone back East who can identify him . . . I don't know what we're gonna do. He may have brung us a pack of trouble!"

He gave the reins a little flick of his wrist and coaxed the horses over a patch of bumpy ground.

I decided it was best for me to keep my thoughts to myself for a while. For the life of me I couldn't figure why any of what he said made it right for him to ignore us, and not let on he was our pa. I didn't see how it made it right for him to leave Ma and us alone all those years either, or to let us think he was dead.

The clicking of his tongue, the groaning sounds of leather and wood, and the jostling wagon wheels filled in the silence. We certainly weren't off to the joyful kind of start you'd expect from such a family reunion. Ma had been our family, and with her gone we really didn't have one anymore. Pa had never really been part of our family. When he left, he cut himself off from us. Whatever that meant to us kids, it hurt Ma real bad. And I didn't see how we were going to be able to forget it that easily. He may have been our pa, but that still didn't make him part of our family.

I guess Zack must have been thinking some similar sorts of things, 'cause all at once he blurted out, and didn't even try to hide the resentment in his voice: "You still ain't told us why you deserted us and left me with no pa!"

I could see Pa's eyes wince at Zack's blunt question—I couldn't tell whether from exasperation or real pain. He drew in a deep breath, resignation building on his face, and then, without turning his head, replied, "You don't understand how it was at all, boy," he said. "There just ain't no way you can understand!"

He picked up the whip and flipped it. The leather thong at the end of the line gave a sharp crack as it slapped against Snowball's rump. The horse jumped into a trot.

CHAPTER 11

OUR NEW HOME

Pa and Uncle Nick had a cabin on their claim, less than a mile from the clearing where Becky had gotten herself lost. Once we got there, I could see why Pa had gotten so vexed with Mrs. Parrish. I wondered if it *was* an accident we'd had our picnic right there.

The cabin was small and dirty. If Ma had seen it, not knowing it was Pa's, she'd have either called it rustic or just a shack—depending on what kind of mood she was in. I didn't want to say anything negative right away, but after spending two days at Mrs. Parrish's, I suppose our faces showed our disappointment once we were all crowded inside.

"It ain't much, I admit," said Pa. "But Nick and I didn't build it with five kids in mind. I'll add a room on in the mornin'," he said matter-of-factly, like it was nothing.

At least it sounded hopeful. In fact, he decided that since it was still early in the day, he'd go right out and start cutting some timber. He told me to bring our stuff inside and take care of the young'uns, and then turned to Zack. "Let's go . . . Zachary."

Zack glanced toward me, and I nodded for him to go along.

"You got a nickname like your sister, boy? What do folks in a hurry call you?"

"Just Zack, sir."

"That's always what I figured to call you when you got bigger. Well, Zack, you're pretty big now, I reckon, so you grab that axe there and come with me."

Zack had been completely quiet since his outburst on the wagon. I'm not sure if Pa was trying to be nice by taking him. But at his age, there was nothing Zack wanted more than to be treated like a man. So even though I could still see the silent anger on his face, I knew he was pleased.

"You keep them young'uns outta the creek and away from the mine," he sternly admonished me, and then he tramped off into the woods, with Zack hurrying to keep up.

Emily and I, with a little help from Becky and none at all from Tad, spent the day cleaning and trying to make a place where the five of us could sleep. We had our sleeping gear out in the wagon, but finding a place to bed down, especially as disorderly as everything was, became a chore. I'd never seen a place so in need of cleaning as that one-room cabin!

By sundown we had the house as close to shining as a bare-wood cabin can get, with a pot of beans bubbling over the open fire in a big black pot. I even got a tablecloth from Ma's things to put on the coarse board table set in the middle of the floor. Becky completed the look of civilization with a bowl of wild flowers. I'd been so busy I didn't see her slip away. I didn't ask how far she'd gone or where she'd gotten them. But at least she hadn't gotten lost this time. I gave her a big hug and smiled at her. I could tell the flowers were her way of trying to make Pa glad we were there. All of us were a little scared I think, still not knowing if Pa was going to be mean or nice to us. All we really knew of him was what Ma had said, but we couldn't help wanting to make him like us.

When Pa walked through the door, I tried to read the reaction on his face. I had already begun to figure out that he wasn't likely to say what he felt in so many words.

He glanced at the flowers, turned toward the fireplace to smell the beans, then set his gaze on me.

"What have you gone and done with my place?" he said, his voice sounding gruff. Then I caught the faint spark of fun in his eyes. When I didn't respond, a smile broke on his lips—just a tiny one. "Why, I'd grown right attached to all the dirt and clutter around here!"

"I hoped it would be all right if we cleaned up some," I answered finally, swelling with pride inside. Somehow I could tell he was pleased.

"Guess I'll have to learn to live with it," he answered, the smile gone now.

Zack followed him in, then Pa set his rifle in a corner and unbuckled his gun belt. It was the first time I'd noticed that he wore a gun. He slung the holster on a hook by the door, then strode over toward the fire, took a closer look at the beans, and nodded in approval.

"Looks like your ma made a right good cook outta you, too," he said. " 'Course I guess you been doing the mothering yourself since . . . Aggie died."

I nodded. I'd never heard anyone call Ma that before.

"Let's see, Corrie you'd be what—hmmm . . . fourteen? No, fifteen?"

"Fifteen," I said.

"I ain't likely to forget that winter of '37. Coldest dang January I can ever remember, and your ma swellin' up real big carryin' you. I cut up more logs that month to feed that fire and keep her warm. . . . No, I ain't likely to forget that!"

We all stood there kind of aimless and awkward, wondering what to do.

"Well," said Pa finally, breaking the silence, "what about supper?"

He helped us get everything on the table. We had to go out to the wagon for some bowls and utensils, because I hadn't gotten everything unloaded. Then we all sat down to eat. Pa didn't say a prayer, he just started eating. So we all did the same. No one said much. We just ate quietly, staring into our bowls of beans and munching at my attempt at cornbread. It wasn't too good. I'd have to get used to cooking over Pa and Uncle Nick's fireplace.

We were about halfway through our meal, when all of a sudden Pa noticed the tablecloth. He put down his spoon deliberately, and took the edge of the white linen between his fingers, rubbing it gently. Then he spoke—his voice sounded soft and faraway—"The minister's wife back in Bridgeville gave this to your ma the day we was married. It was always real special to her 'cause it was nicer than anything we could ever afford."

We just listened in silence. It was hard to know what to say at times like that. One minute Pa would seem real friendly, then the next he'd get that gruff look again that seemed to say, "Get outta my way!" It was going to be a while before I knew how to respond to either of his two sides.

When we were done with the meal, I took the two girls with me outside to wash up the dishes. There was no water pump, only a crude table with a couple of buckets on top of it, filled with water from the creek.

When we went back inside, Pa was sitting on a stool oiling and cleaning his gun. There weren't any chairs, only two stools and the bench we kids had sat on while we ate. Tad was sitting in a corner silently watching Pa. Zack busied himself poking at the fire, and then finally laid on another log. We three girls just sat on the bench and folded our hands in our laps.

We were all tired, and would have liked to have gone to bed, but I didn't want to say anything. We were all going to have to sleep in that one room together.

Tad finally got up, walked over to Pa, and as bold as you please said, "I have to go to the outhouse."

Pa looked up with a blank expression, then glanced from me to Zack.

"We have an outhouse back home," said Zack.

"Guess I'll have to build that tomorrow too," Pa muttered. "Well, Zack, take your brother out to the woods."

"I'm big enough to go by myself," Tad insisted. But when he opened the door and stared out into the night, he hesitated.

"You afraid of the dark, boy?" asked Pa, a bit roughly.

"No . . . sir," stammered Tad. "I ain't afraid of nothin'."

"Well boy, you'd better learn a thing or two about California," said Pa. "Why there's wolves out there, and bears, and . . ." He winked in my direction, but Tad didn't catch the humor.

"Really?" Tad whispered seriously.

"Yep. Didn't your ma tell you? We Californians gotta be tough."

Tad cleared his throat nervously, "Could *you* take me out?" he asked.

Pa's expression changed. This was not what he expected. No doubt he would have preferred taking his rifle and going outside to face one of his imaginary bears. But with resolve, at last he laid down the gun he had been cleaning, got to his feet, and, glancing around kind of helplessly, headed for the door.

When they returned about five minutes later, Pa's only words were, "It's time to be bedding down."

I think he'd had enough of his kids for one day.

CHAPTER 12

THE FIRST FEW DAYS TOGETHER

After that first awkward day, we were kept too busy to worry much about how strange we felt about everything. We tried to get the place livable, and Pa kept talking about winter coming on and all we had to do.

Some men came from town on the third day, and helped with the building of the extra room. It wasn't very big, but it fit us kids fine. There were five beds—two bunks, one for the girls, one for the boys, and a single bed for me. We each had our own place to sleep, and we hadn't even had that back home.

Pa built a bigger supper table, too, with sturdy benches on both sides. After being cooped up in a covered wagon for so long, all these changes were heaven to us. Pa kept muttering little comments about "making do till winter's past" and that he'd "have to see about things when Nick gets back." As much as I didn't want to think so, it almost sounded like he was planning on our being there only temporarily, until he could find some reasonable way to send us back home. But then it did seem that he was going to an awful lot of trouble just to put up with us for a few months. I had to try to be happy for the present and not think too much about the disappointments that might come later.

On the fourth day, Pa took the canvas canopy off our

wagon, and took it into town for supplies.

"Bye, Snowball," Emily called out after him as he disappeared down the road; then she and I turned back toward the cabin to join the others. It was a strange moment, but pleasant in a homey way, walking up to a cabin we'd laid eyes on only a few days before, all alone now, with our Pa trusting us to stay by ourselves.

Late that same afternoon he returned with that big wagon loaded down. We ran out to meet him rumbling up the road, and when he stopped, Zack and Becky clambered up into the wagon. There were straw mattresses for all the beds, and lots of extra blankets. We had been sleeping on the rough, cold boards with our ragged, moth-eaten blankets from the trip west.

But that wasn't all! Besides the bedding, he had dishes and some pots and pans. The equipment I had been using from the wagon was old, charred, and broken. To my delight, there was also a small pot-bellied stove and two new chairs! It was just like Christmas unloading all the new things! All the while Pa kept a gruff look on his face, and kept saying things like, "Now you be careful with that!"

But even with those new chairs and benches, new beds and dishes and all that stuff, it seemed to me that there was something missing. When I closed my eyes, I could still see us as a family back home. But Ma was in the picture in my mind, instead of Pa. Maybe she was sitting by the fire sewing, or reading a book to us, or maybe we were all singing hymns together. Sometimes we didn't even say much, just sitting there listening to Ma's rocker creak back and forth, or lying in bed hearing her humming softly to herself until we fell asleep.

But when I opened my eyes, everything was strange and new. Ma wasn't there, and Pa sat fixing a harness, sharpening a tool, or cutting a piece of leather for something. Everything was quiet. There was no singing, no humming. Just quiet. I was pleased with what Pa had done, but there's something about a ma that can't be replaced by any man, even your own pa. And it seemed as we sat around in the cabin that we just weren't a real family, even with all the homey new things Pa had brought back from town.

Besides all the stuff that was in the wagon, Pa brought with him the old prospector we'd met at the General Store, Alkali Jones. He helped Pa and Zack and me unload. For such an old man he was strong enough, but I guessed from the look of him that he was tough. Tough like an old buzzard. And his voice did nothing to make the similarity in my mind go away.

He was a peculiar fellow. An ornery old cuss, folks called him. After a while I got kind of used to the creak of his voice and that cackling laugh. I had plenty of practice. Everything seemed to amuse him.

After the wagon was unloaded, the girls and I busied ourselves getting dinner. In the several days we'd been there, Pa'd never given us many chores or jobs. Every once in a while he'd tell Zack to bring in some firewood, and the night before he said, "Best be getting some dinner started for the young'uns, Cornelia." I guess he was so used to living alone that he figured we'd all know what to do. He never seemed to realize that except for me and Zack, the kids were young and needed a lot of tending. I guess he figured I'd do all that, too. I had done it, after all, since Ma died.

Tad traipsed along with Zack to cut up some firewood. Pa and Mr. Jones went into our bedroom to finish up the beds, so we could use them that night. I went to fetch some of the new pans that were sitting in a box over on the side of the cabin where they were working, and I overheard Pa and Mr. Jones talking. I knew eavesdropping wasn't proper, but I couldn't help myself. Besides, their voices were so loud that I likely would have heard anyway.

"You make a new strike or somethin', Drum?" asked Mr. Jones.

Pa told us not to call him *Pa* when Mr. Jones or anyone

else was around. When Becky asked why, he just said he'd have to talk to Uncle Nick first to see what they ought to do. I didn't know what Uncle Nick had to do with it, but Pa seemed to have some pretty strong reasons for still wanting folks in town to think he was Mr. Drum. But whatever they were, he wasn't telling us.

"Why you askin'?" said Pa.

"You practically bought out the General Store. Hee, hee! Where'd you get money like that?"

"I got the stuff on credit."

"Why, you'd think them kids was yourn! Hee, hee!"

"What'd you expect?" said Pa, a little too defensively, but Mr. Jones didn't seem to pay any heed. "They're my partner's kin, after all. Couldn't just leave 'em out in the street."

"Well, I figured you ain't got no cash. That game the other night cleaned you out."

"The mine still produces a few ounces a week, if I work it."

Alkali Jones let out with that cackle of his again. "That's the rub, now ain't it? Kids'll take a heap o' *ounces* to bring up, I 'spect."

"Where do you leave off knowin' so blamed much about kids?"

"Don't know nothin', thank the good Lord! But five extra mouths to feed is five extra mouths. An' even that pie-eyed Bosley at the store will be expectin' his money by and by. Hee, hee!"

"I got it all figured out," said Pa confidently. I couldn't tell from his voice whether what came next was part of his Mr. Drum act, pretending to be indifferent toward us, or whether he was confiding his real feelings on the matter to Mr. Jones. "Come spring," Pa went on, "them kids'll be gone. You know Nick, Alkali. Even if he gets himself cleared with the sheriff over this mess with Judd, you don't think he's about to take up as no pa to a passel of kids his sister sent him, do you? Nah, come April, we'll be free men again. But I had to take 'em in 'til then or that Parrish woman might have made things too hot for me. I'll hang on to all this stuff I bought 'til late summer when the new wagon trains arrive, and then I'll sell—at a nice profit, to boot. I'll pay off Bosely and have a little extra for myself!"

Quietly, I grabbed the pans I needed and forced myself away from the door. At that moment, I knew why eavesdropping was wrong—if nothing else, it makes the listener miserable! The part about leaving in the spring didn't bother me as much as all the talk of money, and thinking about Pa having to go into debt because of us. I'd almost forgotten that he wasn't a rich rancher like we'd expected Uncle Nick to be. He must not have had any money at all, and it didn't seem like he had much of a regular income from the mine. And to make it all worse, it sounded as if he was pretty familiar with poker games and gambling tables. I'd been thinking so much about all the changes in my own life that I hadn't stopped to consider what our coming meant for Pa and Uncle Nick.

Right then and there I whispered a little prayer. It might be wrong to listen to someone else's conversation, but maybe it was good I heard this one, because I needed to know these things so I could *do* something about it. I didn't quite know exactly *what* I would do. But I asked God to show me, and I finally got an idea after we were done eating that evening.

We were sitting around the blazing fire listening to Mr. Jones tell story after story about his life in the West. He sure livened up the evenings! I'll never know how much truth there was to his tales, but they were interesting.

"Danged I wish I had my fiddle with me!" he said, turning toward me with a big grin, "But since I don't, let me tell you about a time, Miz Corrie, when I hugged a bear to death."

We were all listening with huge, open eyes.

"Me an' my companions was all sittin' about our campfire eatin' our vittles, when we heard a growl so deep we practically jumped clean outta our boots. We didn't know what that dad-blamed noise was, but I told the other green-horn prospectors, 'Leave it to ol' Alkali here, an' he'll take care of it.'

"So I got up and walked a little deeper into that there box canyon we was camped on the edge of. I was lookin' all 'round and didn't see nuthin', when all of a sudden I turned around and there was a great big brown bear standin' face to face with me."

"Were you scared?" asked little Becky innocently.

"No, Missy! If you think starin' down a bear's hard, why you jest wait 'til I tell you 'bout the time I jumped clean across the lake to get away from the pack o' wolves that was after me! Hee, hee!

"Well, I tell ya, I jest stood there for a minute eyein' that mean ol' cuss of a bear. An' then the story 'bout ol' Davy Crockett came to my mind, so I grinned real big at him, made a leap toward the varmint, an' grabbed him and hugged him hard 'til he couldn't stand it any longer, and he jest dropped to the ground." I saw Pa look at Zack and wink.

Another one of Alkali's stories took place in '48 just after gold had been discovered.

"Me an' a handful o' others was gettin' mighty 'xasper-ated by the pickin's down t' Coloma way," said the old miner when he had us all listening again. "By then, Californians an' Mexicans was pourin' into the mine fields an' things was gettin' mighty close. Hee, hee! If we'd only knowed what was a comin' in the next year! Well anyways, we moved upriver a spell, an' puttered around fer a few days but didn't hit no payload. An' then ol' Charlie Pelham up and got hisself bit by a rattler an' just plumb died. Jest like that! Well, Charlie, he was a good friend so we gave him a right fine funeral. We even had an ex-preacher in our gang, so's it was as official a layin' to rest as you ever wanna see. Now we was all standin' round that open grave, an' preacher

Jones, he was a prayin' his heart out fer the departed soul o' ol' Charlie. But he went on and on with them sentimental notions an' my mind began to wander some. I guess I was starin' down at my boots an' was a diggin' my toe absent-mindedly in the dirt, without even payin' no attention to what I was doin', when suddenly I seen somethin' sparklin'! Prayer or no prayer, I fell down on my knees an' grabbed at the little pebble like thing, an' before I realized what I was sayin' I yelled out, '*Gold*!' Hee, hee!

"Well, I can tell you this, that was the end of that there funeral. I mean, it was plumb over! The preacher, he left off his prayin' pronto, an' we all commenced diggin' quicker than a polecat's spit can hit the ground. Without no disrespect to poor ol' Charlie who missed all the fun, he didn't get right proper covered up fer two days! Hee, hee! Why, I drew two hundred dollars worth o' dust an' nuggets that first day alone, and the others was close on my heels! Turned out to be one of the richest strikes on the American River. We drank to Charlie Pelham that night an' thanked him fer the right nice inheritance he done left us!"

CHAPTER 13

MY IDEA

Mr. Jones was a fine spinner of tales, and I right enjoyed them. But on this particular night I could hardly wait till he was finished, 'cause I wanted to get Pa alone and tell him my idea. But even after Alkali finished up and ambled out to the tool shed for the night, I still had to get the young'uns ready for bed.

That seemed to take forever, especially with the excitement over the new beds and all. When everyone had finally settled down, I peeked out the door of our room to see if Pa was still awake.

"What're you doing?" asked Zack.

I closed the door. "I had a mind to say good night to Pa, that's all," I whispered back to him.

"Why? He don't say good night to us."

" 'Cause I want to, that's why. Now quiet, Zack, and go to sleep."

I opened the door again and crept out.

The kerosene lamp was turned down low, but the fire still burned bright and sent out odd-shaped shadows against the walls. Pa was on his knees, bent over the hearth laying on another oak log, and his shadow looked like a giant's.

I cleared my throat shyly, because I still felt a little timid around him. He turned at the sound I made. Maybe it was from the warm reflection of the fire on his face, but all of a sudden he didn't seem quite so terrifying.

"Could I—" I began, then hesitated.

"Somethin' the matter?"

"No, sir. But if it ain't too disturbin', I wanted to talk to you."

He finished with the fire, wiped his hands off on his shirt, and pulled over one of the new chairs.

"You ain't disturbin' me," he said finally. "Come and set yerself down."

I did that, and he sat on the stool just opposite me.

"What's on your mind, girl?" he asked. He sounded like he really wanted to know.

I took a deep breath.

"I done something today that I knew was wrong, and I'm real sorry. But I don't think I'm altogether sorry, 'cause maybe it was something I needed to know—"

"Hold on, child!" he said. "I ain't quite following you. Slow down a mite and tell me what happened."

"Well, sir, I heard you and Mr. Jones talkin' before supper about money. I know it wasn't right of me to listen, but—"

"Don't you think nothing of it."

"Well, to tell you the truth, I never gave it a single thought before then, but we'll be costin' you plenty to take care of."

"I'm sorry you heard that," he replied earnestly. "but it's nothin' for you to worry about."

"But we barged in on you uninvited."

"Don't pay that no mind, Cornelia," he said, a hint of his old brusqueness coming back into his voice. "What's done is done."

"But I want to give you some money. It's only fair we pay our own way."

"Ridiculous!" he said with a wave of his hand. "I'm your pa, and it's my duty to take care of you. Besides, you got less than I do."

"That ain't true," I answered as respectfully as I could. "You see, Ma had some money. She left that to me. And it seems only right that—"

"Don't tell me what's right! Besides, I ain't about to take no money from the kids I ran out on nine years ago."

It was the first mention he'd made of his leaving us. I don't think he meant to say it either, because just hearing himself say it seemed to sober him, and he sat staring into the fire for a long time. Neither of us said a word. We just listened to the fire.

Finally, I ventured to say something more. "In a way, maybe it's really your money after all," I said, "or else Uncle Nick's."

He cocked a bushy eyebrow toward me. "How'd you figure that?" he asked.

"The money came from Grandpa Belle's estate," I answered. "That's how we had money to come here. Ma herself said it was real odd Grandpa never left nothin' to Uncle Nick, and she said that as soon as we got to California she was going to give him his due. I forgot all about it until now, but there's near two hundred dollars put away. And if it ain't your's as Ma's husband, then what about Uncle Nick? I'd feel real pleased if you could find a way to put it to use, for us to pay our way."

The mention of the sum seemed to sober him further, but only for a moment. Then he replied firmly. "And it'll stay put away, too. Nick'd gamble away that money in one night and then it'd be gone. And I ain't none so sure I want it in my hands neither."

"You could pay off your bill at the store," I suggested.

He looked at me, half amused, I think, and half perturbed. "Cornelia," he finally said, "you ain't struck me as an impertinent child 'til now. Don't you know better than to argue with grown-ups? Now, I want you to listen to me good. Your grandpa willed that money to your ma. So it was *hers*. And unless she left something in writin', it's now *yours*, not Nick's. That's the law. He wanted your ma to have it, not Nick, and with good reason, too. And it's God's truth your ma wouldn't have wanted me to have my hands on it! Maybe with just as good a reason."

"But why would Grandpa—or Ma, for that matter—not want their son or brother to have his share?"

"There's plenty neither of them knew about Nick," he answered. "And about as much your Ma *thought* she knew about me, but didn't."

He fell silent for several moments, gazing steadily into the fire. I began to think the conversation was over, when he looked back at me and spoke again.

"You know, I was here in California in '48. Most of the men that were here then are wealthy men today, 'cept them that was still doing nothing but fightin' the Mexicans, or doing what I was doing. I heard someone say once that you had to be either a fool or an idiot not to make a killin' back then. Well, Sutter and Jim Marshall are fools, and I suppose that's why they ain't made a dime off the gold rush. I don't know which I am—probably a fool, too, for getting mixed up in the kind of deals I did, 'cause I don't have nothin' to show for it neither."

He stopped and took a deep breath. I hardly dared make a sound. It was so strange for him to talk like that. As if he'd forgotten I was there. He gave the log in the fire a kick with his boot and then started talking again.

"I remember one week back in '49 when I had ten thousand dollars in dust and nuggets in my saddlebags. It lasted me one trip to San Francisco."

He paused and sighed. "You ever hear the saying, 'Throwin' good money after bad,' Corrie?"

I nodded, but now that I think about it, I'm not so sure I had heard it before. I just nodded without knowing why.

"Well, your Grandpa Belle knew what he was about. He knew me and Nick well enough to know what was the right thing to do with his money. So I don't want to hear no more about it. You keep that money. Put it someplace safe—one day you'll be needin' it. Now get you to bed. It's late."

I stood right up and walked back to our new room. At the door, I paused and took another look at Pa. He was staring right at me with the most peculiar look on his face. But when he saw me looking, he quickly jerked his head away and stared back into the fire.

I crawled into bed still thinking about that look—a sad, faraway expression, as if he was feeling some ache in his heart that had nothing to do with me or our talk.

Seeing his eyes for that brief moment, I felt as if I was eavesdropping again, seeing a little part of Pa that he had wanted to remain a secret.

CHAPTER 14

THE INDIANS

Before winter set in for good, my brothers and sisters and I wanted to get to know our new home and all its surroundings as best we could. Pa was always admonishing us about getting lost or running into a den of foxes or a mother bear or a bee's nest. But he didn't keep us from wandering out and doing some exploring, so we took advantage of it.

"This ain't no New York farmland," he said, every time we were about to go for a walk up the hill, through the woods or along the creek.

That, it certainly wasn't. In fact, just a few short years ago, no one but Indians had roamed this part of the country—except for a few Mexicans that may have wandered this far north. My mind was full of the possibility that there were still a whole lot of paths and sections of forest that had never been explored. There could even be new gold to discover somewhere! It gave me goosebumps to think that perhaps I might be the first person to lay eyes on a meadow or a particular formation of boulders, or to climb to the top of some hill and be the first to look out on the valley beyond. It was such a new and exciting land, with so much to learn, so many possibilities for adventure, I didn't want to miss a thing. Yet the growing chill in the air told me that time was running out, and that soon I'd be forced indoors.

On one of those crisp, chilly fall days we went hiking

along the creek just east of Pa and Uncle Nick's claim. The creek had been one of our unspoken boundaries. We had more or less grown accustomed to our particular side of it, and knew how to find our way up and down its length and back to the cabin. But on this day, I found myself looking across to the woods and fields on the eastern bank, thinking how lovely it all looked and wondering what lay out beyond. I had no doubt that there, just past the rise which cut off my view, I would discover true virgin territory. And right then I determined that if I were still here next spring, I would make it my project to strike out and explore over there, maybe even spend a night alone under the stars. I would be sixteen by then, and surely capable of spreading my wings, as Ma would say, farther afield.

But on this day, especially since I had the young'uns with me, I had to content myself with the western side. The others had run off to survey up and down the creek. I had been standing there for quite a while, gazing into the distance, alone on the little bank with only the sound of the water gurgling along in its stream bed at my feet. I was thinking about one of Alkali Jones' tales about the strike that had given the creek and the town its name.

"I was standin' right aside him, hee, hee!" he cackled, "right when he fished out that big nugget!"

According to Mr. Jones, nothing in the whole of California had managed to happen without his help.

"Big as a man's fist, I tell ya!" His eyes shone, just telling the story. "Pure gold, it was! Biggest nugget I ever seen! 'It's a miracle.' I yelled, an' all the others came runnin'. A downright miracle it was, too, an' afore long all the folks for miles around began callin' the stream Miracle Springs, an' the town grew up right on top of it."

So there I stood on the bank of Miracle Creek, just a couple of miles downstream from the spring where Mr. Jones and his friend had supposedly found that first big nugget, and maybe four or five miles upstream from the town. I didn't see any gold sparkling in the water that day, though I had no doubt there were still fortunes to be had from this stream, and I hoped maybe someday I might have a share in one. I bent down and took a scoop of the clear, cold, sweet water in my hands, still thinking about gold, and noticing nothing but the water rippling along beneath me.

But when I glanced up, not a stone's throw away stood two Indian braves. My heart nearly stopped! In my surprise I almost toppled head first into the water.

Somehow I managed to keep control of myself, and held back a strong urge to jump up and flee. Yet the sight was so fascinating I didn't really want to run away, either. I was overcome by such a feeling of wonder at actually seeing two Indians so close, face to face, looking like . . . well, just like two ordinary people. Not savages, like the ones that attacked our wagon train in Wyoming, nor like the ones we'd seen back East in books, all made up with paint and fake head-dresses, but like other people . . . only Indians.

Ma always said my curiosity was going to get me killed like the cat some day. I only hoped today wasn't going to be that day!

I suppose the two Indians were father and son. The younger one was about my age. He was tall and brown, like the older man, and both were dressed only in buckskin loin-cloths reaching almost to their knees. Their long, black hair shone—glistening in the sunlight, but was otherwise plain. I think coming upon a white girl out in the middle of the woods, kneeling all by herself at the edge of the stream, had surprised them as much as they had surprised me.

I especially noticed shock in the boy's face, but the man's was as solemn and unmoved as a rock. They had bows and quivers of arrows strapped to their backs, but I didn't notice that at first. Even if I had, I don't think it would have wor-ried me. Though I was taken aback by their sudden ap-pearance, for some strange reason, after the first instant I wasn't afraid. They looked kind of wild, but not mean. The boy was staring straight at me with a look—curiosity, interest, possibly a hint of unspoken friendship, but certainly no menace. Maybe he'd never seen a white girl his own age up so close either.

All those thoughts went speeding through my brain in only a few seconds; then I could feel my legs going numb beneath me. So I slowly rose to my feet, smiling so they wouldn't get the wrong idea. The man's face did not even flicker in response, but the boy's started to soften into what I hoped might be a smile too.

"Good morning," I said, not even knowing if they would understand me. But before they could respond, all at once there was a rustling in the brush behind me, followed by the laughs and calls of my four brothers and sisters.

As they broke into the clearing where I stood, the two Indians leaped back, then turned and ran away like two frightened deer. If they'd only waited another second to see that the cause of all the noise was nothing but four little kids!

I was perturbed at the rude interruption, and gave Zack and Emily a long scowl, though later I realized they couldn't have had any idea what they had done.

My anger with them dissolved as we walked home, but I was still quiet, and the disappointment lingered with me. I wondered if the two Indians might have talked to me if given the chance, and what they might have said. All I could think about was finding another chance to go back to that same place in hopes of finding them again—this time alone!

We took a different way back, and I got a little confused about where we were. We strayed past the southern boundary of the claim, and there we had our second interesting encounter of the day.

There were three men on horseback riding toward us.

They were coarsely-dressed white men, maybe miners, but definitely not farmers or city fellows. They looked rough and wore guns at their sides.

The appearance of these men didn't startle me like the

Indians did. In one way they were friendlier, smiling as they paused before us and tipped their hats. But I was immediately afraid. Their eyes didn't smile with their lips, and their voices seemed filled with mockery. I clutched Tad to me.

"How do, young folks," said one of the men.

"Hello," I replied, giving a tight smile.

"Ain't too common to find kids in these parts." He looked us over with just a slight squint. "You must be Nick Matthews' kin that ol' Drum's taken in?"

I nodded, wondering how he knew. Though I suppose in an isolated place like this, when five kids show up on a man's doorstep, word gets around.

"Well, you kids better skedaddle on home. We seen signs of Indians a way's back an' it ain't safe to be out."

"We can take care of ourselves," said Zack.

I could have kicked him for his insolent tone. The last thing I wanted was to rile these men.

But the man who had been speaking just laughed and turned to wink at his companions. I didn't altogether like the look of that wink either. As he turned, I noticed an ugly scar on his cheek, making him look all the nastier.

"Thank you, sir," I said, then nudged my brothers and sisters on. The instant the men were out of sight we took off as fast as we could go.

We found Pa up to his knees in the creek, shoveling gravel from the trenches into the sluice box at his mine. We were all red-faced and sweaty from running so hard, and even his untrained eye could tell we'd seen something to throw a scare into us.

"What's wrong?" he said in the gruff tone I was learning was his way of covering up a real concern. "You run into a bear or something?"

"Corrie seen Indians!" burst out Becky excitedly.

"And *then* we seen three mean-looking men on horses!" put in Emily.

"What's this?" he said, setting down his shovel and looking at me.

I told him about the Indians. "They looked friendly," I said, as I finished.

"It was plumb foolish of you not to run," he said. "There might have been more of them."

"I didn't want to upset them," I said lamely.

"You're just lucky they didn't try nothin'."

"I'm sure they wouldn't have harmed me."

Pa rubbed his hand through his beard thoughtfully. "I don't know, you may be right. California Indians are generally the most friendly of the lot. Why, back in the old days they worked right beside us in the mines, even though most of the miners cheated them bad. But that's changed in the last couple of years—most white men just couldn't abide having Indians as friends, much less equals. They drove the Indians away and made them downright hostile. It's best to steer clear of them now."

"I wanted to talk to them so bad."

"Well, you get a fool notion like that out of your head pronto! If we leave them alone, they'll leave us alone. Now, what about those other fellas you was talking about?"

"Aw, they just wanted to warn us about the Indians," said Zack.

"They looked mean," Becky added.

Again Pa looked at me. "They *do* anything?"

"No, sir," I answered. I couldn't help feeling a little proud that he seemed to respect my judgement, though it was probably just because I was the oldest. "But they were pretty stern-looking and carried guns."

"Everyone in these parts carries a gun. They give their names?"

"No, sir, but one of them seemed to know we belonged to you."

"One of them had a big wide scar on his face," piped up Becky.

"On his cheek?"

"Yes, sir," I said.

Pa frowned and rubbed his beard again.

"Well, you stay clear of them, too, you hear?" he added with a finality that indicated the discussion was over. Then he hoisted up the shovel and went on with his work.

It wasn't too many days before I'd nearly forgotten about the scar-faced man and his companions. But I could not get the two Indians out of my mind.

I felt sorry for them after what Pa had said about the gold miners' treatment of them, and I wanted a chance to prove that all whites weren't like that. I thought the Indian boy and I might even be friends, and it would be especially nice for Zack to have another boy near his own age.

Of all of us, I think everything that had happened was hardest on Zack. I had my writing in my journal to occupy me, Becky and Emily had each other for companions, and Tad was young enough to adjust without too many problems. But Zack really had nothing much to keep him busy. For some reason I didn't understand, Pa wouldn't let him help at the mine.

But having an Indian brave for a friend probably wouldn't have solved the problem anyway.

CHAPTER 15

AN EVENTFUL DAY IN TOWN

The next day it rained, and the day after that, and the day after that. It hardly stopped long enough for us to go outside for ten minutes without it starting up all over again.

We all got pretty bored and restless.

I especially noticed it in Pa. He couldn't go out and mine or work much outside, and I suppose he'd about had it with the company of a cabin full of kids. Every once in a while he'd question me again about the three riders we saw, and always afterwards he'd get real quiet and thoughtful, almost sulky.

As the hours of the dreary days passed, he grew more and more sullen and short-tempered. By afternoon on the third day of rain, he was hardly saying a word—not that he ever said much, but now he was downright glum. The rain finally stopped, but it was still dark and gloomy with heavy clouds overhead. I was starting supper when all of a sudden Pa, who had been sitting hunched up in front of the fire, suddenly hitched himself to his feet and half muttered something like, "Well, I'm a fool, but I gotta know if he's hanging around . . . and my fingers are itching for some action, anyway. . . ."

He strode to the door, taking a minute to put on his gun belt and pull his coat over his shoulders. In the doorway, he spoke almost as if it were an afterthought. "I'm going to

108

town," he said matter-of-factly.

I just stood there, not knowing how to respond, as usual.

"For how long?" I finally asked.

"No telling."

"What about us?" I said.

"Do what you like," he answered. "You're welcome to come along if you want."

"We're needing some things," I suggested.

"Suit yourself," he replied, still not looking up.

I watched him another minute, but realized he'd said all he was about to say. So I turned and called inside to the kids. "Come on, you all!" I yelled. "On with them coats. We're going to town!"

"Ya-hoo!" shrieked Zack and Tad.

While the kids were getting themselves ready, I grabbed some bread and apples for us to eat on the way. I didn't want to keep Pa waiting. But when I ran outside to tell him we'd all be going with him, he'd gone up the creek to check something at the mine, so I figured we weren't in such an all-fire hurry after all. Besides, the wagon and team still needed hitching up.

About half an hour later, we all piled in the back of our wagon. Zack sat up front and handled our two horses, while Pa rode along on his bay. We made a jolly crew, laughing and talking, and I could almost imagine that everything was going to work out fine for us in our new home. But Pa didn't enter much into our jovial spirits. He just sat there silently on his horse and plodded along behind us.

It was getting well on toward evening when we finally arrived in Miracle Springs. Pa took us to Mrs. Gianini's, with a stern reminder that we weren't to call him anything but Mr. Drum, and he ordered us some supper. He didn't eat with us. He said he'd be back later and left. I thought about going to see if Mrs. Parrish was back from her trip, but it was pretty late by the time we finished eating. In fact it was too late to do much of anything. I wondered why I had wanted all of us to go along in the first place.

Sitting around in Mrs. Gianini's boarding house, we played a few games of checkers and she showed us some travel books. But pretty soon Tad started to nod off. I kept glancing toward the door wondering when Pa was going to come back. When Becky and Emily started to doze, Mrs. Gianini clicked her tongue disapprovingly, and shot a glance first at her clock and then at the door. Finally, she rose and told us to come upstairs where she had made up some beds for us.

Next morning we were all up at first light. I helped the kids get dressed, and brushed Emily and Becky's hair, and then we went downstairs. There was still no sign of Pa. We found Mrs. Gianini singing to herself in the kitchen.

"Ah, did the bambinos sleep well?" she asked when we walked in, giving Becky's pudgy little cheek a soft pinch.

"Yes, Miz Geeneene," said Becky. The plump woman laughed heartily.

"Where's our—where's Mr. Drum?" I asked, glancing around the room, still seeing no evidence of his return.

Mrs. Gianini clicked her tongue in the same way she had last night. Her thick jowls shook in a comical way.

"Your-a uncle's partner . . . he no come-a back," she said in her heavy accent.

"Did he—leave word about what w-we were to do?" I stammered.

"*Santa cielo!*" she exclaimed. I didn't understand any Italian, but from the expression on the lady's face, her answer didn't seem too hopeful. "You poor little bambinos. When I get-a my hands on that Drum, or that Nicolas Matthews for getting himself into trouble, with you coming—!" Rather than finish her sentence, she just waved her arms above her head in frustration.

Breakfast didn't taste nearly so good as last night's supper, though that was not the fault of Mrs. Gianini's cooking. We kids started at every sound outside, looking up expecting to see Pa. It was like that first day we came to Miracle, only now it was even worse, because things had started to look promising. We cleaned our plates, then went outside.

"Where's Pa?" asked Tad.

"I don't know, Taddy," I answered.

"You know as well as I do he's down at that drinkin' house," said Zack. And he was all for marching right down there and walking in on him. But I couldn't quite bring myself to agree to it. Even if I was a little angry that he had gone off and left us without so much as a word, I didn't want to hound him so much that he'd start to hate us. Besides that, it still didn't seem quite proper.

I was anxious to see Mrs. Parrish. When I suggested we go to her place, everyone cheered—everyone except Zack. He just followed behind sullenly.

Emily, Becky, and Tad ran right for the livery where Pa had left the rig. They were anxious to see Jinx and Snowball. Zack said hello to Mrs. Parrish, then ambled off aimlessly down the street. I hoped he didn't plan on looking for Pa.

"Well, Corrie!" said Mrs. Parrish with a friendly smile. "How are you?" She took my hands and looked me over. "You seem a bit pale. Are you eating well? Is your father—"

"Oh, our Pa's taking real good care of us, Ma'am," I answered quickly. But Mrs Parrish could tell I wasn't saying everything there was to tell.

"Come and sit down," she said in her gentle voice.

She led me into the Freight Office and sat in a big leather-covered chair by her oak desk. "I've got some water boiling," she said. "I'll fix us some tea."

She went about getting cups and saucers, sugar, cream, and a little plate of cookies, while she continued to talk. "How have you all been adjusting—if you don't mind my asking. It must be quite a change. I've thought about you and prayed for you often, and wanted to visit—"

"Oh, I know you're an awful busy lady, Mrs. Parrish."

"It wasn't that at all. I've been back in town several days

now, but I thought it was best to leave you all to yourselves for a while. I didn't want to appear the meddler."

"We would never have thought that, Ma'am."

"You might not have, but such a thought might well have come into your father's mind. It's nice that you all came into town together."

I looked down at my lap. I didn't think I was going to cry, but I wasn't going to take any chances. I felt about for my handkerchief just in case.

"What's wrong, Corrie?"

I didn't say anything for a moment or two. "I just don't understand," I finally blurted out, even though I hadn't wanted to say anything. "Things were going so well, it seemed. I really thought he didn't mind too much our being there."

"What happened?"

"I don't know, maybe nothin'. I just don't know where Pa is, that's all."

"Doesn't sound to me as if that's quite all."

"Well," I fumbled, playing with my handkerchief and hoping I didn't have to use it, "I don't want to speak ill of Pa. He's trying real hard. But this does take a lot of gettin' used to, I reckon. It's just that I thought when we all came to town we'd be together. I didn't figure on him runnin' out on us. But now it seems he's gone just like before. I don't know what to think."

"When did he go?"

"He got us supper at Mrs. Gianini's last night, then left. He didn't even have any supper himself."

"And he left no word?"

I shook my head.

"Why that—!" Her voice rose and her eyes flared, but then she seemed to think better of herself and went on in a milder tone. "I'm sure there must be an innocent explanation. Some business probably has detained him."

I nodded. That's what I had thought first, too. At least

that's what I'd hoped. But somehow I think we both knew we were "buildin' castles in the sky," as Ma used to say.

"But I almost forgot! I have some exciting news," said Mrs. Parrish in a light tone. I could tell she was trying to cheer me up, but I didn't mind. "Two days ago I received a letter from back East in response to an inquiry I had made. I wrote to the pastor of the church I had attended in Boston, asking if he knew any ministers who might feel the call to come west. Miracle is still a pretty wild and woolly place, but I don't think it need always be that way. When the mining plays itself out, this could well become a respectable town—with a school and a church, and lots of nice people putting down their roots. More and more families are coming to California. We need to grow, and our towns and western ways need to mature to accommodate civilization."

I could tell from her voice that she was excited, that this all meant a lot to her.

"That sounds real nice, Mrs. Parrish," I said.

"And now it looks like we are well on our way toward that goal! A preacher is coming to Miracle. According to this letter, he ought to arrive in a few weeks."

"But how's he going to cross the Sierras so late in the season?"

"He's coming by the Panama route. I'll meet his ship in San Francisco. Isn't it wonderful, Corrie? We will have our very own church!"

"Is the town going to build a church?" I asked.

"We don't need a *building* to have a church. The early Christians often met in one another's homes."

"Don't seem like even your house would be big enough."

Mrs. Parrish smiled, then gave a little chuckle.

"Oh, to have the faith of children!" she said. "Or, young ladies, I should say! But perhaps you are right, Corrie. We may just have a big turnout, if only for curiosity's sake. I will have to give all of this more thought."

"Does seem that a town with five saloons ought to have at least one church," I said.

"Truly spoken, Corrie," she replied. "And I believe in time it will. But until then . . . you have given me an idea."

She tapped her finger thoughtfully against her lips. "I wonder what the new preacher would think. . . ."

If Mrs. Parrish's intention had been to make me forget my troubles with Pa, it almost worked. I found myself caught up in her enthusiasm. It was so nice the way she treated me, as if I were a lady just like her. I wasn't even close to being a lady, but I couldn't hide my pleasure at how nice she was to me. I never had anybody talk to me quite like that.

But our nice conversation ended suddenly.

The office door burst open, and Becky, her face red from running hard, burst in jabbering excitedly.

"They're gone! They're gone! A man took 'em, and Emily's cryin', and nobody can stop her!"

CHAPTER 16

THE HORSES

It took a minute to get Becky calmed down, and even at that we still couldn't understand what she was trying to say. Finally Mrs. Parrish led her outside by the hand. By that time Becky began tugging at her arm, leading us to the livery stable behind the office.

There we found Emily perched on a bale of hay with Marcus Weber seated beside her. His big, black muscular arm was wrapped around her sobbing frame. He looked up, both helpless and relieved at our arrival.

"What happened, Marcus?" asked Mrs. Parrish.

"I 'spose I shoulda come fo' you, Miz Parrish," said the gentle Negro, "but you's allas sayin' fo me to take charge o' the stable, an' . . . well, it all seemed legal-like, an' that there feller was wearin' a gun, an'—"

"What man, Marcus?" interrupted Mrs. Parrish, patiently but firmly. "Tell me exactly what happened."

"He took Snowball!" shrieked Emily beside him, and then burst into a new fit of crying.

"The hosses, Ma'am. The feller done took the chil'en's hosses."

"What man, Marcus?"

"I don' know, Ma'am. This here feller, he done had a bill o' sale signed real official like—signed by Mr. Drum hisself. So the man, he jest took off with the hosses an' now

115

this here young'un's jest about to break her po li'l heart! I guess it's all my fault."

I hurried over to sit on the other side of Emily to try to calm her, while Mrs. Parrish did her best to comfort the miserable blacksmith.

"It is not your fault, Marcus," said Mrs. Parrish. "This man, did he say Mr. . . . er—Mr. Drum *sold* him the horses?"

"Yes'm."

Mrs. Parrish was about to say something. But all at once she stopped, her mouth hanging half open, staring straight ahead.

I turned my head around and followed her gaze. There in the doorway of the livery stood Pa, with Tad and Zack behind him.

I had almost forgotten about Tad. I guess when the commotion started he must have run off after Zack, and somehow the two of them met up with Pa. Anyway, there he was.

All of a sudden, I guess something inside me just kind of popped, because I jumped up off that hay bale and ran over to him.

"How could you?" I cried.

He looked back at me with genuine shock at my reaction. "They was just horses," he said.

"Just horses!" I said. "They were our . . . our pets . . . they'd come all the way with us! Snowball was Emily's special friend!"

My voice was shaking, all the frustration I'd been feeling coming out all at once. I'd never before in my life spoken to an adult like that. "You had no right!" I yelled.

"I was up against a wall," he replied, still bewildered at all the stir he'd caused. "I needed some quick capital."

Mrs. Parrish turned to Marcus Weber. "Marcus, will you please excuse us?" He quietly left the stable. When he was gone, Mrs. Parrish turned her glare right on Pa.

"Did you gamble those horses away, Mr. . . . ah . . .

Mr. Drum?" she asked angrily.

"Things just got out of hand."

"You could have had Ma's money!" I cried. Tears of anger and anguish were streaming down my face. I had tried so hard since the beginning to see things Pa's way and to stick up for him. But now I felt he had betrayed us. "I was going to give you that money!" I said again. "But why the horses?"

"I don't take money from kids!" he shot back, his voice rising. I couldn't tell if he was angry or just frustrated.

"But you would sell their horses, Mr. Drum? Not only their pets and friends, but the only link they still possess to a past that has been torn away from them—a past full of a great deal of pain at your hand!" she added, glaring at him as she spoke.

"Oh, for criminy sakes! You're makin' me out to be some kind of thief!" retorted Pa. " 'Sides, it ain't none of your affair, Miz Parrish. We're kin, an' kinfolk stick together, ain't that right, kids?"

None of us said anything. I don't guess we were feeling too much kinship right then.

"Someone has to look after the interests of these children!"

Still she scowled at him, but he just glared right back. For an instant I thought he might strike her, he looked so mad. But finally he just let out a sharp breath.

"What's done is done," he said finally, in a tight, strained voice.

A stifled sob from Emily made us all painfully aware that Pa was right—the horses were gone. It *was* done, and it wasn't going to be so easily resolved. All our eyes turned momentarily toward her.

"Ain't a one of you thinkin' about me and the tight spot I was in," said Pa. "Listen here—if I hadn't come up with them horses, I might've taken a couple of slugs. I had no choice."

"That doesn't make it right," I said, sinking helplessly back on the bale next to Emily.

Pa looked around at all of us. "Since when is a man answerable to a bunch of kids and a busybody woman that's got nothin' to do with his affairs? If you don't like the way I do things, just remember it wasn't me that asked you to hitch up with me. I told you from the beginnin' it wouldn't work!" He spun around and strode out of the stable.

Mrs. Parrish ran right out after him. I had never seen a bolder woman, nor a braver one. I figured my pa'd been pushed just about as far as any man was likely to go.

By the time she caught up with him he had rounded a corner and I couldn't see them. But their voices came through the wide-open stable doors as clear as gunfire through cold, night air.

"You are not leaving those children again!" said Mrs. Parrish, and it wasn't a question but an order.

"Since when is it your business to tell me what to do?" shot back Pa angrily.

"You have a responsibility."

"So do you, lady, and it ain't pokin' your nose into my life!"

"Now look here, Mr.—"

"Now *you* listen, Mrs. Parrish," interrupted Pa, and his voice was cool, almost calm—but not like the calm of a spring day, more like the dead quiet before a thunderstorm. "You may run half this town," he said, "*but you don't run me*! I'll do as suits me best, and I'll thank you to mind your own affairs!"

"And what about the children?" Mrs. Parrish was just about as cool. I knew if I could have seen her as she spoke she wouldn't be flinching a muscle.

"It seems apparent to me that they've had it up to their eyeballs with me, just as much as I've had it with them!"

I heard the sound of horses hooves and a jingling harness.

"And so you intend—" Mrs. Parrish began, but whatever she meant to say was lost in the sound of clopping hooves.

In a moment she returned alone. Pa was gone on his horse. Mrs. Parrish looked sad for our sakes, but inside I could tell she was boiling mad at the same time. She seemed used to having her way with how things went.

I felt awful. And it didn't help when Zack lit into me.

"Now look what you've done!" he said. "Yellin' at him and driving him away like that."

"Don't blame your sister," said Mrs. Parrish. "Whatever blame there is to be dished out belongs to your father and no one else." She was infuriated with him. "Well . . ." she added, "and some to me, I suppose. I should have guarded my words more carefully."

Tears ran down my cheeks. Deep down I couldn't help but think Zack was right, that it was my fault Pa had run off. Mad as I had just been with him, part of me still wanted to believe in him. Part of me kept thinking that if only I had kept still like a proper, obedient child, things would have been okay. We would survive somehow without the horses. But we needed our Pa and I hoped he needed us a little too. Having to grow up so fast was awfully confusing at times!

"Come now," said Mrs. Parrish after a moment. "You children can stay with me."

The stable was silent a minute, with only the soft shuffling of the horses in their stalls. Then all of a sudden I found myself speaking up boldly again.

"Thank you kindly, Mrs. Parrish," I said, "but we best be gettin' home."

"I doubt your father will return there tonight."

"I know, Ma'am, but that's where we belong now. It's our home. We'll manage. I can take care of the young'uns, and Zack can handle a rifle if need be."

She let out an exasperated, yet not unfriendly sigh. "It seems determination runs in your family."

I couldn't help smiling a little. More than once I heard Ma observe that the stubborn streak was most strong on my *father's* side.

"I'm afraid that's probably true, Ma'am."

"But you don't even have horses to get you there now," she added.

Now it was my turn to sigh. I had completely forgotten the cause of this hubbub in the first place. Jinx and Snowball were *gone*. Mrs. Parrish walked quickly outside to find Mr. Weber. When they returned she was talking to him. "Marcus," she said, "will you hitch up a couple of our horses to the children's rig and drive them home?"

"Yes'm! Be most glad to!" He jumped up, obviously eager to make amends for his part in the misunderstanding.

Mrs. Parrish went over and conferred quietly with him while we stood glumly about. In about ten minutes the wagon was ready and we were off, saying good-bye to Mrs. Parrish, who promised to come up to see us the next day.

CHAPTER 17

ALONE AT THE CABIN

We'd never been alone in the cabin at night.

In fact, I can't remember us five kids being alone at night anywhere before. I recalled my conversation with Zack when we first got to California about fending for ourselves. It seemed pretty silly. I felt like a little girl, not a woman.

I could hardly sleep. Every little sound jerked me wide awake.

Luckily, the little ones slept. But I heard Zack tossing and turning in his bunk over Tad's.

I thought I should just get up and go into the other room and light a lamp so I could read or write in my journal or something. I'd been wanting to make a drawing of the cabin. But then I was afraid the light might attract attention. And when I thought of that, I began to think of Indians, and pretty soon I was imagining that all the sounds outside were the padded noises of moccasin-clad feet!

Then I started to think about what it would be like to be massacred. If something like that happened, Pa would sure feel awful then. But that thought didn't make me feel any better. I wasn't angry at him anymore, especially now that I realized more than ever how much we needed him here with us.

But now he was gone.

Would he ever come back? Especially after my outburst

121

made him think we didn't want him?

No, he had to come back. He was our pa, after all, and I could never stop trying to believe in him.

Suddenly a sharp explosive sound shook the quiet night. *Crack! Crack!*

Twice it came, and I knew it was gunfire!

It echoed deafeningly through the night, then all was still once more. The silence seemed even deeper than before, though it lasted only a second or two, for we were all wide awake now.

"What was that?" said Zack in a tremulous whisper.

"Gunshots," I whispered back.

"Ma . . . Ma. . . !" came three smaller voices.

Shaking all over, I folded back the blanket and crept out of bed. I tiptoed over to a window. Zack was at my shoulder a second later.

"What do you see?" he said.

Peering out, I could see nothing but darkness. I found myself wishing for those small night sounds I had been listening to before; it was dead still outside now.

All at once I heard a sound at the front door. My blood froze. I glanced at Zack, hoping it had been my imagination. But the look of terror on his pale face told me the sound had been real enough.

Clasping one another by the hand, we crept into the other room. As quietly as I could I took down Pa's rifle that hung over the hearth and handed it to Zack. He would have been happy to know that at that moment he looked more a man than I had ever seen him before. Though he was only thirteen, I was sure glad to have him beside me! But I was too distracted to say anything just then.

Now someone was pounding on the door! My heart was in my throat.

"Who's there?" I said finally, in a voice barely more than a squeak. Behind me Zack cocked the rifle and held it steady.

"It's me . . . you chil'ens all right?"

The voice sounded familiar, but wasn't the one I expected. It was Marcus Weber.

"W-we're safe, Mr. Weber," I said in a voice of tremendous relief. "Let me unbolt the door."

The big Negro blacksmith was indeed a welcome sight when I swung open the big wooden door. But his usual congenial look was replaced with serious concern. He came in quickly, shut the door, and told me to bolt it right away, which I lost no time doing. Then I lit the lantern.

"What's going on out there?" asked Zack, lowering the rifle, relieved he hadn't had to use it.

"There was prowlers about," said Mr. Weber.

"Indians?" exclaimed Becky and Tad together. Emily was still too frightened to speak.

The black man's brow creased into deep furrows. "No, siree . . . them weren't no Indian tracks I seen out dere—an' if they's one thing I knows, it's tracks. Someone else be prowlin' 'roun' yo uncle's mine."

But who could have been out there, nosing around so close to the cabin?

"Was it them that fired the shots?" I asked.

"No, that was me, Missy," answered Mr. Weber, patting the pistol now tucked securely in the holster at his side. "I seen 'em creepin' roun' suspicious like, an' so I fired in de air to scare 'em off. I was afeared they might be Indians too, but a close look at their tracks showed it had to be white men. But thank the good Lawd, they didn't put up no fight."

"But what brought you here, Mr. Weber?"

Now the worried look on his face turned into a sheepish grin. "Well . . ." He hesitated a moment before plunging ahead, "Miz Parrish, she done asked me to stick aroun' after I brung you kids home. She didn't want to say nuthin' 'cause . . . well, she figured yo might not take to the idee too well."

I *had* been acting a bit contrary this afternoon. I don't know what got into me. Ma would have said I was being too ornery for my own good, and she would have been right. If

Mrs. Parrish hadn't been so wise, I don't know what would have become of us tonight. So now it was my turn to look sheepish as I spoke.

"I sure am glad you turned up, Mr. Weber. And I thank you kindly for putting yourself out like that to protect us."

"Aw, it's my pleasure, Missy, an' that's a fact!" The blacksmith's worried creases softened into one of his warm smiles.

"You're welcome to stay in here the rest of the night," I said.

"Please stay, Mr. Weber," added Becky in a sleepy, innocent voice. He laughed, and it helped clear away the last of the fear to hear his merry voice echo through the cabin.

He knelt down on one knee, took Becky's tiny, soft white hand in his huge, rough black one, and said, "I'm much obliged fo' yo' kindness, Missy. But iffen it's all the same to you, I think I'll jest bunk down in that tool shed out dere by the mine. That way, I'll hear any unusualness right off."

"Okay, but come in for breakfast in the morning," I said.

"That I'll do right gladly, Missy!" he said to me, rising.

So we all got settled down into our beds again. I tucked the little ones in and tried to pray a prayer with each of them like Ma might have done. Then I crawled back under my own blanket.

I slept a lot easier after that, knowing I wasn't the oldest person around anymore, and feeling the safety of Marcus Weber keeping watch over us.

As I snuggled down into my bed, with the words of the prayer I had just prayed with Tad still in my mind, I realized that Someone greater than the blacksmith was looking over us kids too, just like Ma'd told me. I guess I'd been forgetting that lately. Sure, things had been confusing, and weren't going so smoothly. But it could have been much worse! We had food and a place to sleep. And we'd already met people who were kind to us. I decided to start counting my blessings, starting with Marcus Weber's presence out in the tool shed—even including our pa, because down inside, I still had the feeling he might turn out to be a blessing in the end.

CHAPTER 18

BREAKFAST WITH MARCUS WEBER

The events of the next morning muddled my notions all over again about Pa being a blessing.

We were all eating breakfast and having a good time. Marcus Weber was there with us. I fixed a special meal in appreciation for what he had done last night—fluffy buttermilk biscuits, heaps of scrambled eggs and sausages that Mrs. Parrish had sent back with us, and gravy from the drippings sprinkled over everything. Mr. Weber said that biscuits and gravy were his favorite southern meal and he missed them. I probably didn't make them just like he remembered, but I did my best, and he seemed real appreciative. He made his own coffee on the stove, and the fragrance from the fresh-brewed pot, mixed with the sizzling sausages in the skillet, filled the cabin and made it seem cheerful and homey. We were laughing and talking together, and Mr. Weber was doing his best to entertain the younger kids with stories. I suppose we looked a pretty contented lot for the first time since we got to Miracle.

"Why, Miz Corrie," said Mr. Weber, "you is one fine cook! You's gwine t' make some feller a right fine missus one day."

I blushed and giggled. "Not me, Mr. Weber. I figure I'll just be a schoolteacher."

"Ma says Corrie's too interested in books to get a husband," chimed in Becky impudently.

"Stuff an' nonsense!" exclaimed the blacksmith. "Meanin' no disrespec' to the dead, that is. Why look at Miz Parrish! She's one of de smartest people I knows, an' she got hersel' a right fine husban'—I knowed him person'ly. An' they is plenty o' fellers like him, eben in dese parts—jist you wait an' see."

"Are you going to get married, Corrie?" asked Tad.

"No, Tad, don't be ridiculous," I said, but the others had a good laugh over his question. It felt so good to see everyone laughing that I didn't mind that it was at my expense.

Then without warning the door opened and in walked Pa.

His clothes were all dusty as if he'd been riding a great distance. His beard was scruffy and his hat had dirt caked on it. He strode in as though he'd only been gone an hour, took off his coat, unstrapped his gun belt and hung it up on its peg, then came over and sat down in the chair at the head of the table where he usually sat.

"I'm starved," he said just as normally as you please, "what's for breakfast?"

I got him a plate and he helped himself freely to several biscuits. There were still plenty left.

"Well, Marcus," he said after taking several large bites, "what brings you out our way?"

"Miz Parrish, she sent me up t' keep an eye out fer the kids while . . . while yo was gone, Mr. Drum."

"Oh, she did?"

His eyes narrowed some, but then he seemed to change his mind about what he wanted to say. "Well, that was right neighborly of her," he said. "I'll have to thank her next time I see her. And thank you, too, Marcus."

"Much obliged, sir." Marcus looked down at his plate as if he wasn't sure about something. Then he lifted his head and looked straight at Pa, "I scared off some prowlers here las' night," he said.

"Oh?" For a moment, the easy-going nonchalance Pa had been demonstrating seemed to slip, revealing a flicker of real concern. "You kids okay?"

"Yes, sir," I answered simply.

There was so much I wanted to say to my pa. But I could find no words. Yet when were there *ever* words to say what I was feeling? When was it ever easy to say things straight from the heart? Maybe never. Seems we were all trying so hard to protect ourselves from facing any more hurt, that we just couldn't let ourselves be honest with each other. I wanted so much for Pa to like us and accept us. And maybe he was suffering hurts I didn't know about. More than anything, I wanted us to be able to get to know one another. That's the way families were. Yet that was the one thing we didn't seem to be doing—getting to know each other. It was a reminder all over again that we weren't really a family.

Pa finished his breakfast, then he and Marcus Weber went out to take a look at the footprints and horse tracks from last night.

Nothing was ever said about what happened at Mrs. Parrish's; not about what I had said to him, not about the horses, not about Pa's leaving. Maybe it was better that way. What good would a lot of talk have done anyway?

Pa didn't act angry toward any of us. He was just the same as always. Things just went on as if nothing had happened.

Emily kept mostly to herself for a few days. I could tell she was heartbroken over Snowball. I tried to interest her in other diversions, and a time or two I thought I caught Pa making a special effort to talk to her. But she was pretty silent. What he'd done had really hurt her and it wasn't going to be easy for him to win back her friendship.

CHAPTER 19

AN UNEXPECTED VISITOR

The next few days went by uneventfully.

Pa didn't say much, kind of stayed out of our way, and spent most of his time up by the mine. Although I think he was embarrassed by what he'd done, he never brought it up, and neither did we. Zack was real sullen.

About three days later, when we were sitting around in the evening, the next big change came in our lives. It was pretty quiet, I had just finished putting Tad to bed and was coming back out into the main room of the cabin, when all of a sudden the door burst open and in walked a man we'd never seen before.

It didn't take longer than a second or two before we knew who it was.

"Nick!" Pa exclaimed, jumping up from his chair. "Where in tarnation you been?"

"Down t' Yankee Jim's," replied our uncle, flipping his hat onto the vacant peg by the door, and walking over toward the stove to see what he smelled in the pot.

"I went down there looking for you after you left," Pa said. "I scoured the countryside from Auburn to Shingle Springs, but no one had seen hide nor hair of you."

"I hid out down at Grizzly Flats for a spell. I didn't get to Jim's 'til after you was gone, but—"

He stopped and glanced around at the open mouths and wide eyes all staring at him.

"Hey, Drum," he finally said after he'd eyed us all, "who're all these kids?"

"Let me just ask you one thing first," said Pa, eyeing him intently. "Did you see a feller from back home some time last year?"

"Last year? How am I supposed to remember that?"

"You don't remember?" Pa returned sharply. "After all we done to hide who we are, you don't recall if you seen someone who can identify us? I always knew you was dim-witted, but this takes the cake. You just can't keep from gettin' us into a peck of trouble!"

"Come on, Drum, I don't see what—"

"Well, I don't suppose there's an easy way to tell you other than just saying it."

"Telling me what?"

"Aggie didn't make it," said Pa slowly. "Your sister's dead, Nick."

The men just looked at each other a second or two. The cabin was silent.

"These are your nieces and nephews, Nick," said Pa finally. "Me and Aggie's kids. They was all on their way out here when Aggie took a fever. But the kids made it—got here two, three weeks back. Kids," he said, turning to us, "say hello to your Uncle Nick."

I stood up and curtsied. Zack went over and silently shook Nick's hand. The younger ones just stared. Tad had gotten out of bed and stood watching in the doorway.

Uncle Nick just glanced around, first at one of us, then the other, all around, and finally back at Pa, without saying a word. Finally he slumped down into one of the two rocking chairs in the room and let out a long deep breath.

As I watched, I wondered what he was thinking. His face, beneath the scraggly several-day's growth of brownish whiskers, showed no apparent emotion. He stared vacantly ahead. Were his thoughts ones of sorrow about Ma? Or annoyance that we kids where there in his place? Or was he thinking about his own trouble with the sheriff and what he should do?

He was a handsome man, several years younger than Pa. Pa must've been thirty-nine or forty. Ma said he was twenty-two when they were married, and Ma a year younger. So I'd guess Uncle Nick to be thirty-three or thirty-four.

His hair was kind of a curly golden-brown, falling down into bushy sideburns around his ears. I saw Ma's family right off in the eyes, and in the prominent nose, too—a straight nose, not too big, but what they call the Roman look, I think. He had a strong resemblance to Zack. Even though he was kind of gazing off into the distance, his face had a lively appearance. Just from looking, I figured him to be more talkative than Pa. He may have been in trouble, but he didn't look anxious or upset about it. In fact, in spite of whatever his difficulties were, he looked like the kind of fellow who enjoyed life and didn't let too many things get him down.

All of a sudden I realized I was staring. I looked away hastily, then went over to the stove. The least I could do was be hospitable, I thought. After all we were in *his* home.

"Would you like some stew and bread, Uncle Nick?" I said, getting a plate.

He jolted himself out of his reverie. "Why, that sounds mighty nice," he said. "What's your name, girl?"

"Cornelia," I answered.

"Yeah, o' course! How could I forget little Cornelia! You musta been two or three when I left New York."

"I last saw her when she was seven," put in Pa, "and you only left a year ahead of me."

"I guess you're right," laughed Uncle Nick. "You lose track o' time out here, you know."

"Speaking of names, Nick," said Pa, "the young'uns here know all about the *Matthews* dodge."

Uncle Nick nodded thoughtfully.

I set the plate down on the table. He sat down at the

bench and tore into it like he hadn't eaten in a week.

"Corrie," Pa said, "why don't you get the young'uns bedded down? Me and your uncle's got some things to talk about."

I motioned to Becky and Emily to come with me. Zack just kept sitting, and Pa didn't say nothing more. I took the girls into the bedroom and got Tad back into his bunk. When I came back out about ten minutes later, Zack was still sitting there listening, and no one paid much attention to me. Pa's voice sounded serious.

" . . . but don't you know what a blame fool thing it was to do?"

"I didn't think," Uncle Nick replied lamely. "Anyway, that fella recognized me first."

"You should've ignored him, denied who you was—anything."

"I didn't think there'd be no harm. It was Pete Wilkins. I grew up with him. It was awful good seein' someone from home, from the old days."

"You're telling *me* about home, about the *old days*!" Pa burst out. "At least you didn't have to leave a wife and kids!"

"Maybe you're right. But I'll never get to see Aggie again, either."

"I guess we made a mess of our lives," said Pa more sympathetically.

"You mean *I* made a mess, Drum."

Pa didn't answer, and I couldn't tell if he was agreeing or just didn't have anything to say.

Finally Uncle Nick went on, "What's done's done, anyway. What's the use of gettin' all riled at me now?"

" 'Cause maybe it ain't done with yet," answered Pa. "Didn't you hear what I just told you about them men the kids seen? Then that Parrish woman's Negro, he scared someone off the other night prowlin' around here. I tell you, Nick, Aggie ain't the only one who found out from that fella where we was."

"Pete wouldn't of said nothin'."

"They could've been watchin' the house, and Aggie."

"But everyone thought we was dead."

"Maybe the law did, though I'm not even sure about that, anymore. But the Catskill bunch . . . they wouldn't give up so easily. More'n likely they got wind of Aggie's leaving and tailed her."

"Followed her all the way out here? Come on, Drum. You don't really believe they coulda done that without some-one seein' 'em?"

"Aggie didn't know them. They coulda been part of the wagon train and no one would have been the wiser. All they had to do was see where she lit, and they'd have us."

"Na, I can't buy it! You said yourself you didn't see 'em in town."

"Well, somehow they got to us after all this time. You heard what I told you the kids saw. With a scar like that, who could it be but Krebbs?"

"Plenty of fellas has scars."

"Prowling around here at night . . . askin' questions about us. We never had no trouble all this time, till the kids showed up."

Uncle Nick said nothing in reply. He just sat thinking over Pa's words. "I jest can't believe they coulda trailed the kids so far."

"Men'll do anything for that kind of loot, and as long as they still think we got it, they'll never give up."

He stopped for a minute, then shook his head and muttered in exasperation, "Blast it! I thought we'd finally shaken that bunch of scum! Now the kids're gonna be in just as much danger as ever."

He thought a minute more, then something new seemed to occur to him. He looked up at Uncle Nick with renewed anger. "Which reminds me," he said, "it sure don't help none for you to keep gettin' yourself into fresh trouble. What were you thinking pulling your gun on Judd like that? Sometimes, Nick, I think you're still that fool trigger-happy teen-aged kid I pulled outta that free-for-all back in Schenectady."

"Just 'cause you saved my hide once doesn't mean you gotta treat me like a kid the rest of my days. I can take care of myself."

"You can take care of yourself like the hothead you are! I'll treat you like a man, Nick, when you stop needing me to nursemaid you! Now on top of the kids, and being found out by the Catskill Gulch Gang, I suppose I'm gonna have to get you outta this latest scrap and somehow make things right with the sheriff."

"Judd was itching for it. I told you that—it was his doing!"

"Just 'cause a man wants to start something, doesn't mean you gotta pull your gun and oblige him, right in front of the whole blamed town!"

"He called me a cheat."

"Judd's a bigger fool than you are and everyone knows it. So what if he called you a cheat. Besides, he was more than half drunk. Nobody was payin' heed to a word he said."

"I don't like a man spreadin' lies about me."

"So you pulled your gun on him, and then an hour later Judd is found dead in the alley next to the saloon, and everybody's wonderin' where you are! What good did it do you to protect your honor? If you'd a just kept your mouth shut and your gun in your holster, you wouldn't be in this fix."

Uncle Nick just sat where he was, sulking. Finally he burst out again, getting in one last argument in his defense. Funny, it almost reminded me of Zack whining back at Ma when he didn't want to do something.

"I didn't do it, I tell you!"

"I believe you," said Pa, with a sigh of frustration.

"It was that half-brother of his, Kile."

"Proving that and clearing you's not gonna be easy."

"There's bad blood in that family," said Uncle Nick.

"Everybody knows it, including the sheriff. And he knows Kile's been layin' for him, too."

"I know it, and you know it. But until the sheriff gets proof, you better just lay low here, and me and the kids'll not let on we seen hide nor hair of you. It'll do you good to keep out of the saloon and your hands off a deck of cards!"

CHAPTER 20

THE SHERIFF PAYS A VISIT

When we woke up the following morning Pa was gone. I didn't find out until later that he'd ridden off before daybreak north across the middle fork of the Yuba to some place called French Corral. Uncle Nick told us later that he'd gone looking for some old mountain man called Brennan, who was supposed to be distant kin to the fellow they'd been talking about named Kile.

At the time, however, all we saw was that Pa was gone, "on business," as Uncle Nick put it.

As a result we kids got to see more of Uncle Nick than we might have otherwise.

As I guessed, he was more talkative. Pa was still a little threatening to us all, but Uncle Nick was so friendly and good-natured he almost seemed like one of us. Before the day was out, he had Becky and Emily laughing and chasing him around the cabin with Tad up on his shoulders hanging on for dear life. Zack still hung back, but Nick even managed to coax a smile or two out of him, wrestling around with him on the floor of the cabin before dinner. He was just so lively we couldn't help having a good time around him.

After dinner, Pa'd always just sit down and everything'd get real quiet for a spell. But Uncle Nick didn't seem the sitting-around type. He always had to be doing something.

135

" 'You ever shot a Colt, boy?" he said as he got up from the table.

"Who, me?" said Zack.

"Who you think I'm talking to, your kid brother? What about it, have you ever?"

"Uh, no sir," Zack answered.

"How about we give it a try?"

Still bewildered, Zack wasn't sure what to think. Uncle Nick pulled his pistol out of its holster on the wall and, with an inquiring look on his face, waved it butt first toward Zack. Gradually it began to dawn on Zack what he meant.

"Yes, sir!" he said, jumping up and following Uncle Nick outside.

They walked up toward the mine together. I couldn't hear what they were saying, but I could tell by the excitement in Zack's voice that he was feeling good about the interest Uncle Nick was showing in him.

For the next half hour or so we could hear shots firing from up the creek, followed every so often by an excited yell from Zack.

Later that night, before bed, Uncle Nick sat with all of us and told us stories about himself and things he'd done. He never mentioned the trouble we knew he was in, but we still enjoyed it. We went to bed that night happier than any night since we'd got there, and all of us were really glad Uncle Nick had come back.

Pa got back about ten the following morning. He didn't say much, just got Uncle Nick aside and the two of them talked seriously for a while. Uncle Nick seemed to protest what Pa was telling him, but in the end they seemed to reach some agreement. Then Pa got back on his bay and galloped off again.

This time he was gone about two hours. Uncle Nick was quiet the whole time, fidgeting around nervously. After a while, he went out and saddled up his horse, then came back into the cabin and packed up some things in his saddlebags, as if he was planning to go someplace. Finally, he got his gun belt down from the peg by the door and strapped it around his waist. He had a determined look on his face, completely different than the carefree expression of the day before, when he'd been playing and laughing with us and showing us things all around the claim. He looked like I imagined a gunfighter would look, and I couldn't help wondering if he was an outlaw after all.

When Pa's horse came into view down the road, he had another rider with him. Uncle Nick told us to get inside the cabin. We obeyed, but as we were going I saw him loosen his horse's rein where it was tied on the hitching rail, as if in readiness for flight. But still he just stood there in front of the cabin as the two riders approached.

We went inside and closed the door. Zack and I were too curious not to know what was going on. So we went into the bedroom and watched from the window.

Pa rode up and got off his horse. He was the first of the three men to speak.

"Nick, I told the sheriff here that you'd give yourself up, long as he talked to old man Brennan first."

"That right, Matthews?" the other man said, still sitting in his saddle and looking down at Uncle Nick.

Uncle Nick nodded without much enthusiasm.

"You're in a barrel of trouble, Matthews," said the sheriff. "I've a good mind to run you in and slap you in jail right now. But this partner of yours seems to think he can clear you."

"I didn't shoot Judd," said Uncle Nick.

"Well, we'll see. That's not what the folks that heard you and him arguing in the saloon think."

"We may have argued. That don't mean I killed him. I never killed a man, and that's God's truth."

"Maybe you did and maybe you didn't. But I got to go on evidence, and the evidence all points toward you. In the meantime, is what Drum tells me true? Are you willing to place yourself in his custody and promise to stay put 'til I talk to Brennan, and give yourself up and face trial if it comes to that?"

"I ain't about to go to jail," said Uncle Nick pointedly.

"Be reasonable, Nick," put in Pa. "If you run again, they'll have to put a price on your head. Then you'll take a slug in the back."

"Listen to the man, Matthews," said the sheriff. "Running away just says to everyone that you're guilty. If you give yourself up willingly, I can try to make things easier for you, and it'll say to a jury that you know you're innocent. I'm inclined to believe your story, but you got to do your part."

"It's the only way, Nick. I talked to Brennan yesterday, and he'll tell the sheriff that Kile slept out at his shack for two nights after the incident. He'll tell what Kile told him, too."

"Okay, I'll stay put," replied Uncle Nick at length. "But old Brennan better not double-cross us."

"Good," said the sheriff, looking relieved. "Now you two stay where you are. I'll ride up to French Corral tomorrow and see if I can't get Brennan to corroborate your story."

He spun around on his sorrel, then galloped back the way he had come.

Pa and Uncle Nick tied up their horses and walked slowly inside, hanging up their guns by the door.

"It's the only way you're gonna get out from under this," Pa was saying.

"I still don't like it," said Uncle Nick. "Though it's not that I don't appreciate what you done for me."

"Yeah. Maybe next time I'll just let you dangle from your own rope."

Uncle Nick didn't answer, just plopped down in a chair like he'd had a tongue-lashing from his own pa, and stared straight ahead. Nothing more was said about the incident the rest of the day.

CHAPTER 21

MIRACLE SPRING'S BIG DAY

Three days later the sheriff returned. Zack heard the conversation that Pa and Uncle Nick had with him outside.

"That man Brennan told the sheriff that Kile had been around and confessed to killing Judd!" Zack said. "As soon as the sheriff said that, Uncle Nick let out a big sigh of relief. The sheriff was upset though," Zack went on. "Because when he asked Brennan where Kile was, the old man just replied, 'I ain't about t' turn one o' my own kin int' the law. I told ya what he said, but I ain't gonna tell ya where the varmint is!' "

"Then what happened?" I asked.

"The sheriff just told Uncle Nick to watch out and not to get himself involved in any more trouble. He said he wouldn't go so easy on him next time."

"And what'd Uncle Nick say?"

"Oh, he sorta thanked the sheriff for being so under-standing," said Zack. "But he didn't like saying the words. I think Pa made him do it," he added.

The next few days passed peacefully enough. Now that the cloud over Uncle Nick was gone, at least for a while, he seemed even more fun-loving than before.

In those days of quiet, I did a lot of thinking. We had been in Miracle Springs for a month. The reflection of the setting sun each day on the gold, red and yellow leaves said that fall was truly in the air. Already many of those colorful leaves had fallen to the ground and were decaying underfoot.

So much had happened since the previous spring, when those same leaves were growing from tiny buds. Then, I was three thousand miles away from this place. Now, here I was in California, with my brothers and sisters, our ma gone, and a whole new life before us.

On the outside I was still the same fifteen-year-old girl who left New York. But inside I felt like I'd aged twenty years. I could hardly imagine more adventures—good and bad—happening to one person in a single lifetime, although books I've read about people like Robinson Crusoe and Leather-Stocking in *The Last of the Mohicans* make what's happened to me seem a bit tame.

But, I suppose that especially here in the West, lots of things are bound to happen to everyone—some happy and exciting things, and some tragic things, like losing our ma. I guess she would say that's what life's all about.

One of these fall mornings began with a surprise when Pa woke us all bright and early. That in itself was unusual, for he'd never gotten us up a single day since we'd been there. Usually I'd rise at first light to find him out of the cabin and already at work somewhere about the place. But on this morning he called us out of bed while it was still dim and gray outside. Bacon was frying in the skillet on the stove and coffee was already brewing when I came out.

"Thought you young'uns might like to go into Miracle today," he said in a voice more chipper than usual. Uncle Nick's return and the temporary clearing of the trouble with the sheriff seemed to have raised his spirits.

"Oh, we'd love it!" I replied as I began to stir up some buckwheat batter.

"Big doin's in town today," he went on. "Why, history's likely gonna be made. You kids won't want to miss that."

Just then Uncle Nick walked in from outside. "You going to town today, Nick?" asked Pa.

"You think it's safe?"

"Judd's kin ain't gonna bother you none. They know you didn't do it as well as I do. And if you keep yourself outta trouble, the sheriff ain't gonna do nothin'."

"I wasn't thinking of that," said Uncle Nick. "I was thinking of the other trouble that you think mighta followed us here."

"Oh, yeah," said Pa. He lowered his voice as he continued. "But if it is Krebbs that's nosing around, our staying out of town's not gonna stop him. If that was him the kids seen, he already knows our place. And if we can spot him in the crowd in town, then it might even be to our advantage. At least we'd know for sure he was here."

"Yeah, but he ain't actually laid eyes on either of us yet. It could just be a coincidence."

"If it's Krebbs, it's no coincidence. He's out for our blood, I tell you. That is, if he can't find the hundred grand. And we sure ain't got it!"

Uncle Nick sighed. Neither of them were paying much attention to me, but I was straining every nerve to hear what they were saying.

"I shoulda listened to you in the first place," Uncle Nick said. "Them was a bad bunch to get mixed up with. But all I could think of was how easy that bank was gonna be and how much money there was inside."

"Well, like you said the other day, we done what we done and we can't undo it. So we just gotta watch ourselves now."

When there was a lull in their talk, I asked, "What's going on in town?"

"Newspaper's coming to the area, that's what," answered Uncle Nick as if he had struck El Dorado. "You especially oughta be interested in that, Corrie."

"Me?" I said, and stopped stirring to glance over at him.

"Sure. I seen you night after night scrawling in that there journal of yours. What're you raising here, Drum?" he said to Pa as he flashed a wink in my direction, "Some female Bill Shakespeare?"

I blushed. "I'm just writing down my experiences, that's all—Ma said I should."

"And your ma was right," put in Pa to my defense. He thought Uncle Nick was giving me a bad time, and he hadn't seen the twinkle in his brother-in-law's eye.

"Well, around these parts," Uncle Nick went on, "just being able to write proper puts you up there with them author fellers."

I still didn't see what he was getting at.

"What does a newspaper coming to town have to do with me?" I asked.

"Well, even a no-account ignoramus like me knows that them newspaper fellers write. Seems like with all your writing in that there journal, you'd have something in common with them. Or at least that you'd be interested in them coming to Miracle."

"Yes—yes, I am, Uncle Nick," I said. "I guess I never thought of it in that way before."

"I expect your ma'd want to see you get some kind of education," added Pa, "even in this uncivilized country, where there ain't so much as a school for you." He mumbled the words almost as an apology, as if he was embarrassed at saying something thoughtful. "The newspaper'd be a good thing for you to know about and get involved in."

I smiled. It was nearly the first time he'd shown any real interest in any of us. So newspaper or not, I knew this was indeed a special day!

After breakfast we all loaded up in Pa's old buckboard, hitched to his own bay mare. It was not as comfortable as our old wagon. Emily still missed Snowball, and the bay showed in no uncertain terms that she did not appreciate being put to this kind of labor. But none of us said a word. We all silently realized it was a subject best left alone.

When we got to town there was almost a carnival atmosphere in the air.

Uncle Nick said he hadn't seen it this lively since the actor Edwin Booth had performed in town. "It ain't just the paper, you see," he explained. "As hard as these fellers work around here, anytime they can turn somethin' into a celebration, they'll do it. The paper's just an excuse to whoop it up for a day or two."

A raised platform had been built in front of the largest saloon in town where the two main streets intersected. It was draped in red, white, and blue banners just like election day back home. There was no one on the platform yet, but Uncle Nick said there'd be plenty of speeches before the day was done.

We stopped and piled out of the wagon while Pa tied the horse to a hitching post. Some of he and Uncle Nick's friends came up, and there was a flurry of back-slappin' and guffaws. When Pa turned to us and said they had some business to attend to, his friends all winked and chuckled. Then he told us to have a look around. They walked off down the street toward the Gold Nugget, and we were left gaping at the sights and wondering what to do.

Down near the livery stable there was a sharpshooting contest going on in a big corral. Not far from where we stood, down one of the other streets, several Indians in war paint were doing some dances to the steady beat of the tom-toms. Then down the same street in the opposite direction was a fellow holding a "medicine show."

The boys wanted to see the sharpshooters. They didn't even wait to ask but just dashed off excitedly, Tad running to keep up with Zack.

I was curious about the Indians, wondering if one of them might be the Indian brave I'd seen out by the stream. But Emily was afraid, and I can't say I blame her, for they did have a rather alarming appearance at first. So finally we decided on the medicine show.

I'd never seen anything like it before. A big box-like wagon stood in the middle of the street, painted all over with pictures and banners, and the words "Dr. Aloyisius P. Jack's Famous Miracle Rejuvenator" printed in fancy, colorful letters on the side. A man I figured was the famous Dr. Jack stood on a little platform at the back of the wagon. He was dressed in a bright yellow frock coat that hung to his knees over tan pinstriped trousers and a red vest. If he meant for this outfit to attract customers, it worked, for there were twenty or thirty men, mostly miners, gathered around. He wasn't a big man, but standing up on that platform in those bright clothes and his black stovepipe hat, he looked mighty impressive. His eyes glinted and shone when he talked, and his long, brown beard wagged to give just the right emphasis to his words.

"I can see the town of Miracle Springs is not short of intelligent men . . ." he was saying. "Men of vision! Men of wisdom! Men of. . . ."

He seemed to falter as he scanned the crowd. Then to my horror I realized he was looking right at me!

" . . . and young ladies, too!" he went on in a merry tone. "Ah, yes, I can see this is a town of no mean populace!"

The audience chuckled and applauded, and all at once Emily, Becky, and I found ourselves being jostled nearer to the front.

"Welcome one and all!" Dr. Jack went on. "Ladies—" he winked at us as he said the word, "and gentlemen! With great pleasure I present to you the most stupendous medical discovery of this century! My very own 'Miracle Rejuvenator'! And is it not appropriate that it should be named as your fine town?"

"What's it do, Doc?" yelled someone from the crowd.

"A most intelligent question!" shot back the doctor. "Most intelligent, indeed. The secrets of my Rejuvenator are vast, to be sure. It contains herbs and potions that I, myself, procured at great peril and personal danger from the great Cherokee Indian Chief Oouchalatah. Tell me, my friends of Miracle Springs, have you ever seen an Indian with gout or ague? The prevention of these two maladies are but two of the marvelous feats of Dr. Jack's Rejuvenator. Stomach ailments too will be a thing of the past. Regular use of my elixir improves vision and strengthens the blood—and you all know what that can mean on those cold nights at the diggin's!"

I didn't know what it meant. But lots of others seemed to, for several started waving money and yelling.

"Gimme a bottle of that!"

"One dollar, folks," Dr. Jack was saying again. "One slim dollar to possess the benefits of youth again!"

He glanced down at me. "And, young lady, surely there is someone you know who can benefit from this wonderful tonic?"

"I haven't got a dollar," I said.

"I got ten cents," piped up Becky. I felt like stuffing a sock in her mouth.

"Do you now?" mused the doctor. "Well, little lady, I just happen to be running a special for ladies such as yourself—ten cents a bottle!"

But before Becky could get her fingers around her money, one of the onlookers who had already made his purchase yelled out, "Ooo-wee! This here's one-hundred-proof whiskey!"

Dr. Jack cleared his throat deprecatingly. "I must admit that one of the ingredients does happen to be a small amount of alcohol—to enhance the flavor only!"

I waited no longer, yanking Becky and Emily away from the so-called "medicine" show. As we broke through the crowd we nearly ran headlong into Mrs. Parrish.

"Hello, girls," she said cheerfully. "I just saw your brothers, and was hoping to run into you. I'm so glad your father brought you."

"Uncle Nick's here, too," chimed in Becky proudly.

"Ah, so your uncle's back?" she asked, looking at me with a worried frown.

"Yes, Ma'am," I said. "Pa brought the sheriff out to the cabin and got Uncle Nick's problem all straightened out."

"That's wonderful," she replied. "I just hope it stays straightened out."

"Pa said this was an important day for Miracle," I said.

"Indeed it is. Every influence that brings civilization more and more to the wilds is to be enthusiastically welcomed." She paused thoughtfully. "I am a bit surprised he saw it in that light, however. Surprised, but still pleased."

"Why do you say that, Ma'am?"

"I just thought that men such as your father and uncle, you know, from their *background*—"

But she let her words trail away unfinished. I guess she didn't want to speak ill of Pa or Uncle Nick in front of us, though her look didn't suggest she was going to say anything bad. Actually, she looked pleasantly surprised, just like she'd said.

Anyway, she started up again on a different subject almost in the same breath. "Well, girls, the formal festivities are about to begin—mostly long-winded speeches—but historical, nonetheless."

She cast down her eyes almost timidly—a very uncharacteristic gesture for her, then added, "I myself will be delivering a few short remarks as well."

"How wonderful, Mrs. Parrish!" I said. "We wouldn't miss it."

"It won't be much. Many of the town fathers, so to speak, thoroughly resent having a woman up on the platform with them. But since I operate the second largest enterprise in town, they had no choice—especially when I insisted. I have an ulterior motive, however. I want to advertise for another historic event which will be coming up shortly."

"Ma'am?"

"Don't you remember? The preacher will be here in less than two weeks—almost any day now."

"Oh, yes."

"Come along," she said, taking Becky's hand. "I'll walk you over. But I'm afraid after that you'll have to be on your own."

The throngs of people scattered around town were beginning to migrate toward the raised, banner-covered platform. Mrs. Parrish found us a place near the front. Seated at the back of the platform, a band was playing "Oh, Susanna." Four men were seated on chairs in front of the band, all looking very important in their brown and black frock coats and matching trousers, silk ties and waistcoats, wearing stovepipe and derby hats.

One of the men I recognized as the sheriff who had come out to the cabin about Uncle Nick. Mrs. Parrish said his name was Simon Rafferty. He was a big, barrel-chested man, and his general size, solid build, and huge cigar, made him look more like a locomotive than a speech maker. I guess since Miracle had no other officials, he was the most important dignitary we had.

Next to the him sat a tall, younger man whom Mrs. Parrish told me about as we approached the platform. His name was Franklin Royce, and he looked very important. But whereas the constable seemed to be *trying* to look important, Mr. Royce just did. You would never mistake him for anything but an important man. There were two other men with them—the General Store owner, Mr. Bosely, and another man I didn't know. I thought he must be the newspaper man, for surely he would have to be on the stand. I liked the look of him immediately. He had kind eyes behind his spectacles, though his thin, taut lips seemed unaccustomed to nonsense. Maybe he was just a little frightened about the speech he was going to have to make. He must have been about forty, though his thinning hair was more blonde than gray. His skin was pale and looked soft to the touch—a sure sign of someone who hadn't been long in the West.

Mrs. Parrish joined the men, who all stood and tipped

their hats to her as she took the fifth and last chair on the platform.

I must say, Mrs. Parrish looked just as important as the men as she sat up there. In fact, she was almost regal in her gray silk dress and the matching hat with its pink feather tilted just so on her brown hair, all pinned up on her head in soft ringlets. I wondered if I'd ever look *half* as lovely as she did.

The band was striking up "Old Dan Tucker" when Uncle Nick came up beside me. I was beginning to wonder if we'd see him again before it was time to go home. But here he was seeking us out! I smelled a faint whiff of whiskey on his breath as he spoke.

"You kids having a good time?" he asked.

"Oh, yes, wonderful, Uncle Nick!" I answered.

"Now comes the boring part," he said.

"Where's Pa?" I asked.

"Shhh!" he replied with a finger to his lips. "You remember what he told you on the way in—he's still just Mr. Drum! Can't nobody find out who he is 'til we take care of this little problem we have with the fellers from back home." I don't know if Pa'd have wanted him saying all that to me. Always before when they talked, they were very secretive. But I'd heard enough to figure they were in some kind of trouble from home, too, and that men were looking for them—dangerous men, by the sound of it.

"But Mrs. Parrish knows," I whispered.

"Yeah, and your pa said he was a fool to tell her. But he told her to keep quiet."

"She won't tell," I said. "She's a real fine lady. Look, there she is up on the stand getting ready to make a speech. Doesn't she look grand?"

Uncle Nick gave a more interested look, then rubbed his stubbly chin. "Well, by Jove, you're right, a handsome woman at that!" he finally said.

"So, where's Pa—er . . . Mr. Drum?" I asked again.

"Over with some of the boys. He'll be here pretty soon."

The speeches started, and mostly what followed *was* boring, as Uncle Nick had predicted. About halfway through the first speech, Pa wandered over to where we were all standing.

The speakers all talked about "this fair town" and the "flowering of civilization" and the "wealth not only in mineral, but in human resources, also."

I never heard a town get so many compliments, and wondered if they were really talking about ramshackle Miracle Springs with its sprawling, ragged conglomeration of tents and claims and cabins, its five saloons and rough inhabitants. But maybe they were speaking in terms of what they hoped Miracle would one day be like.

When Mrs. Parrish got up, she finished off her speech by reminding everyone that Miracle would "truly come of age when we receive our first man of God." She told everyone to set aside Sunday, November 27, for that very auspicious occasion when the first services would be held. There was scattered applause as she sat down, but I had the clear impression there would not be nearly so good a turnout on that day as this.

"What's that woman thinkin'?" grumbled Pa. "Sunday's our day of rest from work, not a day to fill up with meetin's!"

Somehow, though, I had the feeling Mrs. Parrish would see to it that there was a decent showing for the preacher's first Sunday!

After the speeches were over, and the crowd gave several cheers for the newspaper's editor, Mr. Culver Singleton, everyone began to disperse back toward the various sideshows or the saloons. Mrs. Parrish stepped down off the platform and walked toward us. With her were Mr. Royce and Mr. Singleton. Introductions were made, and I couldn't help feeling quite honored at the nice things Mrs. Parrish said when she told Mr. Singleton about us. The man named

Royce already seemed to know Pa and Uncle Nick. They tipped hats and shook hands, but no smiles were exchanged. What a world of difference there was between my rough-looking, quiet Pa and the two city-bred men in their fancy suits! But it didn't make Pa any less in my eyes.

"Well, Drum," said Mr. Royce, "how's that little mine of yours doing?" His voice sounded almost condescending.

"Fair to middling," answered Pa.

"Have you reconsidered my offer to sell?"

Hearing the words, Uncle Nick, who'd been on the edge of the conversation not paying much attention, now angled his way to the forefront and answered the question directed at Pa.

"We told you last month, Royce, our claim ain't on the market."

"Even though I'm offering you more than what it's worth?"

"Not more'n what it's worth to us."

"What do you say, Drum?" said Mr. Royce, looking at Pa. "Does your partner speak for you?"

"He does. The claim ain't for sale." He didn't seem to like the other man's tone, and his eyes narrowed and seemed even harder than usual.

"I heard you lost it in a card game not long ago," persisted the banker.

"Got it back."

"I simply don't understand your attachment to the place. Some of the other men to whom I've made offers have been more reasonable."

Mr. Royce spoke casually, but I could tell he was driving at something.

"I've had geologists all over that area, you know, and the scientific conclusion is that the gold for several square miles is played out."

"Then why are you so all-fired intent on gettin' your hands on it?" said Uncle Nick heatedly. The whiskey must've begun reaching his brain.

Royce chuckled—a little nervously, I thought—but quickly regained his composure.

"I'm a banker, Mr. Matthews. I'm pledging my future to this area. I'm interested in acquiring good land, land with water and timber, for the future settlers who will come to Miracle Springs to make their homes here. Of course a banker must keep abreast of mineral developments in an area such as this, but I assure you, gold is of secondary concern to me."

"And that's why you're buying up whatever claims you can, for the streams and the trees?" asked Pa, hardly hiding the sarcasm in his voice.

"Well, that's putting it a bit simply perhaps, but I suppose that catches the gist of it, Mr. Drum."

"You say the gold is played out for several miles, Mr. Royce. Just how far exactly?" asked Mrs. Parrish.

"Not to worry, Mrs. Parrish," the banker replied. "The Parrish mine is well out of that range and should have a few more profitable years left."

"This is a simply fascinating conversation," said Mr. Singleton enthusiastically. Until then he had, though silent, been keenly observing the speakers. "*The California Gazette* will want a feature article on this subject."

"I should be glad to supply you with an interview," said Mr. Royce.

"Thank you kindly, sir," replied the newsman. "But a woman's perspective might be a novel approach. In fact, I can see *two* articles, one featuring the big mining operation like yours, Mrs. Parrish, contrasted with a small two-man partnership. Might you consent to an interview, Mr. Matthews?"

"What?" said Uncle Nick, rubbing his face like he had just awakened from a deep sleep. "You mean you want to put what I got to say in that newspaper of yours?"

"I believe you are representative of a large percentage of

my readership, and thus your perspective would lend greater appeal. You must give it some thought, and you too, Mrs. Parrish."

Then the newspaper man smiled weakly at Mr. Royce who seemed suddenly to have been edged out of the proceedings. "And in the future," he said to him, "I'm sure I shall also want to run an article on the banker's view in all this."

Then some folks came and led Mr. Singleton away.

Mr. Royce used the opportunity to return to the subject of Pa and Uncle Nick's claim. He turned to Uncle Nick, who had begun sauntering away.

"I understand, Matthews," he said, "that the population around your little cabin has grown considerably of late." As he spoke he nodded in our direction. "In light of that, I can understand your reluctance to part with the only roof over your head. Because of these new developments, I am prepared to double my previous offer for your land. It would give you the opportunity to move into town and start a new life for yourself and the young folks here—your long-lost kinfolk, as I understand it."

"We told you before, Royce," said Pa, not even giving Uncle Nick a chance to reply, "our mine ain't for sale. We'll do just fine where we are—all of us."

"I only thought for the children's sake—"

"The children will be here only through the winter anyway."

My heart sank as Pa said the words, but I tried not to show my disappointment.

"Oh, I see. I understood they had no other family but your . . . uh, your partner here, and that—"

"Well, you understood wrong! You may be able to smooth-talk Pickins and MacDougall outta their claims, and I ain't heard what Larsen's decided to do about your offer. But Nick and I ain't selling!"

Mr. Royce said nothing further, merely tipped his hat and ambled slowly away.

"There's something about that man I don't like," Pa muttered. "I don't think I altogether trust him."

"I hope you don't take Mr. Royce's words completely to heart, Mr. Drum," said Mrs. Parrish. "Geology reports can be misleading at times."

"Oh, I don't," Pa replied.

"You and the children's uncle have put a great deal of labor into your claim. I would hate to see you give up on it."

"Royce can keep his geologists," said Pa.

Then followed an awkward silence. It was Uncle Nick who broke it. "Mighty fine speech you gave up there, Ma'am."

"Thank you. I hope it inspired you to attend our first church services here in Miracle Springs." She said the words addressing my uncle, but I could see her glancing over toward Pa as she spoke.

"Well . . . uh, let me see—when was that again?"

"The children need to have their spiritual education enhanced, you know, Mr. Matthews . . . Mr. Drum." Now she looked over at Pa.

His mood changed abruptly. I don't know if he didn't like Mrs. Parrish meddling with us kids, or if he just wanted to be left alone to do his own thinking about religious matters. But he clearly didn't much like her giving him counsel about us.

"The kids'll get along just fine," he said, "without no one telling me what kind of education I oughta be giving 'em. Now if you'll pardon me, Ma'am," he added stiffly, touching the brim of his hat, "I gotta git along."

He spun around and strode off down the wooden sidewalk. Uncle Nick just stood there a moment longer, then walked off in the other direction toward the Gold Nugget. We stayed with Mrs. Parrish and she never mentioned our pa again.

CHAPTER 22

DINNER WITH ALKALI JONES

Over the next several days, mining and the status of gold in the streams and rivers and hills about Miracle became a major subject of conversation. Pa never discussed the mine with us kids. But when he was talking to Uncle Nick, or to anyone else whenever we'd go into town, that's mostly what they talked about. And I could tell he was more concerned about it than usual. He seemed to spend every spare minute either at the mine or at the stream.

I wanted to learn all I could about gold digging. It was such an important part of everyone's life around here. Pa was short on details, but Uncle Nick would answer my questions whenever I'd ask him.

I did learn a little about the two basic kinds of mining—placer and quartz. Most of the small claims around Miracle were placer operations in the rivers and streams. They used sluice boxes of many types, and lots of water. Pa and Uncle Nick had several sluice boxes situated on the stream at places where the water would run swiftly through them and sift out the gold as they dredged up dirt and gravel with a shovel and threw it into the top of the box. Watching them shovel and sift the dirt, and then pick through the bottom sections of the wooden chute looking for the specks of gold left behind, I could tell it was a lot of work for what little they found. I tried to draw a sketch of them working to put in my journal.

A person could find a lot more gold with quartz mining, but only rich men and mining companies could afford to do it profitably. Instead of above ground digging in streams, quartz miners dug and blasted their way into the side of a hill where they figured gold might exist, hollowing out a cavern that went inside the mountain. They searched about, hoping to run across a whole vein of the ore.

Pa and Uncle Nick began placer mining in the stream, but they dug out a cave up there at the mine, too, so I guess they had been trying their hand at both methods. They were digging it out by hand with a pick rather than dynamite, and Uncle Nick said it was slow going because it was just the two of them. But he said that's where the real gold is— inside the mountains, not in the streams. Pa warned us several times to keep away from the mine, especially the younger children.

"You gotta stay clear of the cave," he'd tell Tad and Becky every day. "You never can tell when one of them roof timbers'll give way." Then turning to me and Zack, he'd add, "You keep 'em outta there, you hear?"

One day, Alkali Jones came out to the cabin and stayed for supper. I learned more from the talkative old miner in that one day than I might have in weeks from our tight-lipped pa and carefree uncle.

"I tell you, Drum," said Mr. Jones, "that's jest stuff an' nonsense about the gold bein' all dried up."

"Franklin Royce's geologists come all the way from Harvard College in Massachusetts," said Pa. "Leastways, that's what he claims, though I don't believe them neither."

"Aw, what do they know about minin' way back there?"

"If they was workin' for anyone but Royce, I might have to pay 'em some heed. But like the Indians say, Royce tends to speak with a forked tongue."

"He's a snake, is that what yer meanin'?"

"Maybe that's a mite harsh, Alkali. I don't like him much neither, but he is a banker."

"One an' the same, iffen ya ask me."

"I gotta agree with Alkali," put in Uncle Nick. "I think the varmint's up to no good around here. I wouldn't put nothing past him."

The talk lulled as I brought a plate of fresh biscuits to the table. Pa lifted two from the dish, buttered them, ate one in two huge bites, and then spoke as the other two men did likewise.

"Well," said Pa, "our placer operation on the stream is slowing down, and there's no denying it. What do we get, Nick, an ounce, maybe two a week, if we're lucky and work at it? That is if I can keep you here working at all!"

Uncle Nick grinned half-sheepishly and looked over at Mr. Jones.

"Weren't it the underground potential you was lookin' for in this claim when ya got it in the first place?" asked Jones.

"Wasn't really looking for nothing," Pa answered. "Not long after we got here, Nick won it in a Monte game from old Phil Potter."

"Phil was always talking about a bonanza vein and such like," said Uncle Nick. "But I think all that was just so we'd let the claim cover the pot on the table, which was worth more'n we ever took from this stream. Probably nothing but talk."

"I don't know," mused Pa. "He was from the coal mines over in Cornwall, England, and all his friends hereabouts said he knew his stuff." A slow smile spread over his face as he recalled the incident. "That was some game," he said. "You had them cold, and they never knew it."

Uncle Nick laughed. "And now they got their revenge—sticking us with a dead mine!"

"Potter'd be bound to know more'n any blamed Harvard geologist!" said Mr. Jones.

"Too bad Phil ain't around no more," said Pa. He popped the second biscuit into his mouth in one piece. The talk slowed while he chewed and the other two men concentrated on their plates.

When the meal was finished, Pa leaned back in his chair and lit up a cigar. Mr. Jones put his feet up on a log and filled up his pipe, and then lit it with deliberate satisfaction. Uncle Nick threw a quick tickle toward Tad and Becky, then shadow-boxed a couple punches in Zack's direction. The resulting giggles from all three contrasted with the serious talk always coming out of Pa's mouth. I think Uncle Nick might've liked to be more involved with us kids, but was just a little afraid of what Pa might say. Even though he was a man to us, every once in a while I'd catch a look in his eye that made me think he almost looked on Pa as a pa too, more than just a big brother—or brother-in-law. But the talk soon settled back again around the topic of the future of the mine.

As the smoke curled silently up in the air from the cigar and pipe, the girls and I started to clear the supper things off the table. But I moved quietly, hushing the little ones up every so often so I wouldn't lose the thread of the conversation.

"So what're ya aimin' t' do, Drum?" Mr. Jones finally asked, punctuating his words with a wisp of smoke. He talked mostly to Pa, more or less acknowledging him as the head of the partnership, even though it seemed to be common knowledge that the claim was in Uncle Nick's name. Folks in town called it the Matthews claim. To all but their best friends, Pa tried to pretend he was just in the background. I still didn't know why.

"That's one of the reasons I wanted to see you, Alkali," replied Pa. "I know you're bound for Marysville—and you'd find better pickings over yonder on the Feather. But we were thinking—and me and Nick's talked this over and are in complete agreement. If you wanted to stay in Miracle, you could work here with us and help us get the mine deeper into the mountain. Three men could do a lot of things two men just can't."

"There's lots of fellers who'd jump at the chance o' teamin' up with the two o' ya, Drum—younger an' stronger than me. Hee, hee!"

"Yeah, but none we'd trust like you. Nick and me, we've got . . . well, let's just say there's some of those fellers you mentioned who would be a mite too inquisitive to suit us, and we got some things we just can't let get out."

"Nobody can stop that mouth of yours," laughed Uncle Nick from where he stood by the fire, "but you know when to keep it shut, too."

"Thank ya kindly—that is, if yer meanin's what I think it is!"

"Don't worry," added Pa, chuckling himself. "Nick was paying you a compliment."

Mr. Jones might have blushed his pleasure at my pa's words, but it was impossible to tell for certain since so little of his skin showed through the hair and grime. His beard was at least four inches longer and two inches thicker than Pa's.

"It might turn out Royce's eastern fellers are right," Pa went on. "I'm guaranteeing nothing. All our efforts could be for nothing—"

"Pshaw!" exclaimed Alkali Jones with a wave of his hand in the air. "That's the least of my worries. I been workin' all my life fer nuthin', anyhow! Hee, hee! No reason to stop now!"

"I'm going on nothing more than Phil Potter's word and my own gut instinct."

Mr. Jones winked coyly. "Ya may like t' keep it quiet, Drum—an' I know ya got yer secrets houndin' ya from wherever ya come from—"

Pa shot him a keen glance. But a moment's look apparently satisfied him that Mr. Jones knew nothing more than he was saying, and meant no harm by the statement.

"—but I know you! You know yer own share o' that geology stuff."

"I may know a thing or two," consented Pa, "and I'm trusting to that."

"That strike o' yers, when ya went over t' Rough an' Ready by yerself back in '49—that was more'n pure luck."

"Maybe. Though it didn't do me much good, and here I am still scratching the soil for nothing more than dirt."

"The gold's here," said Uncle Nick. "I can *feel* it!"

"There's no cash in feeling it in a lame-brained head," said Pa with a wink in Mr. Jones' direction. "You gotta feel it in your hand!"

Mr. Jones took the opportunity to let loose a high-pitched cackle.

"And we still gotta account for Royce's statement," Pa went on, serious again. "What reason would the man have to spread false rumors?"

"To scare folks off and buy claims up cheap!" said Uncle Nick.

"He could never get away with it," Pa replied. "If there really was much gold left, he'd never pull a swindle like that off. This ain't '49 or '50. We're not just a batch of greenhorns anymore."

"Don't ya believe it, Drum!" said Alkali Jones. "You and I and Nick may be too smart fer that. But there's still enough of the other kind around."

There was a long pause while the two men smoked in silence, rocking back and forth on the legs of their two chairs. Uncle Nick still stood with his back to the fire. I guess Zack had been listening to the conversation, too. Now he looked over to where Pa and Mr. Jones were seated.

"Mr. . . .uh . . . Mr. *Drum*," he said hesitantly, his high-pitched voice both cracking and lowering as he spoke. "I could work at your mine."

Pa stared up at him as if it was the first time he had even noticed my brother. But before he could say anything in reply, Mr. Jones spoke up.

"Hee, hee, Drum! Looks like you don't need me after all! Hee, hee!"

I could see a cloud come over Zack's face. Right then there was nothing he hated more than being treated like a child.

"I'm a real good worker," he said defensively.

"The mine ain't no place for kids," said Pa, exactly as he had a hundred times before.

"Hey, Drum, hold up a minute," said Uncle Nick, with a hint of fun in his voice. He saw an opportunity to speak up for us kids when Pa couldn't say too much to contradict him. "Watch how you're talking about my sister's boy! He's no runt—even a mite big for his age."

"If I'm t' be one o' the princeeples in this here operation," chimed in Alkali Jones, "well, I figure we need jest about all the help we can git."

"He's just a boy, Alkali," said Pa. "Blastin' and pickin' our way into that hillside is man's work."

"Why, jest look at them muscles shapin' up in his arms," Mr. Jones went on. "Drivin' a rig across them plains got him in fine shape fer gold minin'. 'Sides, he's yer partner's kin. So ya can trust him better'n ya can trust even the likes o' an ol' coot like me! Hee, hee!"

Pa saw he was out voted. He took a long, agonizingly slow puff on his cigar, all the while looking Zack over from head to foot as if pondering his friend's words. Finally he spoke again.

"You know how to do what you're told, boy?" he asked sternly.

Zack nodded.

"Well then, maybe we'll give you a try one day. But mind you, there ain't going to be no larkin' on this here job!"

I found that last statement a strange one considering what a hard time Pa was always giving Uncle Nick for getting into scraps that took him away from the work. Yet working the mine seemed to have suddenly become more important to everyone. I wondered if it had anything to do with us being there, or if something inside Pa just wanted to prove Mr. Royce wrong.

Whatever the reason, activity at the mine began to pick up. The buckboard, drawn by Alkali Jones' mule, made several trips into town bringing back loads of mining supplies and cases of dynamite. Meanwhile, Tad insisted that he was almost as big as his brother and should be allowed to work, too. And Becky's natural recklessness and curiosity kept her constantly in the way. It was all I could do to keep Tad and Becky out from under the mens' feet.

But winter was coming on too, and days of rain kept halting the work altogether. Uncle Nick said that in the spring they'd really be able to get going.

I couldn't help thinking that if Pa had his way, by springtime we Hollister children might be on our way back East.

CHAPTER 23

SOME TIME ALONE

One of my favorite diversions during those chilly days of late fall was to sneak away from the cabin for a walk in the woods.

Taking care of the young'uns, and trying my best to put a decent meal on the table for Pa and Uncle Nick, and sometimes Mr. Jones, every night, tired me out from morning till bedtime. I wasn't a ma yet, but being those kids' oldest sister made me wonder sometimes why anybody'd *want* to be one. I didn't understand it back then, but now I know why Ma used to collapse in a chair and let out an exhausted sigh.

So I didn't get a chance to get away by myself too often. But sometimes I'd leave Zack or Emily in charge, or convince Tad and Becky that it was time for a nap or "quiet time," and then slip away for thirty or forty minutes—or even an hour, if I thought I could get away with it.

One morning, Pa said he had to go into town for some things, and Uncle Nick soon had everybody else loaded in the back of the wagon to go along. Pa didn't seem to mind, and finally looked around at me where I still stood by the cabin. "Ain't you coming, Corrie?"

I hesitated a moment. "I thought maybe I'd just stay home this time."

He looked at me kinda funny, then turned back and

snapped the reins and took off, while Uncle Nick and Tad ya-hoo'd in the back.

Five minutes later, there I was—*all alone* at the cabin! There was nothing but silence inside, and the sounds of the wilderness outside, to keep me company for several hours.

I could hardly contain my delight! But what should I do with this precious time?

Almost before I'd stopped to think about it, I tucked a copy of Sir Walter Scott's *Ivanhoe* under my arm and wandered out toward the creek. A month before the woods had been pretty with all their bright colors. Yet now, even with most of the leaves brown and dead and fallen to the ground, it was still lovely.

The air was crisp and chilly, and I pulled my winter coat tight around me. The chill stung at my cheeks even as my feet crunched over the dead leaves all over the ground. *This is just what I need*, I thought to myself. *Some time alone.* I didn't worry about myself all that much, but every once in a while I found myself thinking about grown-up things—or maybe I should call them growing-up things. I was starting to become a young woman, and there wasn't anybody to talk to and share with, no one who truly understood the new and sometimes frightening feelings that were coming and going inside me. I suppose Zack was feeling the hurts and uncertainties of trying to grow up, too, but he was only thirteen. And then, of course, he was a boy, and boys just don't feel things the way a girl does.

I didn't mind the cold as I walked along. In fact, it seemed to suit my mood just fine.

Pa was very much on my mind; he always was these days. It had been hard enough getting used to Ma's dying. But then all of a sudden to have Pa back in her place—that was some change to reckon with!

At first, with the horrible uncertainty and aloneness, I'd been so happy to find out about Pa. I remembered that first day, when he told us who he was, and I walked over and put my arms around him. I couldn't believe it was really him, and I wanted so much to love him! I began to feel a little hurt, though, when I thought about his not wanting to claim us. What that might have to do with him keeping his name secret, I still wasn't sure. But I still thought we might somehow make the best of it, even though he was quiet and sometimes gruff and didn't seem to want us around much.

When he gambled away our horses, and caused all that hurt to Emily, it made me downright mad. He had no cause to do such a thing, and it made me start thinking about everything Grandpa'd said about him—how he'd brought trouble and hardship to his family thinking only about himself, what a poor example of a husband and father he was, leaving Ma to fend for herself. Ever since the incident with the horses, I'd wondered if maybe Grandpa had been right in everything he said. Pa wasn't treating us much better than he had Ma, and now he was even talking about sending us back East somewhere.

I was angry at him—even bitter, I guess—on account of Ma. I tried to keep it inside. And having Uncle Nick around the place had helped, because if he hadn't been there, I'm afraid I might have said some things I shouldn't have to Pa. He treated Zack so badly. I wouldn't have blamed Zack if he hated him. He didn't act like a pa at all to him.

As I walked along in the woods, Ma came to my mind. In the daily effort just to do what had to be done, and in trying to figure out how I was supposed to feel about Pa, I'd more or less forgotten how much I missed her. But now, with the anger rising in me against Pa, I realized that maybe Ma'd still be alive if it hadn't been for Pa's deserting her.

Oh, Ma, I found myself thinking, *I wish you were still alive, and it was you we were with—not Pa!*

Tears began to sting my cheeks, and all of a sudden the urge to run came over me. I took off and raced over the uneven terrain. It felt good, almost as if I could run the pain out of my heart by making it pump faster and faster. The ground was uphill; I was running up the creek, and after about a quarter of a mile, I finally collapsed in a breathless heap against the trunk of a huge old oak. I half-giggled, half-cried, struggling to catch my breath, still not sure which of my mixed-up emotions was going to get the upper hand.

The sudden sound of my own voice surprised me and made me feel all the more alone. Crying can be done alone, but laughing isn't much good unless you've got someone to share it with. And laughing and crying together doesn't feel quite right any time. I leaned my back up against the tree and sat, still breathing heavily from my run. I was too keyed up to read, so I laid my book aside for a while.

I could hear the gurgling of the creek only a short stone's throw away. I peered over at the opposite bank, still and deserted. It brought to my mind that day several weeks ago when the kids and I had been out here and had seen the Indians. I'd just about given up seeing them again, when all of a sudden, I heard a sound!

It hadn't come from across the creek where I might have expected, but from *behind* me—so close it rang in my ears!

I started to my feet. Terrified, the first thing that came to my mind was Alkali Jones' story about the bear!

If it was some wild animal, trying to flee would do me no good. I froze, still pressed against the oak. All I could think of was how awful it would be to get eaten by a bear. Hastily, I brushed a sleeve across my wet eyes.

Then the sound came again. It was a snapping twig. But only one twig, not anything like what you'd expect from a charging bear. Gathering up all my courage, I turned my head and twisted my body as quietly as I could, and then leaned to the side and peered around the tree trunk.

It was *him*!

The Indian boy had come back! I was so relieved not to see a bear that I forgot to be afraid. I stood up, though my knees were still a bit wobbly, came out from behind the tree, and smiled at him.

"Hi," I said. "Do you remember me?"

He stared at me. I thought maybe he couldn't understand English, but then he gave a little nod.

"I remember," he finally answered. Just the sound of his voice was music in my ears!

"My name's Corrie," I said. "What's yours?"

"I am Little Wolf."

"How did you learn English?" I asked, wanting to inch closer to get a better look at him.

"I must go," he said, and started to leave, almost as if he sensed my intent.

"Please!" I called out quickly, "don't go yet."

He paused.

"I'm—I'm new here," I said again. "Would you . . . would you be my friend?"

He half turned back toward me, with the most peculiar expression on his tanned face.

"I am of the Nisenan tribe—Indian," he said, as if that was the only answer necessary.

"What does that matter?" I replied.

He studied me for what seemed a long time. His dark eyes were filled with intelligence and thoughtfulness, as if the notion of such a thing had never occurred to him. I couldn't tell whether his hesitation was the result of my being a girl and he a boy, or because we were from different races.

"You are strange for a white girl," he said finally.

"How do you mean?"

"You do not show fear. You do not run away or scream."

"I'm not afraid. Why should I be?"

"I have been taught that white men fear us."

"From the first time I saw you with your father I knew you would not hurt me."

"But there is trouble between my people and yours."

"Not between you and me."

"My father says there will always be strife between us."

"I don't hold with any of that," I replied. "My pa doesn't either. He says white folks have been unfair to the Indians."

"White man is our enemy."

"But *I* am not your enemy. It doesn't seem right that you hold against me what others have done."

He didn't say anything for a minute. It was clear this kind of talk wasn't going to get us anywhere, and I didn't want him to run off. So I decided to change the subject.

"How did you learn English?" I asked again.

Still he did not speak for a moment. I couldn't quite make out the look on his face. It seemed that he might want to be friends, but that he felt he ought not to be. Finally he answered.

"My father learned it in the mission school. He said it is good to know the white man's tongue to keep from being cheated by him."

"Does your father hate the white man, Little Wolf?"

"They have been my father's friends. They have also cheated him and stolen from him. White men killed my father's brothers."

"I am sorry."

Our eyes met as I said the words. We looked at one another, maybe even into each other's eyes, for a long time. I felt as if I had finally made him believe that I was sincere.

But he never said another word. As quickly as he came, he turned and ran off, disappearing into the woods. Maybe nothing more needed to be said, right then. The look in his eyes told me that if he had the chance, he would be my friend. I hoped my eyes had told him that I would try to be worthy of his trust.

I'd had enough of a walk. Taking up my unopened book, I slowly headed down the creek the way I had come.

When I got back to the claim, I went to the big rock that sat about fifty yards from the cabin, scrambled up, and sat down. I'd gone there several times—it was my thinking place. Today as I climbed up and perched atop it, my mind was full of Little Wolf, Ma, and Pa. The thought of the one brought happiness, the other sadness, and the third anger. If I wasn't careful, I'd start crying again!

I decided not to say anything about Little Wolf when the others got home. Maybe something inside wanted to hold onto my own personal secret, but I was partly afraid it'd rile Pa if he knew.

I'd tell them sometime. But for now I would just keep quiet about my walk up the stream.

CHAPTER 24

A TALK WITH UNCLE NICK

All the rest of that day I was moody and glum. I guess I was feeling homesick, realizing all over again how terribly far from home we were and how much life had changed for us. I missed home, I missed the way it used to be, and I missed Ma.

I was so afraid I'd start crying and not be able to stop, that I kept to myself after the others got back from town.

A little while after supper, I looked around and realized I hadn't seen Tad for a while. I put down the skillet I was scrubbing, and went into the bedroom. He was lying face down, alone on his bunk. I walked over and sat down beside him. "What's the matter, Tad?" I asked, laying my hand on his head.

"I miss Ma!" he sobbed. He was only seven, and trying hard to be like his older brother, but he sat up and threw his arms around me. As much as I wanted to be brave and grown-up, I felt the tears trickling down my own face.

I didn't know how to comfort him. All afternoon I'd been thinking about Ma, too—and all the familiar things I'd never see again: the swimming hole down on Elway Creek where we spent so much time in the summer, the woods, and the delightful hours spent with my sisters picking berries. And the sweet-smelling hay in the barn and my special hiding place in the loft where I'd while away the hours playing make-believe games. And, oh, the smell of Ma's bread filling the whole house on baking day!

"I know," I said, my voice choking. "I miss Ma, too." I couldn't think of anything else to say.

Then I heard the door creak on its new hinges. I looked up and was surprised to see Uncle Nick standing there framed in the light of the sunset coming through the window from the other room.

"What's wrong?" he asked quietly. His voice was full of sympathy.

"Tad's missing Ma," I answered.

Slowly he walked into the room and sat down on the edge of the bed next to me. Tad was still sniffling.

" 'Course you'll miss your ma, boy," he said, with sincere compassion. "We all do. I miss her myself sorely. It's just that us grown-ups have learned how to keep our sadness from showing. And I reckon the missing'll last a spell, for both you and me. But I knew your ma real well, and I think she'd be wanting you to be a big boy—to be tough about it, even though you're still sad."

"H-how do you know?" choked Tad, sucking in tentative gulps of air.

"I just do."

Uncle Nick rubbed his chin and glanced off in the distance, as if he was thinking. By now Becky, Emily, and Zack had wandered into the room, too. And then Uncle Nick started to reminisce, something he didn't do too often.

"When we was kids—your ma and me—there was this swimming hole, down t' Elway Creek—"

I wanted to burst in right then and say I knew the place. I'd never thought that if Ma had grown up not far from our farm, then Uncle Nick must have too, and would know many of the same spots. It changed everything to think of Ma as a little girl and Uncle Nick as a little boy!

But I kept my mouth closed. I didn't want to interrupt Uncle Nick's story.

"We was swimmin' and divin' and havin' a grand ol' time," he was saying, "until I went and slipped in the mud puddle we'd made with our games. I was probably jist a mite older than you are now, Tad. Well, down I went with a crash and a snap. I didn't know how a busted arm could pain so! I was screamin' and blubberin' my eyes out, but your ma, she put her arms around me and held me 'til I calmed down. Then she says, 'We gotta get home.' I started up my bawlin' again. 'Now, Nicky,' she says, 'you gotta be tough and strong. This is one of those times you gotta act like a man.' And she kept sayin' it 'til we finally got home. And that's how I think I know what your ma might say to you right now, too. She'd want you to be strong. Cryin' won't bring your ma back, but maybe thinkin' of the good memories will help."

"You really think so?" Tad took a long resolved sniff.

"Sure do, son."

By now the other kids had sat down and all five of us were listening intently.

"You knew Ma when she was young?" asked Emily shyly from where she sat nearly concealed behind Becky.

" 'Course I did!" laughed Uncle Nick. "She was my sister—my *big* sister. You don't think a man could grow up like me without being a little runt of a lad once, do you?"

"Oh-h-h," said Emily with awe. I snickered a little at what he'd said, but I think it awed all of us—both to think of Uncle Nick as a little boy, and to think of Ma in a way that made her seem alive again.

"Tell us another story!" said Becky bravely. I knew that's what we all wanted, but only she had the nerve to ask.

Uncle Nick was quiet for a while, and I thought this brief special time together was over. I wished it could be like this always.

But then to my surprise, Uncle Nick spoke up again.

"Well," he said, "you kids all know how big sisters can be." The four younger ones—everyone but me—all nodded.

Uncle Nick winked at me, and I smiled.

"Well, your ma was no different," he went on. "It was always, 'You climb the tree first to get the apples, then I'll take a turn.' But of course her turn never would come. Or, 'You take down the first batch of laundry from the lines, and I'll get the next,' when she knew all along there was only going to be *one* batch. She always managed to sucker me into doing things for her somehow! A right cagey young lady your ma was, I can tell you that!

"Well, one day I figured out how to get her back! We was playing hide 'n' seek and your ma was *it*. I pretended to go off and hide, but instead I went home. The thought of her lookin' and lookin' for me and gettin' worried, 'cause she usually found me right off—why it was enough to make me laugh to myself all the way home. Our ma was baking bread, and so I sat back as comfortable as you please eating a big hunk of bread, grinning from ear to ear, expecting her to come bursting through the door all in a sweat. After a while I got another piece of bread, and soon a half an hour, and then an hour went by. By the time I started on my third slice, *I* was the one getting worried. I could hardly swallow that bread, good as it was. And I sure couldn't tell my ma about my worry, since I'd be sure to catch it then. So finally I got up and ran all in a fever back to the old oak tree in the clearing that was our *free* spot. And there was my sister, sitting under the tree reading a book, as if she hadn't never missed me at all! She was just waiting for me to come back, and was determined to outlast me!"

We all laughed.

"Weren't you mad, Uncle Nick?" Zack asked.

"Maybe for a minute or two," he answered. "But I admired your ma too much to stay mad for long. She was smart. I respected that. She made life interesting for me. She wasn't no prissy china doll, afraid to get messed up. Anyway, even if she could be ornery to me, she was always there when I needed her, too, sticking up for me. I sure could get into a heap a trouble for a scrappy young kid! But your ma never let me down."

He paused and smiled. "I'll never forget the Bible Memory Verse contest in church. Like I said, your ma was smart, and she won the dad-blamed thing most every month. She knew more verses than Saint Peter! Our Sunday school teacher gave a ticket for each verse memorized, and at the end of the month the winner traded in the tickets for a prize—the more tickets, the better the prize. Well, all year I had been admiring one prize in particular—a fine-carved wooden horse. But since the only verse I had ever been able to memorize was, 'Jesus wept,' my chances of ever gettin' it were mighty slim. I didn't tell no one, but I guess somehow your ma found out, because all that month she kept finding ways to give me her tickets, mostly in trade for doing chores. She figured I'd be too proud to take her tickets if she just gave them to me, or if she won the horse and gave that to me. The way she had it figured was for me to feel like I *earned* the tickets, even if it was sort of by what you might call illegal means."

Uncle Nick chuckled at the memory, then continued. "The big problem came during the church service when the winner was asked to come forward before the whole congregation. When I stood up, our Sunday school teacher, Mr. Alexander, couldn't believe it. But all the folks was applauding so hard and praising him so for his amazing progress with a mischievous kid like me that he didn't have the heart to tell them the truth. I won that carved horse, and, even if it was ill-got, so to speak, I always prized it special-like because of what your ma—"

Uncle Nick's voice seemed to catch over the words and he stopped a moment.

"Well, your ma was a fine sister," he finally said.

"Why'd you ever leave Ma and come to California?" asked Tad. By now his tears had dried and he was fascinated with this rare and unexpected side his uncle was revealing.

But Tad's question was as ill-timed as the horse had been ill-gotten, because Uncle Nick's talkativeness suddenly stopped. He drew in a deep breath, then let it out slowly. When he finally spoke again, his voice sounded heavy and far away. All of the lightness and fun was gone.

"Well, son," he said, "that is a hard question. And one I can't answer for you."

He sighed deeply again.

A spell had stolen over us that night, and I felt sad that it had to end. But the tone of Uncle Nick's voice told me that Tad's question had intruded upon painful ground.

"That's something, son," Uncle Nick added, "that you'll have to find out from your pa . . . if he ever decides to tell—"

He stopped short and looked up.

Pa was standing in the doorway glaring at him.

CHAPTER 25

THE ARGUMENT

From the expression on Pa's face, we all knew the instant we saw him that he was furious.

"Nick!" he barked out, "what do you mean fillin' my kids heads with notions of their ma?"

"Nothing, Drum," replied Uncle Nick, bewildered at the outburst and half rising off Tad's bunk. "I only thought it'd make 'em feel better to—"

"Well, I don't want you thinkin' about what's right for my kids! They're *my* kids, you hear, and I'm their pa, not you!"

"I didn't think—uh, there'd be no harm," stammered Uncle Nick. "They was just missin' Aggie, that's all."

"No harm! What do you know about missin' Aggie? It wasn't you that had to leave a wife and kids! And then tellin' me I oughta explain to 'em why we left! That's what caused the trouble in the first place, not being able to say *why*! And you want me to tell 'em now, after it's too late, after all these years—after I've lost my Aggie? You want—"

Pa's voice broke off momentarily. Sitting there listening, I had no idea of the feelings that were flooding through Pa as he stood in the doorway yelling at Uncle Nick. I was only aware of my own anger at hearing him fault our uncle for just trying to be nice to us.

"Curse you, Nick!" Pa yelled again, recovering himself.

"You and that foul breed you ran with. You were nothin'
but a fool kid and I shoulda never tried to help you! You
cost me my wife . . . and now my own kids can't stand the
sight of me. Well, I won't be having you play pa to 'em, you
hear me! Get out, I tell you . . . just get out!"

Pa turned and walked into the other room.

Without another word, Uncle Nick followed him, his
head hanging low. Seconds later, I heard the outside door
shut tightly. The five of us sat still as mice, terrified over
the outburst, though we had no idea what all the words
meant. The only sound in the whole cabin was our breathing.

All the hurt and bitterness I'd felt earlier in the day was
slowly rising to the surface again. When it suddenly boiled
over, I found myself on my feet running into the other room,
where Pa stood with his back turned.

"Uncle Nick was just being nice to us!" I shouted. "You
had no call to yell at him like that!"

Pa stood still as a statue and said nothing.

"He's the only one around here who has been nice to
us!" I continued. "You never say a thing! You treat us like
you wish we'd never come, and like you can't wait to get rid
of us! But Uncle Nick's our friend!"

Slowly Pa turned around to face me. He was full of grief
and anguish, but my eyes were too full of tears to realize it.
I only saw the same face of stone.

"Corrie, I . . . I—" he tried to say, but I lashed out at
him again without giving him the chance to finish.

"Grandpa was right! And now you're treating Uncle
Nick and us just like you did Ma."

"Oh, Corrie . . . you just don't understand how it was.
If only I could make you see—"

"I understand what I heard!" I shot back angrily.
"You're nothing but a mean man! Uncle Nick oughta leave
here like you left Ma! And maybe we'll all just leave too!"
I was crying hard and didn't know half of what I was saying.

"Please . . . don't talk like that," he said, his voice sad. He reached out a hand, and I think he wanted to touch me. But I hit at him and forced his arm away.

"If it weren't for you, Ma'd still be alive!" I shouted bitterly. "You ran out on her! You deserted all of us. And now she's dead—all on account of you! I hate you for what you did to Ma!"

I turned away from him and ran for the door, threw it open and ran outside. Night had fallen by now, but there was a moon up. I ran and ran, sobbing wildly as I went. I had no idea where I was going, I just wanted to get away. Finally, exhausted from my outburst and the exertion of running, I came to a big tree near my thinking rock, and threw myself down at its trunk and wept bitterly.

I must have cried for five or ten minutes. I was in such turmoil over what had happened, angry and sobbing and hurting inside, that I lost all track of time. Love and hate were battling within me and I couldn't even tell the difference.

Eventually I began to breathe easier and stopped crying. But I still lay there, unaware of the night cold, my emotions spent, my heart aching.

I'm not sure what I expected next, but I never could have anticipated what *did* happen. When Little Wolf came upon me earlier in the day, the sound had startled me. Now I remained still, though I knew someone was approaching. I felt no inclination to jump up or run away. I just waited . . . waited until the footsteps stopped and I could feel someone standing behind me.

I knew it was Pa.

He drew nearer and knelt behind me. Then I felt his hand lightly touch my shoulder. It was the first time he had touched me since our arrival in Miracle.

"Corrie . . ." he said quietly, "will you let me talk to you?"

I nodded. But I still couldn't turn around to face him.

"There's a lot of things kids can't understand," he went on, "especially when they're young."

"I ain't so young now," I said, finally finding my voice, "and I still don't understand why you left Ma and us like you did."

"You're right there, Corrie," said Pa. "You ain't young. You're a mighty fine young lady. But you were young then, and I know you were hurt, and your ma was hurt. You were all hurt, I know that . . . and it's my fault. But there was just so much about it you *couldn't* possibly understand."

"So why won't you tell me, so maybe I can understand now?" I said impatiently, looking the other way.

Pa withdrew his hand and sat down with a sigh. It was several minutes before he spoke again. When he did, his voice was different somehow—quiet, filled with sadness and regret. Just the sound of it softened my anger. "Your ma and your Grandpa Belle never knew what was going on with Nick. We all knew he was runnin' with a bad crowd. Your Uncle Nick was a mighty rambunctious lad back in them days. And he finally got himself in so deep over his head that I knew if I didn't try to bail him out, he'd likely either get himself killed or spend the rest of his days behind bars. Either way it would have broken his old pa's heart.

"I ain't tryin' to lay the whole blame on Nick. It was easy, too easy, for me to slip back into my old ways, my ways before I married your ma. An' I shoulda known better than to try to help Nick by goin' into the pit with him. It was stupid, but I got myself mixed up with the gang he was ridin' with. Fool that I was, I thought I'd be able to get him out of the fix he'd gotten himself into, and that we'd be able to just ride away clean and pick up our lives from there.

"And that's where I made my big mistake, Corrie. The thing went sour on us. Real bad! Before I knew what had gone wrong, two men were dead and me and Nick were arrested for bank robbery and murder. So *both* of us were going to have to spend our lives in prison. On top of that, the Catskill Gang got it in their heads that Nick and I had the money from the bank. We weren't even there that night—I swear it, Corrie! I nearly had to sit on Nick, but I managed to keep us both away. Jenkins, one of the gang who was shot that night, found us just before he died, and I reckon the others figured he told us where the money was. The others all made a clean getaway, but Nick and I didn't even know what had happened, leastways not enough to get our hides away before the law found us.

"Your uncle and me was sent to prison, Corrie." He said the words as if he could hardly stand to hear them. "You can imagine how ashamed I was. My own shame was likely enough to make me do what I did, but even then I woulda at least tried to see your ma if ever I got the chance. She was too far away to come to the trial or the jail, thank God for that, at least! I had only one visitor in jail—your Grandpa Belle. He laid the blame for the whole thing on me and I didn't argue with him—I guess I still don't. He said I led Nick astray right from the start and maybe that was right, too. When we was kids, Nick always looked up to me, and I could be a rough one before I met your ma. Grandpa Belle said Aggie couldn't hold her head up no more in the community because of me, and it'd be better if I was dead. All he said made sense at the time, 'cause I hated myself and what I'd done enough to believe it—to believe Aggie'd even think such things. But even if I thought she'd have me back—if I ever did get out of prison, though they'd have probably hung us eventually—I figured I was too rotten for her, anyway. And I thought about what it would be like for you kids to go through your lives having a jailbird for a pa. It didn't matter that I was innocent. No one believed me. It was all the same as if I'd done all I was accused of."

"Ma never said anything about all that," I said.

"I reckon your ma didn't want you to think poorly of me," he replied in a voice full of despair. "She couldn't say nothin' good about me, so she just didn't say anything. I'm surprised your Grandpa Belle didn't say nothin', but she musta made him keep quiet—'bout that, at least. The fracas took place far enough away that I reckon no one else around town knew much about it."

"But then we heard you was dead—what about that?" I asked. I wasn't very angry anymore.

"There was a big riot in prison only a few weeks after we got there," he answered, still with that trapped tone to his voice. "Upwards of twenty-five prisoners escaped. Nick and I were lucky, I guess, 'cause we just got carried along in the thing and ended up outside. We got to the woods surroundin' the prison and found some of the prisoners who had been killed. We exchanged clothes with them. When the bodies were found, the guards thought it was me and Nick who died. We were pretty desperate, Corrie. But now I can see we was just gettin' deeper an' deeper into a life of lies."

"You let Ma—and us—think you were dead?"

"It seemed best, Corrie. I still believed all your grandpa said. I was a jailbird—an *escaped* jailbird, now. I could only bring more shame and misery to your ma. I'll never stop regrettin' what I did . . . I just kept going . . . Nick and I . . . we left everything—"

His voice broke, but he struggled to continue.

"Do you realize what I did? I left my wife, my four kids . . . my God! Becky was just a baby . . . Aggie was still carrying Tad. I didn't even know my youngest son's name before you got here!"

Again he stopped. Slowly, I turned to look at him. Tears were streaming down his cheeks. I could see them glisten in the moonlight. I'd never seen a man cry before, and now here was my own pa, the rough, quiet man I'd just blown up at, the man Ma had forgiven on her deathbed . . . here he was, sitting not two feet from me, sobbing like a child.

Something in my heart gave way. Suddenly I felt full of compassion for him.

"But . . . but Ma would have understood," I said. "She would have come West with you. You could have told her, Pa."

"I couldn't face her, Corrie." He shook his head dismally. "I've fought Indians without flinchin'. I faced down a stalking mountain lion and shot it. You woulda thought I had enough courage—but I didn't. I kept thinkin' 'bout what her pa said 'bout being better off if I was dead. I kept thinkin' of the shame I'd caused her. And I'd never be safe again either. Not even now, I ain't safe, between the law and the Catskill boys that want me."

"But don't they think you're . . . dead, Pa?"

"I don't know no more," he replied. "After Nick let your ma know he was still alive and here in Miracle Springs, anybody could find us. An' I ain't so worried about the Catskill crowd as I am about the law. If they ever find me, it'd be back to prison, and . . . I don't know what'd become of you kids. And now that I got you back, I—"

His voice faded into a strangled sob, and he couldn't say anything more.

I found myself rising to my feet slowly. I put my arms around his big, broad shoulders.

"Oh, Pa!" I said, crying hard. "I'm so sorry . . . I didn't mean what I said back there at the cabin . . . you were right—I didn't understand. I'm sorry . . . I didn't mean to hurt you more."

Pa reached up and clasped one of my hands, then rose to one knee. I took a step back, and for a moment I just stood there looking into his tear-stained face, and he into mine.

Then he released my hand and opened his arms wide. In an instant my head was on his chest. I felt his strong arms close around me and we held each other tight.

"Corrie, Corrie," he said, "I've thought of you every day for the last eight years, prayin' somehow the Almighty would let me see you again."

He paused and managed to take in a deep breath. I was sobbing on his chest, still holding him tightly. "Your ma and you kids had every right to hate me for what I done . . . but . . . but, Corrie, can you forgive me . . . for leaving . . . for not being a pa to you all these years?"

Again the tears streamed down his face, and the agony of regret in his voice was more than my heart could stand.

"Oh, Pa . . . Pa," I cried, "of course I forgive you! Ma never hated you. When she died, she told me she forgave you. I don't hate you either, and I'm so sorry for what I said!"

"It's over now, Corrie," he said, reaching up and gently stroking my hair. "I'll never think of what you said again. If we can just find a way in our hearts to get over what's past, then . . . then maybe we can start over again . . . as pa and daughter."

I stood back a little, and attempted a smile. "I think we can, Pa," I said. "I really think we can!"

He smiled back at me, and I embraced him again, this time not just as a man I called Pa, but as a father I was learning to love.

CHAPTER 26

A NEW BEGINNING

When Pa and I finally walked back toward the cabin about twenty minutes later, he left me at the door.

"There's one more apology I gotta make before I go in," he said, then turned off and headed up toward the mine in the moonlight.

I wasn't quite ready myself to go in and face the rest of the kids. I knew they'd pester me with a million questions, and after what had just happened I needed some time to be quiet. My feelings were still running pretty deep, and I didn't know if I could face their looks without bursting into tears all over again.

So I sat down on the wooden porch and waited.

About fifteen minutes later, I heard Pa and Uncle Nick approaching. I couldn't make out their words, but every once in a while I'd hear Uncle Nick laugh, so I figured it'd been patched up between them. When they came into view, Pa had one arm slung around Uncle Nick's shoulder and was looking earnestly at him. All I heard was Uncle Nick's response.

" . . . think nothing more of it, I tell you. I deserved it."

"You're wrong there—I was out of line."

"Don't matter. It's over. You're always telling me that the stream needs a good storm now and then to flush the gold outta where it's hiding. I reckon people are like that, too."

"Well, however we got here, you've been a good partner to me," said Pa, still serious, "and I want you to know it. And we gotta stick together to get through the rest of it . . . oh, Corrie," he said, looking up suddenly and seeing me sitting there. "Ain't you been in yet?"

"I wasn't quite ready," I answered. "I needed a little more time to settle myself."

"I guess we all did," laughed Uncle Nick, trying to lighten the mood. "After we all blowed up at one another, eh? Nothing like a good rainfall to clear up the air, I always say!"

Pa glanced at me and winked, then I stood up and the three of us went inside where the four younger kids were still silently waiting in the bedroom.

From the looks on their faces, I think their worst fears were that someone was going to wind up getting killed. But after they saw Uncle Nick, whose face had recovered its joviality, and they heard a laugh from me, they began to relax. I think they could see the change in Pa too and that eased the tension more than anything.

I can't honestly say that after that day everything immediately got better between Pa and me. There were still lots of questions, and some hurts remained. Pa didn't completely change overnight, but neither did I. He still had his quiet times when I couldn't tell what he was thinking, but he smiled a little more. And I noticed him taking time with the younger kids more than he used to, calling them by name, and hoisting Emily or Becky or Tad up in his arms.

Kids are quick to forgive, and they returned whatever he gave them in love many times over. It was more difficult for Zack. The more effort Pa made to be friendly, the more he hardened himself against Pa, as if he was determined not to let go of the bitterness he had been holding so long. And Pa didn't know how to win him over. He'd been carrying his own grief and guilt so long, it was all he could do to try to overcome that.

I tried to talk to Zack.

"He's trying to be a real pa to us, Zack," I said once.

"Then why'd he keep it a secret who he was when we first came to town?" he snapped back.

"I don't know," I answered. "But he must have had his reasons."

"Yeah, like when he left Ma and us in New York!"

"I already explained that, Zack," I reminded him. "He'd been through an awful lot."

"It still don't seem fair."

"Think how you'd feel, Zack, if it had been you. Being in prison, thinking you'd brought shame on your whole family."

"There musta been some other way!"

"Maybe so, but everybody does things different." I was getting frustrated with him. "I ain't got all the answers, Zack. Why don't you ask him? Wouldn't hurt if you'd talk to him once in a while, you know, instead of just sulking around."

"I ain't sulking!"

"Well, you sure coulda fooled me."

I didn't know what to tell Zack. I still had a lot of the same questions myself. But I thought Pa at least deserved a second chance. After all, he'd asked me to forgive him, and I figured I owed him that much. He seemed sincere, and I believed him.

I did ask Pa again about that first day, when he came to town and pretended not to know us. I knew Zack'd never get around to asking him, so I brought it up again when Zack was within hearing.

Pa said so much had come at him all at once, it was like being hit with a face full of buckshot. All of a sudden, he said, he was standing in front of kids he'd never expected to see again, not even recognizing any of them but me, hearing that his wife was dead, and wondering down inside if it all was some new trick by the New York gang to get him and Uncle Nick.

"I was battling with grief, Corrie," he said. "If it was all true . . . well, just imagine—I'd just been told my wife was dead . . . the wife that I'd never stopped loving, and it just brought it all back over me like a flood. As I stood looking at you all, a powerful bunch of feelings were going through me all at once! Yet, if I let on you were my kids, and what my real name was, the whole town would know in a second. And I was still having to think about protectin' myself and Nick. And all the while, there was that dad-blamed Parrish woman shoutin' at me about what I oughta do, and then Nick in trouble over Judd's killin'—and off somewhere. And even if what that Dixon feller was sayin' was all true— if I let on I was Hollister, not Drum, and *that* got around . . . well, you'd all be in danger again.

"Can't you see the terrible fix I was in? Why I didn't know what I oughta do . . . and all the time I couldn't help thinkin' of Aggie, knowin' I'd never get a chance to see her again and explain . . . and set things right?"

He turned away and quit talking. I never saw him cry again after that first night. But there were a few times I think he was close, especially whenever we'd talk about Ma. More and more I began to see how much he really did love her and how it had pained him to do what he did.

"So, maybe it wasn't right of me to pretend," he told me later. "But without having the chance to think everything through . . . well, I done it, and I guess it's too late to go back and do different. 'Sides," he muttered, "I ain't at all sure we got that Catskill bunch off our backs, yet. So you just make sure whenever you're in town or there's other folks around . . . you keep them kids from calling me Pa! It may be hard for you to understand all my reasons. I know your brother is carryin' a heap of anger, and maybe one day I'll have the chance to make it all right with him. But . . . well,

I *am* your pa, after all, so maybe you just gotta trust me when I tell you it's for the best."

He was right. I didn't understand everything. And I couldn't very well make Zack think any better of him. But even if Zack was bent on carrying a grudge, I felt like giving Pa the benefit of the doubt, and trusting him as much as I could.

We were trying to make a new beginning of it. Pa was still Pa, and we were still uncertain about a lot of things, so it was bound to take some time before we could all trust one another like we should. But knowing how Pa felt inside sure made it easier.

CHAPTER 27

A TALK OVER BREAKFAST

The 26th of November came quickly.

Alkali Jones was still working with Pa and Uncle Nick at the mine—not every day, but often. Every once in a while, either when a big day of work was planned, or when they'd work till dark, Mr. Jones would stay the night at the cabin. And the Friday night before Saturday the 26th was one of those.

At breakfast that morning, the topic of the next day's events came up at the table.

"Well, I hear that new preacher lit into town right on schedule," said Alkali Jones around a mouthful of scrambled eggs.

"Yep," acknowledged Pa.

"Looks like the town's about to git itself tamed fer sure," Jones went on in a regretful tone.

"Don't be so sure," said Pa. "No greenhorn preacher from the East's gonna be able to keep some of these men from raising a little Cain now and then."

None of us kids made any comment. But I couldn't help thinking how excited Mrs. Parrish was about the preacher's arrival. I hoped I'd be able to see him.

"Can't seem to git away from it, can we, Drum?" said Mr. Jones.

"What's that, Al?"

188

"From dad-blamed civilization, o' course! Why, I left Arkansas in 1830 'cause it were gittin' too full o' settlers. Wandered on down Texas-way an' got there jest in time fer all that fracas with Santa Anna. Luckily, I got my hide outta there before Bowie an' Houston an' Crockett got made heroes in '36! Texas wasn't a bad place then—a man could breathe. But then they went an' turned the blasted outfit into a state, an' I says to myself, 'Can civilization be far behind?' "

"You was sure ahead of us," said Pa.

"When did you leave the East, Drum?"

"Well, let's see . . . what was it, Nick, when we lit out from New York? Forty-four, I think. But we didn't get here 'til a few years later."

"Well," went on Mr. Jones, enjoying telling his tales as much as ever, "I figured California was jest about as west as a man could go. So I joined up with ol' John Fremont. I was thinkin' there could hardly be a more remote an' worthless piece o' land than this, an' nobody here but a few Mexicans. Seemed like no one'd trouble us here. Then blamed ol' Jim Marshall had to up an' discover gold! Why, civilization's jest intent on houndin' me t' my grave! Where are fellers like us goin' to go from here, Drum?"

"There's places, I reckon."

" 'Course, you got yerself all strapped down with responsibilities now, Nick, ain't ya?" He eyed my uncle with a mischievous grin. "The wilds ain't fer you no more, no, siree!"

Uncle Nick only nodded in response, and gave a noncommittal grunt.

"But I suppose ya gotta hand it to this new preacher feller," Mr. Jones went on, as unaffected as usual by everyone else's silence. "What's his name?"

"I don't know—Rutman . . . Rodman . . . something like that."

"Well, I suppose ya gotta give him credit. He musta got a bellyful of guts to come to a place like this an' try to bring religion to a pack o' wild sinners like us! Hee, hee! Don't ya think, Nick?" laughed Mr. Jones, turning to my uncle.

"Ah, them fellers is just fanatics," said Uncle Nick, joining in the spirit of Mr. Jones' laughter. "It don't take no guts when a man's plumb loco."

"I dunno," Mr. Jones persisted, but not poking fun this time, and sounding almost serious, "I heared he come the Panama route."

"What's that got to do with it?" said Uncle Nick.

"Why, *that* takes some gumption, 'specially fer some greenhorn city feller. I'd rather fight redskins or Santa Anna than that cursed yellow fever *any* day!"

"He probably just prayed them mosquitoes away," said Uncle Nick sarcastically.

"Hee, hee!" chuckled Mr. Jones. "I can't rightly remember the last time I was in a real church. Not that I ain't a God-fearin' man! But where's a feller goin' to find a church on the trail? Right, Drum?"

Alkali couldn't seem to interest Pa in the discussion, so he turned back to Uncle Nick.

"How 'bout you, Nick? You ever find many churches along the trail?" Both men laughed.

Their talk about the preacher's coming got me to thinking. Ma always made sure our family was a God-fearing one. We went to church almost every Sunday, except when the weather was too bad. She taught us out of the Bible about what was good and what was bad. And I guess I hardly knew anyone who didn't go to church at least some times.

Grandpa Belle didn't go much the last two years, because his rheumatism got too bad. But he still respected God. He would no more poke fun at a man of God than spit in God's own eye! But, now, here were Uncle Nick and Alkali Jones talking about the preacher as if they thought he was some no-account dunce, and the whole town apparently never thought about church at all. I wondered if all the unbelievers had come to California!

I could still remember our minister in Bridgeville

preaching all about how sinners and heathens would face God's wrath and hellfire. I never was quite sure what a heathen was, though I had an idea they were folks in jungles someplace. But plain sinners were another matter, because he used to talk about them as if they were the people in big cities who went into saloons and who shot people.

And now suddenly I found myself wondering about Uncle Nick. He wore a gun and gambled and drank whiskey. And I couldn't help wondering if he was a sinner too and would wind up in hell someday. I figured he wasn't the best man in the world, but I was getting to like him, and I sure hoped he wasn't a sinner. Pa crossed my mind too. He hadn't really gotten into their discussion, but then he wore a gun and had been in trouble along with Uncle Nick, so I just couldn't be sure what to think.

The subject of the new minister and church came up again later in the day. I guess my worry must have showed on my face.

"What's ailin' you, Corrie?" Pa asked.

"Nothing," I said casually, trying to shake the mood away.

"I 'spect you kids'll be wantin' to hear that new preacher tomorrow," he went on without much enthusiasm.

"Yes, sir, I would," I answered. "If you're planning to go," I added, thinking to myself that somehow I *had* to get him to that service.

"Aw," put in Zack, "the one nice thing about living here was that we didn't have to go to church."

"Zack! What a thing to say!" I must have sounded a lot like Ma, because Zack looked surprised at my outburst.

"I like church," said Emily.

"I'd rather go on a picnic," said Becky.

"So, Corrie," said Pa, turning back to me and looking serious, "you want to go?"

I swallowed hard. "Yes, sir," I replied. "I really do."

"Do the rest of us have to go, just because Corrie wants to?" Zack asked with a sulk.

There was silence then. Even Alkali Jones said nothing. All eyes turned toward Pa. He was facing the first big decision about us kids since he decided to take us in, just because Zack had tossed out that question.

He looked around at all of us, from one face to another. He even looked over at Mr. Jones, who didn't seem about to offer any help at all. Then he took a deep breath and said,

"I reckon if one goes, we all go." His tone made it sound more like he was passing some kind of sentence on us than talking about going to church. " 'Sides," he added, summoning a little more enthusiasm, "it's kinda an historical occasion, like the newspaper comin'. So we oughta be there just for that reason, if nothin' else!"

"Should be a mite interestin' to see the Gold Nugget decked out fer a church!" piped up Alkali Jones. "Hee, hee! I wonder what that ol' bartender Jasper'll do? Hee, hee!"

"Howd'ya suppose that Parrish woman managed that?" said Uncle Nick. "I never knowed Jasper t' put no store in religious things."

"That's a mighty feisty woman," said Mr. Jones. "She gener'ly gits what she's after. They say she's got the preacher out here. 'Sides, maybe Jasper owes her money. Hee, hee!"

"A tough one, all right," said Uncle Nick. "I owed her a little money a while back, and she durned near took it outta my hide!"

I smiled to myself.

Leave it to Mrs. Parrish to turn a saloon into a place of worship! The last time we'd talked, she said she had an idea about the service. That must have been it! She probably feels the same way about a church service as she does about praying—you can do it anywhere.

It made sense, too. If there was one place where there ought to be preaching going on, it was in a saloon. But the folks back in Bridgeville sure would be scandalized by such goings on!

It made me realize again how different California was from the rest of the country.

CHAPTER 28

THE GOLD NUGGET CHURCH

The next morning, when I awoke, it was still almost black out, but after a while I began to see the first streak of dawn through the window. I got up quietly, tiptoed over and leaned my elbows on the sill, looking out just as the shapes of the hills and trees began to become visible.

Just then, I saw two deer nibbling the last of the green grass on the little knoll by the stream. I hardly noticed them at first, because their colors blended with the gray of the early mist. But as I continued to watch, their forms became more distinct. Slowly tiny bits of pink began to show in the east. Two rabbits scurried by and then disappeared into their burrow. Red and orange followed the pink across the sky. The deer scampered off into the woods, and all was perfectly still again. For several minutes more, I gazed on the peaceful scene.

After a while, I crept back into my bed and watched as the light grew more and more dazzling through the window, until at last came the moment when the sun burst out into the new day.

What a wonderful sunrise! Something about it seemed to speak to me, as if God himself had made it just for me to enjoy that morning, saying in His own way that I was His child.

Finally, I pulled myself out of bed. I couldn't just lie

there looking at the sunrise—today was Sunday, and we were going to church!

The night before, I pulled all our best clothes from the big trunk that had carried most of our possessions from home. I ironed out the wrinkles as best I could, then gave the young'uns their baths. Now I just had to get everyone up and dressed.

There were groans and complaints from Zack and Tad, mostly protesting their stiff collars. Zack's pants were about two inches too short, reminding us all how quickly he was growing, and how much time had passed since the last time we'd gone to church in Bridgeville, just before we came west. In fact, all our Sunday clothes were on the snug side. But we had to make do, and I thought we looked pretty fine in spite of everything.

Even Pa put on a clean white shirt for the occasion, tucked into a pair of clean, but worn, trousers. The neck of his grimy longjohns stuck up above his shirt collar, tarnishing the effect a little.

When Uncle Nick got up, he just put on his work clothes, seeming to ignore the fact that it was Sunday. He went outside and was heading off for the mine, when Pa stopped him. Uncle Nick muttered something about having some things to tend to.

"You get in there and change them clothes, Nick Belle," Pa said. "You're going into town with us."

Uncle Nick moped back into the cabin and did as Pa said, revealing again that no matter whose name was on the claim, Pa was still boss around here.

The whole town didn't exactly turn out to hear the preacher. There were no banners or sharpshooters or medicine shows. But still there was a fair showing of folks—maybe just the curious, or those who didn't have anything better to do. When we drove into town, a good number of people were already heading toward the Gold Nugget Saloon, and I discovered that more ladies than I had ever imagined lived in these parts.

Along the streets and sidewalks, men were loitering about, watching the proceedings, obviously without any intention of joining them.

"Hey, where ya goin', Drum?" called out one in a sneering tone. But Pa kept the wagon moving steadily forward.

"Matthews," shouted another, "come join us down at the Silver Saddle after ye've dropped off your brood!"

I thought I detected a forlorn look pass over Uncle Nick's face.

"Don't tempt him, Jim," said another. "He's a family man now."

This brought a rousing laugh from the small group.

We finally reached the door of the Gold Nugget, pulled up, and all piled out. There were a few men standing around there, too, and Uncle Nick sauntered over and began talking to them.

After a few moments, I heard, "Let Drum take 'em. He's a religious sort of feller. Come on with us."

Pa walked over, far from cowed by their remarks, and turned a dark glance toward the men. He didn't say a word, but they seemed to understand and shrank back quickly. He took firm hold of Uncle Nick's arm, whispered something in his ear, and without further conversation Uncle Nick turned away and walked with us up the wooden steps. The other children bounded in. But I couldn't help hesitating. Pa started in too, then he turned back toward me.

"Something wrong?" he asked.

"No, sir," I answered. "It's just that I ain't never been in a saloon before."

A faint smile flickered across his face. Then he quickly turned serious. "I'm sorry there ain't no real church for you, Corrie," he said. I could tell he meant it.

"Do you suppose having church in a saloon is all right with God?"

"How in blazes am I supposed to know, girl?" he said, then put his hand on my shoulder and nudged me inside.

Twenty or thirty people were seated in chairs that had been placed in rows in front of the bar—mostly men, but probably six or seven ladies. There weren't any other children.

I saw Mr. Ashton and Mr. Weber from the freight company, and Mr. Bosely from the General Store. Mr. Rafferty the constable, was also there, and Mr. Singleton the newspaper man, and even Mr. Royce. The rest of the crowd were miners and a few farmers. Mrs. Gianini sat with one of the farmer's wives. Mrs. Parrish played the piano, and it would have been fine playing too if it hadn't been for the tinny-sounding, old saloon instrument.

The biggest surprise of all was to see Alkali Jones there. I guess I hadn't really expected to see him at all. But there he was—standing just inside the swinging doors, leaning against the saloon's back wall, waiting for Pa.

"Hey, Drum," he called out in a loud whisper, "I thought ya'd never get here, an' leave me standin' here playin' the fool. Hee, hee."

I don't know if I'd have even recognized him if it weren't for his laugh!

He wore a brown broadcloth suit that looked as out of place on him as his brilliantined hair and beard. Slicked down, the old miner looked like a wet cat whose fur had suddenly been soaked, leaving nothing but skin and bones.

"Quiet, ya old coot!" whispered Pa right back as we walked toward the back row. But Mr. Jones paid him no heed.

"Why, I ain't worn a stitch o' these duds since. . . ." He rubbed his slick beard. "Lemme see . . . since my brother Ezekiel's weddin' back in Arkansas."

"Didn't you wear it last time you went to church?" asked Tad innocently, not realizing he was supposed to whisper.

Several heads turned toward us, and I could feel poor Pa's embarrassment at being caught in such a situation, helped none by Alkali Jones' high-pitched chuckling over Tad's question.

Finally we sat down, much to Pa's and Uncle Nick's relief.

Mr. Rafferty introduced everyone to the Rev. Avery Rutledge. He was not an old man, like I imagined most preachers were supposed to be. He was probably Pa's age, or a year or two younger.

He was handsome in a rather stiff and severe way, a bit on the pale side, tall and slim with shoulders that slumped slightly forward. He surely wasn't robust and muscular like Uncle Nick, but his dark brown eyes beneath the wire-rimmed spectacles were keen and forceful. When he spoke, his voice showed just a hint of nervousness. But he made up for that by speaking a little louder than I thought he needed to, and the preacher-tone of his voice gave it a commanding sound. I doubted he'd be much good in a fist fight, but one word in that voice would probably be enough to discourage most foes. As he stood in front of us, however, his eyes flitted about from face to face, and that detracted a mite from his otherwise forceful appearance.

Mr. Rutledge handed out papers with hymns written on them. We got off to a good start with his leading, and Mrs. Parrish playing "O, for a Thousand Tongues." The piano was louder than all the voices put together, but the voices you could hear were mostly of the women. Even the few gravelly sounds from the motley-looking group of miners—some in monotone, some wandering about in search of the right key, and others like Uncle Nick, who just tried not to be conspicuous—were something priceless to hear and see. I found myself almost forgetting we were sitting in a drinking house!

During the third verse, just as we got to the words " 'tis music in the sinner's ears," all at once there came a commotion at the saloon door behind us, and three or four men came clamoring in.

"Hey, what's going on here?" one of them said.

"What's become o' this here town?" railed another.

"Can't a feller git a decent drink no more?"

"The bar's closed," someone called out. I think it was Mr. Bosely.

"Well, we want a bottle o' whiskey! Where's Jasper?"

"I'm here," called out a man standing against the far wall. I hadn't noticed him before. "But the man's right," he added, though he didn't sound too happy about it. "The bar's closed for an hour."

Mrs. Parrish gave up trying to keep playing the hymn. Finally, Mr. Rutledge spoke up, leveling his gaze toward the intruders.

"Despite the fact that this is a saloon," he said, "we are conducting a worship service, and there will be no whiskey served. But you are welcome to join us."

"So you're the preacher man who thinks he can take our saloon away!"

"Hey, Joe, this I gotta see. Maybe we should stay."

"Yeah. If Matthews can sit through the man's rantin', I suppose our whiskey'll wait an hour."

I could feel Uncle Nick squirm under the words. He fidgeted in his seat and half turned around toward them. I think he was getting set to shout some wise-crack back at them, when Pa gave him a sudden poke in the ribs with his elbow to shut him up.

The men took several of the empty seats, their hard-soled boots echoing on the oak floor of the Gold Nugget, while Mrs. Parrish resumed the hymn, playing as loudly as she dared in order to drown out the ongoing ruckus coming from the back row.

By the time we'd sung two more verses, things had settled down again. Mrs. Parrish played right into "What a Friend We Have in Jesus," and Mr. Rutledge led us in all the verses of that hymn, too. By the time it was done, he'd got his composure back enough from the interruption to start his preaching.

He just started right in, without a word of introduction,

and carried on with one of the loudest most hair-raising sermons I ever heard. He sounded very sure of everything he said, but I couldn't shake the feeling that he'd already preached the same sermon several times before. Every word sounded like he was reading it. But I knew he wasn't, because he had no papers in front of him. I guess he'd memorized it, like the readings we had learned in the school back in Bridgeville.

"And so, my friends," he said as he neared what I hoped was the end of his sermon, "I admonish you again to turn aside from any evil which encumbers you, and to run with godliness the race of life. Only by laying down the evil of our sinful past will we escape the wrath of God, which is as sure as our own corrupt nature, which was born in iniquity. Repent, I say, and enter into the glory of—"

All at once, without warning, a voice spoke out from the congregation:

"Now, I been sittin' here listenin', Preacher," the man said, "an' what I'd like t' know is what ya think men like us oughta do in a place like this?"

Noticeably flustered, a look passed over Rev. Rutledge's face I hadn't seen the whole morning. It was a look, well . . . almost of fear. But it passed from his eyes in an instant, and he quickly struggled to get his sermon back on track.

"I . . . er . . . as I was saying," he went on, clearing his throat nervously, "I would have all men, myself included, turn aside from any and all evils. The wrath of God will come like a thief in the night, and we must—"

"Are you sayin' we're a lot o' evil sinners?" called out another.

Not to be thrown off again, Mr. Rutledge took this interruption more in stride, and proceeded to shake the very rafters of the saloon with his voice. "Yes, my friends," he answered loudly. "A lot of sinners we all are and you are all included in that! Yes, there is sin in every man's heart, and in the saloons of Miracle Springs! But God will not be mocked! He will—"

"Come on, Reverend! Ye're not gonna tell us we gotta give up our poker an' our whiskey?"

"The Lord will exact godliness—" began the preacher in reply, but the men who were now set to disrupt him didn't let him finish.

"Ah, them religious words may be all right for folks back East where you come from, Reverend. But out here things is different. We ain't got nuthin' to do but have a little fun now an' then. Ain't that right, boys?"

Murmurings and a few calls and whistles erupted from around the room.

In vain Mr. Rutledge tried to speak again, but by now no one would let him.

Mrs. Parrish stood. "Please . . . please . . . you must—"

But her voice was drowned out in boos and catcalls, mostly from the back of the room where the fellow called Joe still sat with his friends. We all sat for a few more awkward moments, wondering what was going to happen. All at once I felt movement in the seat next to me, and before I realized it, Pa was on his feet.

"Let the man finish!" he thundered, and in an instant the room was still. "This man came a long way to preach to us," he continued. "Now I say we heed what the lady was tryin' to say, and let him do it!"

He took his seat; I think more surprised than anyone else at what he had done.

Rev. Rutledge mumbled some words of thanks, and quickly finished his sermon, but without ever quite regaining the emotion and fervor of before. I think he was glad to have the service over with, and he didn't stay around much afterwards to chat.

Pa didn't say anything as we filed outside, only led us back to the wagon with a sour expression on his face. I wanted to see Mrs. Parrish, but we were off and on our way back to the cabin before I even had a chance to look for her.

On the way home I thanked Pa for taking us. But he only grunted in reply.

CHAPTER 29

A SURPRISE

As December settled in, the days moved quickly, and I realized once more what a different spot we were in than back home. We hadn't had snow yet, though it got real cold and frosty at times. But when I strained my eyes toward the high Sierras I could catch glimpses of the expanse of white on their peaks. Back in New York we may have had more snow, but we sure didn't have mountains like that.

I wondered what Christmas would be like without Ma.

One thing for sure, it wouldn't be easy. Holidays were family times, and now, even with things gradually getting better with Pa, it was still pretty mixed up. A holiday like Christmas needs a ma to make it special. It would probably be the most difficult for Zack and me, because we would remember how it used to be back home. I didn't want to start crying in front of Pa. I didn't want to make him think I was sad. He didn't need anything else to worry about, and he was trying hard to do the best he could.

All month I wondered what he would do about the holiday, although I didn't want to say anything. But on the 17th we got an invitation from Mrs. Parrish to join her for Christmas dinner. She rode all the way out from town in her rig to deliver it to us personally. She included all seven of our Hollister-Belle clan, and said she hoped we'd all be able to come.

I got my crying done in bed when I was falling asleep on Christmas Eve, so on Christmas Day I tried my best to make it a special day for the kids. Uncle Nick and Pa got up and went out to the mine, just like any other day. The girls and I fixed breakfast, and they came in as usual about an hour later to eat.

I had made some small presents for everyone—dresses for Emily and Becky's dolls out of an old dress that didn't fit Becky anymore, and neck scarves for Tad, Zack, Uncle Nick, and Pa. After we were finished eating I gave them out, feeling a little awkward when I handed Pa his. It seemed so small.

"Merry Christmas, Pa," I said.

He looked surprised as he took it from me. "What?" he said in confusion, "Is this Christmas?"

"Yes, Pa," piped up Becky. "You didn't forget, did you?"

"Well tan my hide, girl!" he said scooping Becky off the ground, "now that you mention it, there is something mighty familiar-sounding about this date."

He set her down, then sat on a stool and began deliberately scratching his head with one finger. "Hmmm. . . ." he muttered. The three younger kids were watching him with wide eyes, incredulous that he had forgotten Christmas. But I thought I detected a hint of mischief in his eye, and it wasn't long before I knew I was right.

"Nick," he said, looking over to Uncle Nick, "did you hear what these kids are telling me . . . that this is Christmas?"

"I heard it, but I don't believe it," he replied.

"Yes, it is, Uncle Nick," said Tad excitedly. "It is—I promise!"

"He promises, Nick," said Pa real seriously. "Could you and me have lost track somehow?"

"Ain't likely," said Uncle Nick.

Pa scratched his head again. "Well," he said at last,

"there's only one way to find out for sure."

"What's that, Pa?" said Tad, taking the bait.

"Well—I reckon we'll have to find out if ol' St. Nick's been here."

"And he don't mean me!" said Uncle Nick.

"But you know," added Pa, "that a heap of things is different in California." He looked at Tad with a very serious expression. "By the time Santa Claus gets to California, he's plumb tuckered out and anxious to get home. So he don't fool with chimneys and stockings and tiptoein' around trying to stay outta people's way."

"He doesn't?" said Tad, amazed.

By this time, Uncle Nick was having a hard time not breaking into a laugh. But he kept his reaction to a smile.

"What does he do?" asked Emily, who had been listening intently, not quite sure what to believe, but letting her curiosity finally get the best of her.

"Well, blamed if he don't just drop off his packages any ol' place he can, usually off someplace where folks ain't likely to hear him. Hmmm," he said, stroking his beard, "I wonder if there's any place like that around here?"

"How about the mine cave?" suggested Uncle Nick.

"Nah—I don't think he'd use a place that ain't safe for kids. Probably someplace a mite closer to the cabin."

"The tool shed!" shouted Becky.

"Yeah!" yelled Tad. They both looked at Pa.

He returned an innocently questioning look, as if to say, *Who knows? It just might be.* Then he said, "I suppose it's worth a look."

Like a shot, Tad and Becky were out the door, followed by Emily. Zack and I were a little excited by now too and we sort of half-ran out after them. Uncle Nick and Pa came along too, but they walked.

By the time we got to the shed, which wasn't more than twenty yards from the cabin, already shouts and calls were coming from inside. Tad burst out as we approached.

"Santa's been here Pa!" he shouted. "There's presents and everything!"

"Well if that don't beat all!" said Pa, glancing around at Uncle Nick. "Ya hear that, Nick? These kids is right—it *is* Christmas!"

Tad reached up and grabbed Pa's hand, and excitedly led him inside the shed. Emily and Becky were already distributing the brightly-colored wrapped packages.

"There's only five, Pa," said Emily apologetically.

"Oh . . . well . . . that's another thing about California," he said, stooping down to her. "Out West, Santa's only got enough presents left for kids."

Satisfied, Emily turned back to the flurry of activity in the small shed. They were big packages too, but not heavy. The younger ones weren't waiting to be told what to do. They were already eagerly ripping into the pretty paper. I looked over at Pa kind of sheepishly.

"Well go to it, girl," he said. "It's got your name on it, don't it?"

Finally, I let my little-girl enthusiasm go. I sat down on a log and lit into my package. In a few seconds, I was taking the lid off the box, and reaching inside to lift out the prettiest hat I had ever seen. It had a wide straw brim, and was decorated with pink and blue ribbons which tied in the back and hung down several inches. It was so beautiful! I'd never had such a lovely bonnet in my life.

I looked up to see the others trying on hats of their own. Becky's and Emily's were beautiful too, with lace and tiny flowers. Of us all, I think Zack was proudest of his, though he was careful not to show his true pleasure. Very deliberately, he placed the tan leather hat on his head, its brim curled up just slightly—exactly like Pa's and Uncle Nick's. And even little Tad wore a smaller version of the same western hat.

Then all of a sudden, as if the thought had occurred to each at the same instant, the four younger ones tore out of the shed for the house in search of a mirror. I was the last to rise.

Uncle Nick had run off after the kids, but Pa was still standing there waiting for me. I looked up at him, and there was a look in his eyes I'll never forget—a look of pride, like he was feeling genuine pleasure at our happiness. I couldn't help it—even though I had resolved not to, I felt my eyes filling with tears.

"Thank you, Pa," I said quietly, looking deeply into his eyes.

"Don't mention it, girl," he replied. "That's what Christmas—and fathers—are all about."

He placed an arm around my shoulder and gave me a squeeze, then we began walking slowly toward the cabin together.

"You look mighty pretty in that bonnet," he said. "I think your ma'd be pleased!"

I couldn't help wondering and hoping that Ma was somewhere watching all this, our first Christmas without her. And I did hope she'd be pleased—not only with me, but with Pa too.

When we got back inside, Pa gathered us together and told us all to sit down, then said, "There's one other thing we gotta do, this being Christmas and all. Your ma and me started doing this the first Christmas after Corrie here was born, and we did it every year after that, 'til . . . well, you know—'til I had to leave."

He reached up to the mantle above the fireplace and took down Ma's little White Bible, opened it to Luke's Gospel, and began to read. I don't think I'd ever realized what a nice voice Pa had. But now as he read, a deep recollection of *his* voice stirred in my memory—not just Ma's—reading this very scripture. I had heard Pa read this before! Knowing that somehow made this reading all the more special.

"*And it came to pass in those days,*" he read, "*that there went out a decree from Caesar Augustus, that all the world—*"

"Ma always read us this," interrupted Becky.

Pa kept his eyes on the page, but I knew what he was thinking. Usually he was quiet for a spell after someone mentioned Ma.

"Yeah . . . I reckon she did," he said at length, then continued: "*that all the world should be taxed. And this taxing was first made when Cyrenius was governor of Syria. And all went to be taxed, every one into his own city. And Joseph also went up from Galilee, out of the city of Nazareth, into Judaea, unto the city of David, which is called Bethlehem. . . .*"

No one said another word. We all sat quietly, even Uncle Nick, listening to Pa read. When he was finished, he closed the Bible, and stood to place it back on the mantle. I think we all felt, even without Ma, that it was really Christmas. I didn't say much for the rest of the morning. The other kids were running around excitedly, all wearing their new hats, and Emily and Becky dressing up their dolls.

But it was a quiet morning for me. I felt a little like Mary, with a lot of things to ponder in my heart.

CHAPTER 30

CHRISTMAS DINNER

A little before noon we all dressed in our Sunday clothes and headed into town to Mrs. Parrish's.

I was already happy about the way Christmas had turned out, but when we walked into Mrs. Parrish's house, it was like tasting it for the first time all over again. She had a lovely decorated tree in the parlor, strung with fine lace and beads, and covered with delicate glass ornaments. Tiny candles clipped to its branches gave it a special glow. I could have stood there for an hour gazing at it.

Around the rest of the house were garlands of holly and evergreen branches, and the fragrance of cloves and cinnamon filled the air. With these pungent scents mingled the delicious smell of roast goose, fresh-baked bread and pumpkin pie.

It was all too wonderful! I just couldn't help thinking of Ma, and how she would have enjoyed being here with us!

Mrs. Parrish praised the neck scarves I'd made. I blushed, but for once was glad for the color in my cheeks to hide that I was feeling overwhelmed by the day. Then she kindly complimented our new hats and bonnets.

"Santa left them in the shed," said Becky.

"You don't say!"

"Uncle Nick and Pa even forgot it was Christmas," said Tad, still incredulous of the fact.

"My, that *is* serious," she said, glancing up at the two men in mock disbelief.

Mrs. Parrish warmly welcomed Pa and Uncle Nick with handshakes, and they exchanged a few pleasantries. "I hope you won't mind," she said, "but I have taken the opportunity to invite someone else—"

Before she finished another knock came at the door.

"—who would have otherwise been alone today," she added, "and it seems that he is here now."

She excused herself and went to open the door. When she returned, the preacher was with her.

"Rev. Rutledge," she said, "I don't believe you've had the opportunity of being formally introduced to my friends here."

"This is Nick Matthews," she said, turning to Uncle Nick.

The two men shook hands.

"And Mr.—uh, Mr. Drum. Mr. Drum, may I present Avery Rutledge."

"Pleased to meet you," Pa said.

"You're one of the men from our first church service," said the preacher.

"We were all there," replied Pa nonchalantly.

"Oh, but you were more than just *there*, Mr. Drum. Why, you saved my hide! I've been hoping to meet up with you ever since to thank you."

Pa shrugged. "I just thought you deserved a fair shake, that's all. Weren't nothing special."

"On the contrary, Mr. Drum," broke in Mrs. Parrish. "You saved the service. I too have wanted to thank you."

"A regular hero!" said Uncle Nick with a grin.

"Look, it was nothing!" said Pa, a little testily. I could tell this was getting under his skin. If there was one thing he didn't want to be, it was a hero in a church service. I was fairly certain he regretted speaking out like he did.

"Well, nevertheless, we're very appreciative," said Rev. Rutledge. "I'd hoped to find one or two strong men in the community who would ally themselves with me in my cause to bring Christ to the lost lambs in the mining camps."

Pa said nothing more.

"Let me also introduce Nick's nieces and nephews," Mrs. Parrish said lightly, changing the embarrassing subject for Pa. One by one she said our names, and we all curtsied and bowed appropriately to the Reverend.

"I'm very pleased to meet all of you children," he said, smiling.

"Well," said Mrs. Parrish, "as soon as Marcus gets here, we'll be able to—oh, there he is now," she said, just as we heard another knock at the door.

As she went to let in the blacksmith, I saw Uncle Nick sidle up to Pa, give him a jab in the ribs with his elbow, and whisper, "So, you're the preacher's new ally to bring religion to us lost lambs, eh, Drum?"

"You keep your nose outta it, Nick, ya hear?"

"Now, if you'll all gather around the table, we can begin our meal," Mrs. Parrish said.

When we were seated, she served everyone a cup of hot cider. "Corrie, would you like to help me bring out the food?"

"Yes, Ma'am," I answered, happy to be able to help on this festive occasion. Then while the others sipped at their cider, we brought out platters of food from the kitchen, all piled high and steaming.

Rev. Rutledge sat there politely waiting, and if it hadn't been for him, Uncle Nick and the kids would probably have just dug into all that food in front of them. But with the preacher's patient example, everyone else waited too. At last Mrs. Parrish and I sat down.

"Reverend, would you give thanks for us?" Mrs. Parrish asked.

"I'd be honored, Ma'am," he answered.

He bowed his head, and all the rest of us did the same. As he prayed, I wanted so badly to open my eyes and see what Pa was doing, not to mention Uncle Nick. But I didn't dare.

"Almighty God our Father," he began in his solemn preacher's voice, "we thank thee for this most holy of days, when thine only Son Jesus Christ became incarnate, entering the world as a little child. Make us ever mindful, O Lord, of thy wondrous gift to us, on this day and on all days, and let us live lives acceptable in thy sight, always striving to do thy will in all things. We thank thee for this provision out of thy bounty, and we pray thy special blessing on the loving hands that have prepared it for us. Through Christ our Lord we pray . . ." Then after some hesitation he added, ". . . Amen."

Within seconds the table was a commotion of passing plates and reaching hands, the grown-ups doing their best to help the children who were seated next to them. When our plates were heaped with more food than we kids had seen in a long time, we set about to eating. We kept quiet while the grown-ups talked, enjoying every bite of Mrs. Parrish's fine cooking.

"It's too bad about Mr. Larsen's cabin," said Mrs. Parrish as she passed the plate of steaming goose again.

"Was he plumb burned out?" asked Uncle Nick. "I ain't seen him since the fire."

"To the ground, Mr. Matthews," answered Mrs. Parrish. "From what I understand he lost everything."

"I shall have to make a call on him," said Rev. Rutledge. "Perhaps later you might tell me where I can locate him, Mrs. Parrish."

"You're probably too late for that," said Pa.

"It is never too late for a Christian word of comfort and sympathy, Mr. Drum," said the minister.

"I was just meaning that Tom Larsen might already have pulled out."

"Just like that?" asked Mrs. Parrish.

"Royce made him an offer on the place a few days before the fire," answered Pa. "He turned him down then, and from what I hear it was none too friendly a meetin'. Though word is now that he's gonna take Royce's money while he can and get outta town."

"That's a shame. Tom Larsen is the sort of man we need around here."

"Not too bad for Royce. He's gettin' the place for a song."

There was a lull for a few minutes while we all concentrated on the meal Mrs. Parrish had prepared.

"It is so wonderful to have children present for Christmas dinner," said Mrs. Parrish at length.

"It sho' is!" remarked Mr. Weber. "Why, Christmas back home was nuthin' iffen it wasn't a day fer de chillens all scurryin' roun' de place! An' this goose, Miz. Parrish, it puts me in sech a mind o' Christmas when I was a little chile'!"

"I'm happy you are enjoying it, Marcus," said Mrs. Parrish. "And we are all honored that you could join us too, Reverend," she added, turning to the preacher.

"The honor is all mine, Almeda," he returned. "I must say, after the first few weeks I'd begun to think I'd made a mistake coming here. But a festive day like this helps restore my faith again."

"Surely you're not serious, Avery?" said Mrs. Parrish with concern.

I couldn't help noticing that they used each other's given names.

"I'm afraid I am serious, Almeda," he replied thoughtfully.

She continued to look at the minister questioningly.

He acknowledged her concern with a brief smile, but then went on, "I have to admit," he said, in a down-to-earth voice, "that I was quite shaken by what that fellow said the first Sunday—that is before Mr. Drum came to my aid. Do you remember his comment that religion may be all right for the folks back East, but that out West it was different?"

Mrs. Parrish nodded her head.

"Well, what if he's right, and I'm *not* cut out for preaching in this setting? What if the religion I bring isn't going to mean anything to these men?"

This was an altogether different Rev. Rutledge than the man I'd heard preaching that Sunday. Different, too, from the man who'd just prayed before the meal a few minutes ago. His preacher-voice was gone, and he sounded like—well, just like a regular person, not someone who planned everything he was going to say ahead of time. I'd never thought about a preacher having feelings before now.

"Nonsense, Avery!" said Mrs. Parrish. "God's truth must be carried to all men and women everywhere, and it's the same Gospel here and in the East and everywhere."

"I'm sure you're right," he mused, "But I've been doing more thinking this last month than I ever have before in my life. Whatever else comes of it, I realize I'll have to modify my methods some to ever reach men like the wild bunch who have inhabited this place."

I saw Uncle Nick glance quickly at Pa. I guess Rev. Rutledge saw it, too. "The kind of men who were trying to disrupt the service," he quickly added, "nothing like the fine examples of Christian manhood we're blessed with in our midst today."

It was his preacher voice again, and it was Mrs. Parrish's turn to look down at her plate without replying. A brief awkward silence followed.

"Well, Reverend," said Uncle Nick, breaking the quiet, "I hear you came West across Panama way. There's been some discussion as to which be worse—the mosquitoes in them jungles, or the savage Apaches on the plains. I dealt with my share of Indians, and I reckon at least once in a while a body can reason with them, if push comes to shove. But I suppose them 'skeeters bite first and ask questions later, eh?"

Everyone chuckled. Pa broke into a grin at Uncle Nick's humor, and glanced in my direction with a quick wink.

But the minister, who dabbed his mouth carefully with his napkin, seemed suddenly offended after so cordial a beginning to the conversation, and focused his eyes solemnly on Uncle Nick.

"Crossing the jungle was a harrowing experience for many in my party," he said sternly. It looked like his preacher voice was back for a while. "Several of my traveling companions succumbed to yellow fever, Mr. Matthews, so please excuse me if I find little amusement in your comment."

Our laughter stopped at the sharp rebuke, and I could tell Pa was irritated. He pursed his lips and cocked his eyebrow disapprovingly.

"You should have tried your luck with the Apaches then, Reverend," he said dryly.

"I do not believe in *luck*, Mr. Drum," rejoined the minister. "The Lord's divine providence is my stay and my salvation."

Pa opened his mouth to shoot back a reply, and by the look in his eye I didn't think it would be any too pleasant. But Mrs. Parrish broke in.

"Avery, I'm sure everyone would be so very interested to hear of some of your plans for Miracle Springs."

All talk of his doubts had vanished now, and he spoke with that commanding voice we'd first heard at the Gold Nugget church. "This is truly a field ripe unto harvest," said the Reverend. "A man of God should find no end of avenues for ministry. My first project, of course, shall be the construction of a proper place of worship. Meaning no offense to you, Almeda—I know you meant well, and perhaps it *was* the only place available, but it is nothing less than a travesty to be forced to gather for worship in such a vile place as that saloon. It makes me quake within to think of God's displeasure."

"Perhaps," said Mrs. Parrish, with a touch of hurt at his comment, "but you will find that out West we must sometimes make do with what we have."

"But we must never degrade ourselves to the level of the ungodly. The Word of God says, 'Be not yoked with unbelievers.' "

"It does indeed," replied Mrs. Parrish. "But I think the scripture you're referring to says not to be *unequally* yoked, Avery. It seems to me that makes a world of difference. As you quote it, Paul would have been saying not to associate with sinners, and that is something our Lord would never condone."

"I was only trying to make the point—" rejoined the minister, but before he could finish Pa cut him off.

"The lady's right, Reverend," said Pa with just enough edge in his voice to make me feel uneasy at what was coming next. "I ain't no Bible scholar, but it seems to me that Jesus spent a lot of his time out meetin' people where they were. I expect if he was livin' in Miracle, you might find him in the saloons as much as any other place. That's where you're gonna find most of your sinners, Reverend."

"It is one thing to go out on the highways and byways of life to win sinners," returned Rev. Rutledge, his face reddening a bit, "but quite another to expect them to find spiritual succor in the very den of iniquity wherein they first fell."

"I think it was in a church, not a saloon, where *I* first fell from grace," muttered Uncle Nick.

"You are baiting me, are you not, Mr. Matthews?"

"Well, I'll tell you like it is, I seen just as many hypocrites in church as I ever did in the Gold Nugget. At least in the saloon they wasn't pretendin' to be what they wasn't." I was surprised by Uncle Nick's boldness.

"So you consider all churchgoers hypocrites?"

"That wasn't what I said," replied Uncle Nick.

"Would anyone like another helping of anything?" asked Mrs. Parrish, trying her best to redeem the uncomfortable situation.

"This is the best goose I ever et, Ma'am," put in Marcus Weber.

"Indeed it is, Almeda," added the minister. "A mighty fine meal . . . mighty fine indeed! I know we're all very appreciative."

"Yessir," went on Mr. Weber. "The Rev'rend here, he sure be right, Ma'am."

"Thank you, kindly. I'm glad you could all come. And I do believe the pumpkin pies are ready. Avery, would you mind helping me take them from the oven?"

The two rose and left the room, Mrs. Parrish seeming to breathe a sigh of relief that the conversation had gone no further.

But the break proved only temporary. I could feel the tension building as we ate our pie a few minutes later. I didn't follow the gist of everything that was said, but it was clear neither my uncle nor my pa thought too much of all the Reverend's smooth-sounding words.

"I have been quite pleased with the turnout at the services," said Rev. Rutledge as he sipped his coffee. "What with the contributions I brought from the faithful in Boston and the generosity of local offerings, I believe it will not be long at all before we can begin construction on a church building right here in Miracle Springs."

"That's wonderful, Avery!" exclaimed Mrs. Parrish. "And I don't think we will have any difficulty finding a site."

"I've spoken with Mr. Royce at the bank, and he assures me he will be able to help us secure property at a good price, and possibly assist with the financing as well."

"That be land he's stolen from hard workin' sinners, if you don't mind me saying it, Reverend," said Uncle Nick. "If Royce builds your church, you ain't likely to get much of a flock."

"He strikes me as one concerned for the welfare of the community, and as ready as anyone to extend the hand of brotherly kindness. A fine Christian man, I would say."

"A snake is more like it!" shot back Uncle Nick. "If you're wanting to find sinners, Reverend, I'd take that Gospel of yours and preach it in his bank!"

"I'm sure no man is without his faults," said Mrs. Parrish quickly, before Rev. Rutledge had the chance to respond. "Now, who would care for another piece of pie?"

"Iffen you's got plenty there, Miz Parrish," said Marcus Weber sheepishly. "It's de bes' I ever dun ate. And tha's de truth!"

The minister didn't seem sensitive to the fact he was scratching away at a live hornet's nest, because the moment there was a pause in the conversation, he started in again about building a new church.

"Once we do find a location, and come to terms with the financing, I see nothing to stop us. I'm certain if the Lord's blessing is with us, we will see a completed church by next summer. I believe there are plenty of able-bodied men who would be willing to lend their talents to the project, fine men who are not ashamed to stand and be counted for the cause of Christ. Men much like yourself, Mr. Drum—"

As he spoke, he turned in Pa's direction, and it was clear he was attempting to smooth over the recent bumpiness of the conversation with what he felt was a compliment.

"Men of courage, saying to their community, as you did when you stood up and spoke out on my behalf, that they are part of the church's ministry to the lost. Fine Christian men who—"

"Look, Reverend!" Pa suddenly burst out in a loud voice. "When are you gonna get it through that head of yours that I ain't of the same mind as you? I gave up all that righteous stuff . . . well, years ago—when I figured I wasn't fit for it, an' it wasn't fit for the likes of me. Your brain's so filled with old-fashioned talk and Bible verses no ordinary man like me can understand, that you don't have sense to see what's right in front of your nose. I'm one of them sinners you're always talkin' about, Reverend! I may go to some of your meetings, and I may help you build your blamed church, and I'll read my—I'll read the kids here the Christmas story 'cause I believe in givin' the Lord his due. But stop makin' me into somethin' I ain't! I don't rightly know why I stood up to make the boys shut up that day. I half-regretted it ever since, and I sure ain't gonna do it again!"

He stopped and took a deep breath, then turned to Mrs. Parrish. Everyone was absolutely still.

"I thank you kindly for the meal, Ma'am," he said in a softer tone. "But I'd best take my leave—I got business in town."

He stood, then looked in my direction with what appeared a fleeting, unspoken apology in his eyes, then added, "I'll be back for you kids in an hour or so."

Then he turned and made for the door, saying as he went, "You coming, Nick?"

Uncle Nick hesitated a moment, then rose, tipped his hat toward Marcus Weber and the minister, then to Mrs. Parrish, "Ma'am, I thank you too, for makin' this day special for us all." Then he too was gone.

An awkward few minutes followed. At length, Rev. Rutledge sighed, and shook his head with a look of great pity.

"Sometimes, I do not understand the ways of God," he said. "To my limited vision, it seems a deplorable turn of fate that men like that should be given charge of these precious little ones."

"Only a few moments ago you were calling at least one of them a fine Christian, Avery," said Mrs. Parrish softly.

"Ah, but that was before I knew the true state of his heart toward God. He is clearly in rebellion against his Maker."

"Be that as it may, I truly feel they are doing the best they can for the children," persisted Mrs. Parrish. Her defense of Pa and Uncle Nick came as a surprise. She didn't have the best to say for them in times past, and I wondered who was doing the changing—they, or her.

"Yo' betta b'lieve they is," put in Mr. Weber, who had been silent for most of the meal. "Well," he added, pausing for a moment's reflection, " 'ceptin' fer them hosses, that is."

"I fear their best may not be enough," continued Rev. Rutledge.

"There's little other choice, regardless," said Mrs. Parrish.

"Surely there must be some decent family willing to take them in."

"He's our kin!" I suddenly heard myself saying. "Nothing's going to make us leave him—that is, unless he says so." The words were no sooner out of my mouth, and I wanted to sink under the table, for I could feel all eyes turned toward me.

"Yes, child," said the minister, and his voice was gentle and full of compassion. It was his normal voice, not the stern, preachy one full of memorized words. "I truly hope it will work out for you—and for your uncle. I can see that you care a great deal for him, and I'm sure he does for each one of you, too. I will be committing this situation with your uncle and his partner, as well as the souls of the two men, to much prayer."

It sure didn't help matters when, an hour later, Uncle Nick came to the door again with the smell of whiskey on his breath. Pa was sitting on the buckboard waiting, and didn't even get down. Uncle Nick and the preacher exchanged not a word.

Both Pa and Uncle Nick were quite talkative on the way home. Maybe it was the whiskey, maybe it was just their way of letting off steam.

"Some high and mighty cuss, wasn't he!" exclaimed Uncle Nick.

"We ain't exactly saints, Nick, now are we!" laughed Pa, seeming proud of the fact.

"Well, you always said you'd rather be an honest sinner than a dishonest hypocrite. You shoulda told him that, Drum!"

"And I'd still rather be!"

"I'm with you, pard!" laughed Uncle Nick. "I'm with you!"

CHAPTER 31

NEW DRESSES

A week after Christmas, Mrs. Parrish came to call. It seemed every other day was full of surprises.

She asked Pa if she could take us girls into Miracle Springs with her until suppertime.

"A ladies' day on the town," she said with a mysterious grin.

"They're old enough that I don't have to watch 'em every minute," he replied. "If they want to go, it's all right by me." He wasn't exactly friendly. We hadn't seen Mrs. Parrish since Christmas Day and I think her presence reminded him of what happened.

But the girls and I could hardly contain ourselves!

Once Ma took me into Bridgeville. "Just for fun," she'd said. I'll never forget that day, because I felt so much a special part of Ma's life, as if we were friends.

I felt the same way on this day in town with Mrs. Parrish. I hadn't known her very long, but the few times spent with her had been important ones. I suppose in a way she made up a little for the loss of Ma. I don't know what Ma would think if she knew I thought such a thing. But knowing Ma, she would be glad I had someone to rely on. As much as I wanted things with Pa to work out, there are times when a girl needs a woman to talk to.

When we got to Miracle Springs, the first place we went

was the General Store. I would have been content to just *look* at all the fine things, but Mrs. Parrish had other plans.

"Good morning, Mr. Bosely," she greeted the store-keeper.

"Morning, Ma'am. Fine day, isn't it?"

"It certainly is. May I see your new shipment of calicos?"

"Parrish Freight brought them in, Ma'am. I would have thought you'd already looked them over."

"I did, briefly. But now I have three young ladies who will want to look them over."

Mr. Bosely grinned. "I see! I'll be right back."

He went to a back room out of sight. Mrs. Parrish turned to the three of us, knelt down so that she could talk on Becky's level, and then said, "Girls, I hope you won't think me presumptuous, but I want to give you Christmas presents. I thought you might each like a new dress."

I gasped in surprise, and couldn't say anything. But as usual, Becky was not at a loss for words.

"Oh, goody! Just for us?"

"Just for you," laughed Mrs. Parrish.

"What about Tad and Zack?" she said, as if she had discovered a terrible flaw in Mrs. Parrish's idea. "They can't wear dresses."

Mrs. Parrish laughed again. "Don't worry, Becky. I've thought of that, too. I thought they might each like a shirt and vest."

She stood, and now spoke to me. "But before I went any further, I needed to have you come into town for fittings."

Finally I found my voice. "That's so kind of you, Mrs. Parrish. But it's too much. You don't have to—"

"*Have* to, child?" said Mrs. Parrish smiling. "Don't you understand? You are my *friends*! Please, Corrie, allow me to do this, won't you? It's as much a pleasure for me as for you."

"Are you sure, Ma'am?" I asked. I suppose I didn't really understand, at least not quite like she meant it.

"I've always wanted children, Corrie. Especially little girls to do things for. Seeing these dresses on you will give me great happiness."

"Well, if you put it that way. . . ." I began. Then Mr. Bosely returned, and all else was forgotten.

He was carrying five different patterns of calicos. Mrs. Parrish must have ordered them with us in mind, because the minute we saw them, each of us knew immediately which cloth we wanted for our new dresses. Becky's hands went right for the red. Emily took more time with her choice, though I think she knew from the beginning, but was just too shy to announce that she wanted the pink. I chose sky blue.

While Mr. Bosely cut off the needed lengths, Mrs. Parrish explained that Mrs. Gianini was an excellent seamstress and would make the dresses, and that she was expecting us that very morning to measure and fit us. It was all more than I could comprehend. Ma had always made our clothes in the past. But to have a fancy new dress, with the lace Mrs. Parrish was asking Mr. Bosely about even as we looked at the fabric, made by a seamstress—it was all too exciting to imagine! We hadn't had anything new since we'd left New York.

The pleasant Italian lady welcomed us as warmly as ever, and after some time complimenting our choice of fabrics and discussing styles with Mrs. Parrish, she said it was time to get started. She took the younger girls first, and told Mrs. Parrish that tea was brewing in the kitchen, and we could relax and visit. Her dark eyes were twinkling and her pink cheeks glowing as she took charge of Emily and Becky. It wasn't hard for me to see that she felt the same way as Mrs. Parrish about the opportunity to do something for the little "bambinas," as she called Emily and Becky. I watched her plump frame shuffle into the sitting room, an arm around each of my sisters, thankful that they had more mothers than me to help look after them.

CHAPTER 32

A TALK WITH MRS. PARRISH

While the younger girls were occupied, Mrs. Parrish and I remained in the kitchen. She poured us each some tea, and then offered me a cookie from a delicate China plate. Mrs. Gianini called them *biscottes*, and they were something like a sweet biscuit with a faint licorice flavor.

"Well, Corrie," she said, sitting down at the table opposite me and taking a sip from her hot tea, "you are practically a full-fledged Californian now. What do you think of this land?"

"It sure is pretty, I'll say that much," I answered.

Then I paused. Mrs. Parrish could tell I was thinking, and waited for me to continue.

"Back home Zack trapped a baby raccoon once," I went on. "It was so cute and furry. Ma kept saying, 'You kids be careful. That little coon'll grow up one day and'll turn wild just like that.' 'Course we didn't believe her. We figured he'd stay cute and cuddly forever. But Ma was right. One day all of a sudden, he turned savage and bit Zack in the arm. Real bad too. Ma said Zack was lucky he didn't have rabies. And so we had to let our pet raccoon go back to the forest."

I stopped again, and once more Mrs. Parrish just waited for me to think out what I was trying to say.

"I suppose I feel about our new life in California a little

like we was watching a baby raccoon grow up. You just can't tell yet how it's going to turn out. It might turn out good, it might not. Maybe that's not such a good . . . what do you call it?"

"Analogy?"

"Yes'm, that's it. Maybe it's not such a good analogy, comparing California with a baby raccoon. But it's something like how I feel inside. I can't tell yet what's going to come of it all—good, bad . . . or maybe some of both."

"I don't know if it's a good analogy or not either, Corrie. But it is certainly very perceptive. Do you think like that often?"

"Well, I guess I'm always thinking, Ma'am. Trying to make sense of things."

"You ought to write your ideas down."

I felt my cheeks suddenly get warm. "I have been writing down a lot of things lately, Ma'am," I told her.

"Are you writing letters—keeping a journal . . . what?"

"I don't have anybody to write a letter to. And it's nothing very fancy, just a diary, putting down in writing what happens and whatever else comes to my mind. Ma suggested I do it before she died."

"That's wonderful! I would love to read it."

"Oh, I'd be too embarrassed, Ma'am," I replied. "I'm probably a terrible writer."

"I doubt that, Corrie. Besides, practice makes perfect."

"I am trying to write it better all the time. But it sure doesn't sound like the books I read. It's just the way I talk, Ma'am. Nobody'd want to read that!"

"I think you may be wrong about that, Corrie. I'm certain it would be fascinating for a good many people to read about a young girl's life and reaction to the new land of California."

"Well, maybe, but I do know how much I appreciate all you have done for me and my brothers and sisters since we came," I said.

"As I said, this is as much fun for me as for you," replied Mrs. Parrish. She took a cookie. "Mrs Gianini really is a superb cook!"

"I was meaning more than the dresses, Mrs. Parrish," I said. "You've done so much since we came to California. You've . . . well, you know—with Ma gone and all . . . sometimes I don't know what I would have done without your kindness."

She reached over and laid her hand, still soft and smooth in spite of her work, on top of mine. Her eyes looked into mine, and were full of tears. I could tell she knew what I was feeling.

"Dear Corrie," she said softly, "you've made my life richer, too. Each one of you, really, but especially you. You are more than just an acquaintance, Corrie. You are my friend. I want you to know that I will be here for you whenever you need someone. I would never presume to take your mother's place, but there are times when a girl needs the companionship or the listening ears of a woman."

"Thank you, Mrs. Parrish," I said. I guess I was crying by now too. "I think Ma would be thankful you came along in our lives when you did."

"If ever you need to talk about anything, I hope you will feel free to do so."

I looked down at my tea. I think she knew I was thinking hard about something serious, because when she spoke again she was really earnest.

"What is it, Corrie? What's troubling you?"

"I guess I've been confused about both Pa and Uncle Nick," I said, "especially since the preacher came."

"Confused . . . in what way?"

"Well, neither of them makes a secret of their reluctance about church. Since Christmas, Pa's said some—I don't know—negative things, especially about the minister. And then the way he and Rev. Rutledge argued at your house . . . and of course there's Uncle Nick's drinking and gambling. And Pa's too, I suppose. I know Uncle Nick and Ma went to church when they was kids. And Pa read to us from the Bible once. Inside I want to believe Pa's a God-fearing man, Mrs. Parrish. But sometimes I get real scared, and I wonder if he cares for God at all. He's told me he and Uncle Nick were involved in real bad things and that's why they had to leave the east. I don't want to think ill of him, Mrs. Parrish, but Mr. Rutledge, I'm sure he'd count my Pa as a sinner and an evil man and on his way to hell!"

I started to break down, but did my best to hold back the tears.

Mrs. Parrish gave my hand a squeeze, and tried to comfort me.

"There, there, child . . . you just cry all you need to, and then we'll talk some more."

I was quiet for another minute. Mrs. Parrish handed me her handkerchief and I wiped my eyes. She looked over at me with a deep smile on her face. I tried to smile back, but what came out was a half laugh and half cry that made me feel kind of stupid all over again.

Mrs. Parrish laughed with me.

"You love your father, don't you, Corrie?" she said.

"Oh, of course," I replied, sniffing. "I'm trying to, but he's just a puzzling sort of man."

"I know he is, Corrie. But I do think you love him. Otherwise, you wouldn't feel this hurt over him."

She paused, seeming to think over what to say next while I blew my nose and took a deep breath.

"Corrie," she said, "is your concern that you think your Pa might be a heathen . . . a bad man?"

"Yes, Ma'am. I suppose that's it."

"And because he's not a churchman, and spoke rudely about Reverend Rutledge, you're afraid he is a sinner?"

"I guess so. Along with the gamblin', and what they did in New York."

"Ah, yes. Those are rather serous issues, aren't they."

"Do *you* think those are sins, Ma'am?"

"No doubt they are, Corrie. I'm sure you're right there."

"So do *you* think my Pa's a sinner?"

"Tell me first of all what you think a sinner is, Corrie."

"Doing bad things, I suppose, and not going to church and not caring about God."

"But what about a person who *didn't* do bad things, and who went to church *every* Sunday, and who was always saying religious things . . . would that kind of person be a sinner?"

"Oh no, Ma'am."

"What if that same person, acting very good and religious on the outside, had bad attitudes and resentments and unkindness down inside his heart where no one could see it, what then?"

I didn't have a quick answer to give her.

"In other words, what if one man on the outside seemed to be a sinner, but was kind inside, and did things to help people whenever he had the chance; and another man was very religious and never drank or gambled or did anything that looked wrong, but inside he was mean and vengeful?"

"I think I see what you mean, Mrs. Parrish. But it does make it awfully confusing."

"Yes, it is complicated. But you see, when Jesus spoke of sin, he didn't talk so much about the outward things a person did—like the drinking and gambling—but more about the inside, what a person thought in his heart."

I nodded. She was certainly good at explaining things.

"There's one particular place in the Bible where Jesus is talking about sin, and he says that it's not the outward things that a man *does* that make him a sinner, but the things that are *inside* his heart—things like pride and anger and unkindness toward others, and selfishness. You see, Corrie, we're all sinners in that way."

"Everybody?"

"Yes. I am, and Rev. Rutledge . . . and even you, Corrie, and your brothers and sisters. We all have those kinds of attitudes deep inside us. And Jesus says they are just as bad as things your uncle or Pa or any miner in Miracle Springs might do. It's a terrible thing to kill a man, or to steal. But Jesus says it might be just as much a sin to think horrible thoughts about someone, and to want to kill him in your heart."

"That seems mighty hard to believe, Mrs. Parrish."

"To our small minds, yes it does. It's easier to point the finger at someone *else's* sin than try to discover our own. But sin is on the inside, not so much in what we *do* but in what we *are*. We are all sinners—all of us. So yes, your father is a sinner. But so are the rest of us. I need the Lord Jesus just as much as he does."

"I've never heard anything like that, Mrs. Parrish."

She laughed. "There are many who don't seem to have realized these truths, Corrie, even many church people."

"Why don't they talk about that in church instead of all that loud repentance stuff?" I asked.

"Ah, Corrie," sighed Mrs. Parrish, "that is indeed a good question. Too often we are so busy talking *about* the truths of God, that we forget to get around to *doing* them. God wants us to be good, to be the kind of person that Jesus was—not on the outside, but inside. But it's much easier, for instance, to talk about repentance, than to actually go to another person and ask his forgiveness for something you did against him. Being a godly person inside, that can be difficult."

"Rev. Rutledge didn't sound like he was saying the kinds of things you are, Ma'am. Meaning no disrespect, he sounded just like every other preacher I've ever heard, like he was pointing his finger at all the sinners in town."

"I know, Corrie. But I think he's been a little nervous, not really knowing how to preach to the kind of men there are around here. Preachers are growing and learning and even struggling, just like everyone else. He's a good man,

Corrie, and he loves God. He just needs time to grow, as we all do."

"This is all so new to me, Mrs. Parrish," I said.

"I've given you a great deal to think about," she replied smiling. "Enough for one day, I think. But there are other things about living the way God wants us to. I hope I get the chance to tell you about them someday, too."

"Oh, I'd like that," I answered.

"We'll be sure to talk again—real soon."

Just then I heard the happy sounds of young voices, followed by running footsteps heading toward the kitchen. Becky and Emily had been in the other room just long enough. I didn't know whether the Lord or Mrs. Gianini had had the strongest hand in keeping them there, but I was glad Mrs. Parrish and I got to have our talk.

CHAPTER 33

TROUBLE AT THE MINE

I found myself thinking about a lot of new things after my talk with Mrs. Parrish, although I didn't have the chance to write in my journal for days. Pa and Uncle Nick were working constantly at the mine, with Mr. Jones coming out almost every day. So I was extra busy keeping vigil on the children, because the men were setting charges. They let Zack help quite a bit, too, except when the dynamite was set to blow—then they'd make him get way back down the hill. The noise of the explosions was deafening, and many times sent Tad and Emily nearly into tears. If Becky shed any, it was only because I wouldn't let her go near all the excitement.

But just because I didn't write for a while doesn't mean I wasn't busy pondering all Mrs. Parrish had told me.

It's funny how I had started out concerned about Pa. Afterward I found my thoughts turning my own direction. Mrs. Parrish was teaching me a lot about life and how I wanted to live. She said she's had to learn what she knows painfully. But she has a quiet peacefulness now, even with her husband gone. Maybe I won't ever be as genteel as she is. But if I could grow up with some of that same contentment on my face, I'd be satisfied. I wanted to ask her sometime how she got that peace, and whether it was something I might hope to have when I was finally a grown woman, too.

229

When I did find time to start writing about my conversation with her, and what she said about attitudes and kindness and sin and church and all, I found myself really wanting to say things right. I felt that all she said was important, and that I might want to read it again sometime. But so much of it I didn't completely understand. Finally I made the decision to show Mrs. Parrish part of my diary. It was kind of embarrassing at first, because a journal is a personal thing. But I wanted her to help me remember as much of that conversation as I could. So we talked about it again, two or three times, and she helped me fill in what I forgot from the first time I'd tried to write it all down. I think she was a little shy about seeing me write down her words too. But she knew she was doing it as a favor to me, and knew it would likely help me to remember what she had said.

I was still trying to to find time to write about my talk with Mrs. Parrish when Uncle Nick and Pa took the wagon into town to get some more lumber to shore up the roof in the mine shaft. I thought for sure I'd have some spare time then, as soon as I finished baking bread. But so much happened that before I knew it, I had two major incidents in my life to tell about.

Right in the middle of my batch of bread, Tad knocked over the bucket of water. My dough was spoiled, and not only did I have to start all over again, I had to go back out to the creek for water.

I picked up the bucket and started out for the creek up by the mine. About halfway there I heard a strange sound, like chopping, or the sound of a pick against rock, followed by the whinny of a horse. I looked down the road, wondering if Pa and Uncle Nick had forgotten something and were coming back. It was an hour or two too soon for them to be returning with the lumber. But the road was deserted.

The whinny came again—clear, and not far from the mine.

I continued on in that direction.

When I reached the mine, instead of going right down to the creek for water, I made my way slowly toward the mine opening. I saw nothing out of the ordinary. But as I circled around it, on the hillside above, where the top of the shaft sloped down, I saw the horse—a chestnut, tied to the branch of a tree.

The animal looked vaguely familiar, but I couldn't quite place it. Then suddenly I heard a heavy footstep behind me.

I turned sharply. The scar-faced rider we had seen two months ago was walking toward me right from the mine. Only a moment before, I had passed right by the spot. Where had he come from?

"Howdy, Miss," he said in a gratingly false tone. His face was all sweaty and his hands were dirty, as if he'd been working. "Out for another little stroll, are ya?"

"No . . . I was just going for water." He should have been doing the explaining, but I was too scared to ask any questions

"All alone?" he said, an evil gleam in his eye.

"My Uncle Nick's back at the cabin," I stammered, looking toward the ground, "and he asked me to—"

"Now, Miss, you oughta know better'n to tell lies. Fact is, your Uncle Nick's way off in Miracle Springs, and ye're all alone here with them little kids. I watched from up on the hill, an' I seen him go."

"Well, if you wanted to see my uncle," I said, "why did you wait till he was gone?"

He laughed, but it wasn't a pleasant sound at all. Apparently the laugh was the only answer I was going to get to my question. Then he returned to the subject of my errand.

"You ought t' wait for yer menfolk t' get back home. A pretty little miss like yourself shouldn't be fetchin' such a heavy load."

"I can manage," I said.

"Well, I'll help ya. Lemme take that there bucket and I'll go fill it for ya." He stepped toward me.

I shrank back. "I can do it myself."

"Shy, are you, Missy?" His coarse, ugly face broke into a leering grin. "Ole Buck's jest tryin' to be friendly."

He moved quickly toward me and laid his rough hand on my shoulder.

I squirmed out of his grip and tried to run, but before I could get away his other hand shot up and grabbed me. My heart was pounding wildly now. I was really scared.

"You're a supple little thing—an' ole Buck likes 'em young an' willowy. C'mon, I can show you a real good time."

"P-please," I said, "let me go . . . I have to get back." He had me pinned against the rock at the edge of the mine now and I could hardly move. But I was afraid to struggle because he would only grip me tighter with those awful hands.

"Well, I sure can't have you runnin' back an' tellin' your uncle I was here, now can I?"

"He wouldn't care," I answered quickly.

"Ha, ha," he laughed. "There you go lyin' to ole Buck again! You know better'n that, now don't ya? I think maybe I better jist take you along with me!"

"No, please!" I yelled. "The children—they'll miss me and know something's wrong!"

"Maybe I should take the whole brood o' ya," he answered, then laughed again. "That way, I'd be sure no one'd tell!"

"Please—I won't say anything, if that's what you want."

"That's what I want, Missy, but I want more, too." He thrust his face so near to mine that his whiskers scratched me. He tried to kiss me, but I twisted my face away and his awful mouth only brushed my cheek.

I felt sick and faint.

His breath was repulsive. Somehow I managed to keep my legs from giving out beneath me. Yet even if I didn't pass out, I could not fight off this burly, strong man much longer.

He pressed closer and shoved the back of my head against the rock.

"Let me alone—please!" I begged, tears now streaming down my cheeks. "I won't tell no one."

"Don't be scared o' Buck, Missy."

"Help—!" I tried to scream, but his hand quickly shot up and clamped over my mouth.

"Now, Missy, that won't do a' tall—"

But the man's voice cut off sharply when the sound of footsteps could be heard nearby, followed by the light rustling of leaves and pebbles sliding down the embankment above us.

"What in tarnation?" he muttered, but then stopped speaking, realizing his danger. Slowly he loosened his hold on my shoulder, but kept one hand firmly over my mouth to keep me from calling out, while he listened intently.

All was quiet for a moment, then came the clicking sound of a rifle or pistol cocking.

"How in blazes could they have gotten back—" he began, then stopped short.

Again he thrust his face into mine, but all hint of vulgar playfulness was gone, and in its place was pure evil.

"You listen to me, Missy," he whispered in a sinister threat. "One sound outta you, and I'll kill your uncle and that fool partner o' his. I ain't so sure Drum ain't more kin to you all than your uncle. Then I'll come back an' kill you an' the kids too. You hear what Buck's sayin'?"

I nodded in terror.

His hand came off my mouth and went straight to the gun at his side. He let go of me completely, then turned, and with gun drawn and eyes scanning the woods about us, began stealthily moving off in the direction of the noise.

There was another sound, this time from further off. It was like a rock hitting a tree, but I couldn't be sure.

Buck twitched at the sound, uncertain fear replacing the grisly confidence on his face, then he moved off toward it, gun drawn in readiness.

I watched immobile, too petrified to move.

All at once, I felt another hand clamp over my mouth from behind. As I was watching Buck, from around the opposite side of the cave mouth, someone had silently crept up to my side.

My heart beating frantically, I jerked my head around.

It was Little Wolf!

As he stood there in his fawn-colored buckskin, one finger was pressed against his lips indicating silence. Slowly he removed his hand.

"Run back to the cabin," he whispered.

"But—but—who is out there?" I whispered back, nodding in Buck's direction with my head.

"No one," he answered. "The wicked man chases sounds, that is all."

"But the gun? We heard—"

"A trick sound my father taught me with the tongue," Little Wolf whispered with a smile.

"But the sounds came from over there—" I pointed, still puzzled.

"No more questions. The Indian has had to learn many things the white man still does not understand to live from the land. But to make noises and then sneak away is not such a feat. It is something we must do every day when tracking the deer or the bear. Now—you must go!"

"But what about you?"

A smile broke across Little Wolf's face.

"The bad man is not such a clever foe. I will keep him chasing his tail until your uncle returns. I have watched him before and I know his ways. No harm will come to you."

I looked into his eyes, trying to speak a word of thanks.

But before I could say a word, Little Wolf had moved to the other side of the mine opening to glance around the embankment at Buck's retreating figure.

I turned and ran back down the hill to the cabin.

Before going inside, I stopped and looked back. I was frightened for Little Wolf despite what he had said. He was now circling back the way he had come, up the embankment on the opposite side of the mine from where Buck was looking for him. I saw him work his way from tree to tree until he was almost within Buck's line of vision again. Then he stopped, withdrew an arrow from his quiver, laid it into his bow, and sent it toward Buck.

Thwack! The arrow sunk deep into the trunk of a medium-sized pine tree about five yards from the prowling white man.

He turned suddenly. I couldn't see his face, but I can just imagine how fearful he was.

Little Wolf stood still, in broad view, waiting for Buck to see him. I couldn't understand why he didn't hide!

"Why, you dirty savage!" roared Buck the moment he eyes focused on his adversary. In the next instant, the air was filled with gunfire as Buck let off a barrage in Little Wolf's direction. But by now the Indian was invisible once more, and the next moment I heard Buck cursing loudly, and lumbering deeper into the woods after his elusive enemy.

I saw neither of them again, though I heard several more rounds of gunfire, always followed by frustrated swearing and angry threats. But each time I heard Buck's voice, it was farther and farther away.

I had been so frightened for Little Wolf, that I didn't realize until then that he was purposely drawing Buck after him, farther and farther from the mine and the cabin.

Finally, I stepped inside and locked the door.

The bucket I'd taken to the mine was still there, but I wasn't about to go after it. I could wait for my water.

CHAPTER 34

LATER THAT SAME NIGHT

There were no more sounds from the woods for several hours.

In fact, the next sound I did hear was our wagon coming up the road. Pa was alone with the load of lumber. Uncle Nick had stayed in town for a while. As soon as Pa was in the door, I told him what had happened.

I'd never seen him look the way he did when I finished my story. I don't know if it was only because of the threats to me, or if it was anger roused because someone had trespassed on his claim. But his eyes were flashing, and without a word or a moment's hesitation, he grabbed his rifle from the corner and headed for the door, with a stern admonition to keep it locked.

I have no idea what he actually did or where he went. I'll probably never know, because he didn't talk about it when he returned at dusk. Uncle Nick had gotten back shortly after Pa left, and we'd all had supper.

The awful face of the man who called himself Buck was hard to erase from my mind, but almost worse was the look on Pa's face when he'd stalked out of the cabin in the early afternoon. There was such a look of vengeful violence in his eyes! It had me worried the whole time he was out.

After he finished his supper, he went outside again to tend his horse. I felt I had to talk to him, so I followed him

236

out. I found him leaning against the fence staring straight ahead. I was almost afraid to approach him, but he heard me and looked up before the second thoughts I was having allowed me to retreat.

"Kinda cold to be out, ain't it, girl?" he said. His forehead was creased, the muscles in his neck taut.

"I was . . . nervous, Pa," I began.

"Don't worry. That slimy snake ain't gonna git near you again!" His voice was full of hatred.

"I was nervous about *you*, Pa," I said. "You seem—so—"

"I'll be all right," he muttered.

"You didn't find him, did you? I mean, the man's not—"

"Nah," he answered, sounding regretful that Buck was still out there. "I couldn't find him nowhere. But when I do, I'll kill him."

"But that won't help anything, Pa," I said. "It'll only get you into trouble."

It was probably impudent of me to say such a thing, but I could remember Ma saying the exact words to Zack when he wanted to get back at a bully in school. And her admonition had kept Zack from a needless fight, because it made him stop and realize that it would do more harm than good. Though they didn't seem to have the same effect on Pa coming from my mouth as they did when Ma said the words to Zack.

"The trouble I'm in," he mused, almost talking to himself, "I got in long ago. I thought I'd managed to run away from it, turning my back on my family in the process. But now it looks like the trouble's found me out in the end."

I didn't know what to say.

"But don't you worry none, Corrie," he said. "I won't do nothin' foolhardy. Just remember, this is the *West*, and what a man does for himself around here is sometimes the only justice to be had."

"Then maybe *I* should be the one to go after Buck," I

said. It was a stupid thing to say, and I don't know why I blurted it out.

"Don't talk foolishness, girl."

"But it was me he attacked, not you."

"Doing justice is a man's job. And since I'm your pa, it's my responsibility."

"I'd rather you just let it go."

"Well, you don't know the whole story," he added, without offering to tell it.

"Tell me about it, Pa," I pleaded.

"I can't now. Maybe the time will come . . . I don't know."

"I don't want anything to happen to you, Pa."

"Don't worry. Nothin's going to happen to me."

But just hearing him say the words made me more and more worried.

"Now get yourself inside. It's gettin' late. Time for the little ones to be in bed."

I went back inside, a little reassured, but anxious about Pa.

Later that night, I lay awake in bed unable to sleep. The events of the day still churned in my mind. I hadn't said much at all to Uncle Nick about the incident. But as I lay there, I could hear his and Pa's voices in the other room. I couldn't make out what they were saying, but at the mention of Buck's name, my ears perked up, and I sat up straining to listen.

" . . . I still can't believe it could be Buck Krebbs," Uncle Nick was saying.

"Believe it," replied Pa. "You heard what the kids said before—the scar on his face, now this thing with Corrie."

"But if it *was* Buck, and he was prowling around our place, why would he tell her his name? He'd have to know she'd tell us, and then we'd be onto him."

"None of that Gulch bunch was overloaded with brains,

Nick," said Pa. "And Buck was the biggest dimwit of them all."

"You think he's looking for the loot?"

"What else?"

"So, did you get any lead on him?"

"Nah. Everybody's tight-lipped."

"Some of the boys say Royce has brought in some out-of-town low-lifes."

"What for?"

"No one knows."

"I never did trust that shyster," muttered Pa.

"You think the others are here too?"

"Aw, who can tell?"

Just the sound of Pa's boot kicking at the fire told me that he was standing in front of the hearth, no doubt with his hand resting on a hook in the large wooden beam just over his head. That's where he always stood when he was thinking, staring down into the fire's red-hot embers.

"Even if he did follow Aggie and the kids, I can't imagine Buck making it all the way out here alone."

"Yeah, but don't you think that if ol' Buck saw a chance to grab the money on his own and high-tail it to Mexico or someplace, he'd as soon doublecross the others as put a slug in either of us?"

"Yeah, you got a point there," said Pa.

The two were silent again, and before I heard another word, I was sound asleep.

CHAPTER 35

OVERHEAD CONVERSATION

Late in January, we finally got some snow. It was nothing like what we had in New York, but on the distant hills it was heavy, with scattered patches in the valley. Actually, it made a lovely picture—the pure white mounds broken by the rich red earth, evergreens standing tall and fresh all around our claim, the stream winding its way down the hill, and a slate of blue sky overhead.

The weather wasn't bothering the mining too much. The shaft was pretty big now and they were concentrating their blasting in a drift which would be an offshoot from the main tunnel. They were working hard, but hadn't hit any paydirt yet.

Quartz mining with only two or three men wasn't done too often. Hauling up the big chunks of rock was back-breaking for one man, and usually only the bigger operations could afford carts to go in and out of the mine, and a stamp mill to smash and crush the rock to get the gold out. But Pa and Uncle Nick were determined. They tried all sorts of things to separate the ore more efficiently, but so far they hadn't found much.

Then yesterday the three of them spent a lot of time talking about trying to put together what they called a chili mill. Mr. Jones said he knew some Mexicans who could help them get one going and who knew all about the operation.

240

So this morning Pa and Uncle Nick headed into Miracle Springs again, this time for more lumber, rope, and cable. Pa was saying something about the millstones, but I couldn't tell if he was going to get them or if Mr. Jones was going to go down to Grass Valley for them.

Pa looked worn and haggard when they left. I remember thinking that I hoped something would happen soon, for his sake. After all they'd been through, and with the added burden of us kids, I was afraid if they didn't find some gold before long, he might quit, or take to gambling again.

After the sounds of the wagon died away, and the breakfast dishes had been cleaned up, I decided to go for a walk. I told Zack to keep a close eye on the kids.

"Aw, Corrie, you know I don't like to stay in the cabin playin' ma."

"I won't be gone that long," I insisted. "You don't have to stay *in* the cabin. Just keep an eye out for them, that's all."

"But I was gonna go up and work at the mine."

"Did Pa give you permission?"

"Well, not exactly."

"I didn't think so. You stay away from that mine," I said firmly. "And you keep Tad in sight. He's been dying to get up there, and you know what Pa said. Keep him close by the cabin."

Zack just shrugged his shoulders, then asked, "What if that man comes back?"

"He won't," I answered. "We haven't seen any strangers for a month, and Pa says that fellow's long gone by now. But if you hear somebody you don't know, just bolt yourselves inside. I won't be that long."

As I left the cabin, I thought that if I found a good drift of snow I would go back and get the kids so they could play in it. But I didn't want to say anything, otherwise I'd never get my walk alone. As I walked, I couldn't get Zack's words out of my mind. Maybe Pa had only said what he had about Buck to keep us from worrying. I knew that man had to be still on his mind, because this was the first time all month he had left us alone, even for a minute.

The day was so lovely that it was easy to push my nagging doubts aside. I was determined to enjoy myself. The air was clean and crisp, and I didn't mind that the cold penetrated even my warmest New York coat. The snow was starting to melt in places, but there was still plenty everywhere. I walked north at first, then east toward some snow-covered hills. I warmed up quickly under the hazy winter sun.

After about half a mile, I reached a steep ridge. It probably wasn't the smartest thing to climb it with all the snow, but I'd been there before, and I knew that from the top was a spectacular view of the lowlands.

Slipping and sliding, I finally made it to the crest, and the sight today was even more beautiful than usual. I felt like a fairy princess surveying the realm of her winter wonderland. Ma was always so practical. She would probably scold me good-naturedly for my fanciful notions, and tell me not to let my imagination run loose. But I figured that as long as I could be practical when I had to be, it was okay to daydream sometimes. I expect even Ma would have allowed me that much.

I could have stayed there for hours taking in the view, but my practical side started to awaken and tell me I should be getting back. Just before beginning my descent I noticed something I hadn't seen before.

Way down below I could see the road into town. I'd never realized it came so close to this ridge, winding in a great half-circle around the hill. I think the whiteness of the snow made the dark dirt road more visible.

This would surely be a short-cut, I thought, to the claim. Or—and I shivered with the thought—a way to sneak up around to the back of the mine like that dreadful man must have done, without anyone detecting him on the road that passed our cabin.

Even as I stood staring at the road, in the distance a

horse-drawn wagon came into faint view. At first I thought it must be Pa on his way home.

I scrambled down from my perch to descend the hill on that side, thinking to meet Pa on the road, forgetting for a minute that he could not possibly be returning so soon.

By the time I'd made three-fourths of the descent, I could see that the wagon was too small and too fancy to be Pa's. But I hardly had time to think further, for all at once a rider on horseback came into view. I hadn't seen his approach. There was an exchange between him and the buggy driver, who then snapped his reins and drove off the road under the cover of some trees. They were heading right toward me.

My heart nearly stopped! The man on horseback followed, and it was none other than Buck Krebbs! All I could think of was getting away as fast as I could. But they surely would have seen me! So I crouched down in the brush, praying they wouldn't see me and would go on by. But they stopped where they were, and I was stuck.

I held my breath, not moving a muscle. Even with my heart pounding in my ears, I found myself straining to hear what they were saying. In the still, crisp air, I recognized the buggy driver's voice, but couldn't place it. His back was turned to me.

"Well, Krebbs," he said, "I hope you don't botch the job this time."

"Now look here!" he snapped back, "I couldn't help it if that blame fool girl showed up afore I could git it done."

"If a little girl's going to keep you from—"

"She wouldn've kept me from nuthin'! I coulda handled her just fine! But then that crazed Injun attacked me!"

"There are men I could hire who wouldn't be afraid of a lone Indian—a mere boy, I understand."

"It was his arrows that coulda killed me as dead as the next guy! You ever seen one a them sharpshooters?"

"No—no, can't say that I have, Krebbs, but—"

"You couldn't hire a local who'd keep as quiet about

your dirty work better'n ole Buck, an' you know it! 'Sides, I took care o' Larsen's place, didn't I?"

"Well, I just hope you can do as well with Matthews'."

My mind was reeling as I listened, trying to remember where I'd heard the name Larsen before, but the instant I recalled, the man's next words made everything become clearer.

". . . I want their place burned to the ground come sunup tomorrow. You got that, Krebbs?"

"Got it."

"Luckily, my scheme may not hinge entirely on your part."

"Whaddya mean by that? I risked my neck to come back here in broad daylight!"

"I'm paying you well enough."

"No more'n the job's worth. Don't forget, I rode with Matthews back in '43. 'Course that weren't his name then! I seen him in action. That's why when his six-gun comes out, I intend t' be behind him, not in front o' him!"

"I don't care about your personal vendetta against the man, Mr. Krebbs, just so long as you do what I'm paying you for. Whatever else you hope to get out of it, that's your own business."

"I got my reasons," muttered Buck, "I'll get the job done."

"In any case, you won't have Matthews to worry about for long, or that partner of his either for that matter." The icy voice made me shiver, but I just couldn't place it. Suddenly I was colder than ever, and it wasn't from the snow.

"Now, just you wait a minute! If you're plannin' to kill 'em, you just hold onto your hat. They ain't no good to me dead!"

"Relax. I'll let you have the honor. All I want is them outta the way. After that, they're all yours. And when I show Matthews what I got, with his cabin nothin' but ashes and his mine caved in, he'll clear out faster'n them kids can hang onto his coattails. Even that stone-faced partner of his, Drum, won't be able to talk his way out of this one!"

"Whatcha got?"

"None of your business!" came the curt reply. There was a brief pause, then apparently thinking Buck deserved to know at least a portion of his plot, he went on, "Let's just call it a little insurance policy I discovered very recently." And shaking his head, "To think that I've had it all along."

As he spoke, he pulled out a piece of paper and waved it in the air.

"What's a little piece o' paper gonna do to men like Matthews and Drum?"

"Even a man like Nick Matthews has to abide by the law, Mr. Krebbs. And this little piece of paper, as you call it, gives me immediate legal right to his entire property unless he can come up with $150 in cash."

"So why do ya want me to burn him out?"

"Call it double insurance. Matthews is so hot-headed, he would probably try to shoot his way out of this. But if I know that Drum fellow, he'll no doubt think there is some way around this IOU, and I would rather not have to fight him in some Sacramento court. There's something about that man I just don't like. He's too cool for me. I think he's hiding something."

"He's hidin' plenty! I can tell you that! Ya know them kids—"

"I don't care about the kids, Krebbs!" the driver interrupted. "I don't care what name they used to go by. I don't care what your devious scheme may be regarding them. All I want to make sure of is that your little act of sabotage convinces both of them of the folly of trying to resist."

"Just so long as you know I ain't settin' a torch to the place 'til I've gone over every inch o' it."

"Just do the job, Krebbs."

"And I'm warnin' you now, don't git no crazy thoughts o' tryin' to git out o' payin' me for *your* dirty work!"

"You'll get your money. I paid you for the other jobs."

Then like a flash, Buck drew his gun and waved it in the driver's face.

"You'll bring the money to that deserted shack on the ol' Smith claim in one hour," he said in a threatening tone, "or you'll be spending the rest of a very short life lookin' over your shoulder. And you can ask the fellow who *calls* himself Drum how long I stay on a man's trail who double-crosses me! Why, he ain't no more a Drum than Nick is a Matthews! You understand me? You cross me and I'll track you down no matter where you go or how many times you change your name!"

"This is what comes of doing business with low-lifes," the driver said with disgust in his voice.

"One hour! Or I'll be after you!"

With that, Mr. Krebbs swung into his saddle and was gone. The other man remained a moment longer, still shaking his head. Then he walked back to his buggy, got in, and went back the way he had come.

I let out a huge sigh of relief, and waited till both men were well out of sight. My first thought was to warn Uncle Nick and Pa. If I followed the men into town from here, I might be able to get there in less than the hour it would take them to do whatever they were going to do at the Smith place.

But what if the man confronted Uncle Nick *before* going to pay Krebbs his money? What if he forced Uncle Nick to surrender the claim like he said he could?

I just had to get to either Pa or Uncle Nick before he did. I started toward the road, while I thought through a plan.

Then all of a sudden, I stopped short in my tracks. Another idea suddenly occurred to me. I spun around and hurried back the way I'd come down the hill. I *had* to go to the cabin first, even if it delayed everything!

Ten minutes later, I burst through the door, breathless and sweaty. I headed for the bedroom without a word.

"Where you been so long, Corrie," Zack moaned, "You

said you'd only be gone a short time!"

"Zack," I said when I came back to the front room, "I'm sorry, but I can't even stay. I've got to go to town!"

"Why?" he asked.

"There's no time to explain. Now listen, if you see or hear anyone hanging around outside, take one of Pa's guns and get you and the kids out into the woods, but not too far from the cabin, so you can keep a watch on it."

"I thought you said to keep them inside."

"Never mind that. I've just overheard two men talking about burning down the cabin!"

Zack's face was clouded with fear. The younger ones were too bewildered make a peep.

"Corrie, please don't leave us here—alone," he begged.

"I have to, Zack! There's no choice. I don't think they plan to do it 'til tonight, and by then Pa'll be back. But I had to tell you, just in case, so you watch careful, and keep that gun at the ready."

I paused to looked deep into his eyes. I still saw the fear. But he knew I was trusting him with a man's job, and in spite of being afraid, I think he was proud. In that instant, with the lives of our younger brothers and sisters depending on us, I think both Zack and I took several big steps toward growing up.

I hugged him impulsively. "I love you, Zack. You pray for me, and I'll pray for you. The Lord will be with us."

Then I turned and ran out the door before I lost my courage.

"Corrie. . . !" Zack called out after me.

I stopped and looked back.

He was standing in the doorway. I could see tears in his eyes, but he stood tall like a man with a job to do.

"I love you, too," he said, dabbing at the tears with his sleeve.

I smiled and took off with all my strength down the road toward town.

CHAPTER 36

A REVELATION OF FAMILY TIES

I left the cabin at a dead run, but that pace sure didn't last for long. The snow that had been so beautiful before was now a curse, what with the mud and slush slowing my pace at every turn. I slipped and stumbled, mud sloshing up over my boots and stockings and caking all over the bottom of my dress.

I wondered if I'd ever make it. My breath came in frosty gasps, and my lungs hurt dreadfully. Still I kept running, keeping my fingers clutched tightly on the small parcel I had gotten from the cabin.

It must have been the longest I'd ever run in my life. By the time I reached the outskirts of town, I had slowed to barely better than a walk, hobbling and limping on my numb feet. All I could think of was whether I'd be on time!

Then I heard the sound of a wagon coming toward me! I couldn't believe my ears or my eyes. It was Mrs. Parrish!

"Corrie—what is it?" she called anxiously, stopping the wagon.

I ran to her as she climbed down to the road, and nearly collapsed in her outstretched arms. It was at least a full minute before I could speak.

"I've got to find Pa!" I finally gasped, "Before it's too late . . . what'll we do if he loses the claim. . . ?"

She could make nothing of my ramblings.

"Climb up here in the wagon, Corrie," she said. "You need to rest a minute, then you can explain everything to me."

"There's no time!" I panted, climbing up after her. My legs and feet ached. "We've got to find Pa or Uncle Nick!"

Without waiting for further explanation, Mrs. Parrish wheeled her horses around, snapped the reins, and sent them charging back the way she had come. My heart gradually slowed its pounding, my chest stopped aching, and I managed to tell her the story briefly. Whether she caught everything I yelled above the din of the charging horses and the clatter of the wagon, I don't know. But she certainly realized the urgency of my mission once it dawned on her that I'd run all the way into town from the cabin in the snow and mud.

About halfway through town we spotted Pa's bay mare tied up outside a place called Lil's Saloon. My heart sank in despair when I saw the buggy drawn up next to it—the one that had brought the man out to talk to Buck Krebbs.

Mrs. Parrish helped me out of the wagon. My feet were still numb and unsteady, but the moment I hit the ground I took off running again straight toward the saloon's swinging doors.

I ran right inside, Mrs. Parrish behind me. We stopped short in the dim light to take in the scene. All the men were so intent on their conversation they didn't even notice us at first. We heard what was apparently the end of a very heated argument.

The place wasn't very crowded this time of day. A knot of men stood around a table against the far wall. My uncle was seated, his arms folded across his chest, his face hard and drawn. My first thought was to recall what had happened with Uncle Nick and the man called Judd over a poker game. I hoped he had been able to control his temper this time!

Pa was seated with Nick; a bottle of whiskey and two half-empty glasses sat between them on the table. Alkali Jones stood behind them, and three or four men I didn't know were gathered nearby, along with the sheriff. And directly in front of Uncle Nick was the driver of the buggy outside. Suddenly I remembered his voice—it was Mr. Royce, the banker!

"I hate to see it come to this, Matthews—or—whatever your name really is," Mr. Royce was saying.

"Do you?" my uncle replied, his lips so tight they hardly seemed to move.

"I'm a businessman, and this note is due and payable on demand." Mr. Royce turned to the sheriff. "It's all perfectly legal, isn't it, Simon?"

Mr. Rafferty was obviously reluctant to take the banker's side. "I've examined it, Nick," he said, "and it's legitimate. Potter borrowed money and put up the claim for collateral."

"Unfortunately," Royce went on with affected sympathy, "when you won his claim, the outstanding obligation fell to you. And I'm afraid unless you can come up with the $150 on demand, as the note specifies, the claim reverts to the bank."

"I ain't givin' up the claim for no piece of paper that I ain't had nothing to do with!" snapped Uncle Nick.

"The law—" Mr. Royce began to emphasize again.

With that, my frozen feet sprang to action and I stepped forward.

"Pa—Uncle Nick!" I cried. "They're gonna burn up the cabin!"

The group of men parted spontaneously as I ran up to the table. In the confusion, no one seemed to notice that I'd forgotten to call him Mr. Drum.

"Corrie . . . what in blazes!" Pa exclaimed, looking up. "What in tarnation are you doing here?"

"I came to warn you!"

"But how'd you get here?"

"I ran—all the way. You've got to stop them, Pa! The kids are up there alone, and these men are gonna do what they did to Larsen's place!"

"Who, Corrie?" asked my uncle from across the table. I turned to him, but before I could answer, Pa noticed Mrs. Parrish standing behind me, and leveled his gaze upon her.

"Your—I should say, Mr. Matthew's niece has gone to considerable trouble to speak with you, Mr. . . . Mr.—Drum!"

"We can take care of our own business, if you don't mind, Ma'am," said Pa, annoyed at her comment.

"I have no intention of interfering. I just happened to meet Corrie as she came into town a few minutes ago. I think you ought to hear her out."

Pa sighed and pursed his lips together. It was hard to tell if he was mad or worried. But now he turned to me again. Without comment, his eyes told me to speak and get it over with.

"It's him!" I cried, pointing toward Mr. Royce. "I saw him and Buck Krebbs talking—"

"So Krebbs *is* in town!" exploded Uncle Nick, half rising out of his chair.

"I don't know where he is now," I answered. "But I came upon the two of them no more than a mile from our cabin. I was out for a walk, and overheard them talking just off the road—"

"Really, this is—" Mr. Royce started to speak. But Pa shot him a look that stopped his words cold.

"You shut up, Royce!" he ordered. "Go on, Corrie what did you hear?"

"They were talking about a job Mr. Krebbs was supposed to have taken care of the day he attacked me up by the mine. Mr. Krebbs wanted his money, but Mr. Royce insisted he do a successful job first. They talked about Mr. Larsen, but I didn't catch enough of it to make sense of it, until they started talking about burning the place to the ground. And that's when I knew I had to warn you! I don't know where Mr. Krebbs is, but the kids are still at home by themselves, and these men said they were going to do it tonight!"

"Come now," said the banker, "you certainly are not going to believe the fanciful rantings of a half-exhausted child!"

Pa jumped out of his chair, sending it to the floor behind him with a crash. He looked a foot taller than Mr. Royce at that moment, and I could almost see smoke coming from his nostrils.

"Are you calling my daughter a liar?" he thundered. If I had been Mr. Royce, I would have been shaking from head to foot.

At the word "daughter" a general murmuring began to filter through the saloon.

A peculiar smile spread slowly over Royce's lips, as if the revelation of this secret gave him further fuel to use against Pa.

"Your *daughter*, you say? I thought this brood belonged to Matthews—ah, but then that's not his real name, is it?" The part about Uncle Nick's name he muttered almost to himself.

"You heard right!" interrupted Uncle Nick, now rising himself and coming to Pa's rescue. "They *are my* kin—my sister's kids!"

"It's all right, Nick," said Pa softly, "there ain't no sense keeping it quiet any longer. Yeah, that's right, Royce," he said, again to the banker. "This here's my daughter, and she ain't been brought up to tell no lies!"

Still wearing that smug smile, the banker said, "I was merely attempting to point out that sometimes children have vivid imaginations."

My natural shyness was gone and I felt indignant at being called both a liar and a child. I was so proud of Pa for standing up for me that I figured I could stand up as well.

"I did not imagine a word of what I heard you saying!" I said, in the strongest voice I could muster.

"Well," said Royce in a slightly altered tone, a thin line of sweat forming on his forehead. "It may well be that she saw Krebbs and me together. The thieving man accosted me on the trail and we did have words. In fact, he tried to rob me. But I assured him I was carrying no cash, and that I would have him arrested if he so much as touched me. He frightened off pretty easily. But if you want to go after him, I say take the law with you and grab him. Men like him are a threat to our community."

"Me gunnin' down Krebbs would be mighty convenient to you, wouldn't it Royce?" said Uncle Nick in a low growl. "That would eliminate the only verification to Corrie's story."

"It's neither here nor there to me." Mr. Royce sounded smug, despite his moist forehead. "Regarding the girl's allegations, whether Krebbs is dead or alive seems to me to hardly change the fact that you have no more proof than my word against hers. And the word of an upstanding town father against that of a flighty child of—shall we say, of dubious parentage—"

Before he could finish, Pa's fist crashed down on the table. He took two strides toward the banker and it looked like he was about to knock him onto the floor.

Uncle Nick and Mr. Jones jumped out from behind the table to restrain him. "The vermin ain't worth it, Drum," said Uncle Nick, suddenly playing the unaccustomed role of peacemaker.

Restrained but hardly pacified, Pa stood glaring at the banker.

"—whose father's real name we apparently don't even know," went on the courageous Mr. Royce. "My word against hers hardly seems a fair contest. What possible evidence could the child bring? And after all I've done for this town, who would believe it?"

"We'll see, Royce," growled Pa between clenched teeth.

"And all this is beside the point, anyway. The problem of the IOU still must be addressed," said Mr. Royce, attempting to again assume the tone of businessman, ignoring Pa for the moment and turning his focus again toward Uncle Nick. "Even if I were everything this foolish girl says, your claim still legally belongs to the bank. Now, I'm going to tell you one final time, *Matthews*—" He spat out the word with contempt. "I am calling your note due. You must make good on that $150 debt, or I will take possession of the mine. There is no court in this country that would tell you differently."

"Well, I ain't got no $150. And I ain't giving you our claim. You can do your best to come and try to take it from us!"

"The sheriff has the authority to arrest you if you persist in your refusal and cause any trouble over this."

Now Alkali Jones' squeaky voice broke into the conversation for the first time. "Hee, hee! I'd like to see him try! Hee, hee!"

"I want to avoid any violence," said Mr. Royce, his smugness slipping once more, "but the law is the law."

"There's another kind of law in these parts, Royce," said my uncle, "and it stands for a dang sight more'n your babble."

"Come now, Matthews," said Mr. Royce with a smile, "you and the so-called Mr. Drum here—you're family men now. Surely even you, despite your reputation, would not resort to gunplay—"

All at once I woke up and came to my senses. Why was I listening to all this? I held the solution to everything right in my hand!

"Pa—Uncle Nick!" I blurted out. "It's right here! I went back to the cabin for it, and I plumb forgot! I heard Mr. Royce telling Mr. Krebbs about the IOU, too. So I ran back for it."

I slapped the velvet pouch I had been carrying down on the table. "There's your money, Mr. Royce!" I cried. "It's my Ma's inheritance. You can take your $150 from it!"

I flashed a look of triumph at Mrs. Parrish, then smiled at Pa.

He and Uncle Nick just stood staring at the pouch, but made no move for it. Neither did Mr. Royce.

"It's yours, Pa," I said, "just like I told you before."

"What about it, Matthews?" asked Sheriff Rafferty.

Uncle Nick glanced at Pa dumfounded. He had known nothing about the money. All eyes were on Pa, waiting for him to speak. But the real expression to watch was that of Mr. Royce. He couldn't hide his chagrin, and it seemed he didn't know what to do next.

Pa remained quiet, stroking his beard, gazing without expression at the pouch. Finally, he looked up at me, and it seemed a mask fell off his face. It was as if he were letting go of a personality that wasn't really his, part of him he'd been trying to hang onto in order to keep back the secrets of his past. Suddenly, he was no longer a stranger who happened to share my family name . . . but my *father*—the man who had loved his wife and children, and who had suffered terrible guilt over being forced to flee and leave us behind.

"Why're you doing this, Corrie?" he said softly, and it was like we were the only two people in that saloon. Everyone else was silent. "Why—after all I done, after my leaving your ma, after the way I treated you. . . ?"

"All that's past, Pa," I answered. "Anyway, we're kin, and I guess that's reason enough. Please take it. That's what Ma would want, if she knew how things were now. I know it, Pa—I know she would! And—it's what *I* want, too."

He took the pouch slowly in his hand, and dumped out the wad of bills. Methodically, he counted out one hundred and fifty dollars, put the rest back into the pouch, and handed it back to me. Then he gave Uncle Nick the money.

"Here's your payment, Royce," said Uncle Nick. As the

banker took it, he looked as crestfallen as ever I've seen a man. "Take it, Royce, and give me that IOU!"

Royce reluctantly handed him the piece of paper.

Now it was Pa's turn to speak again. He looked him coolly in the eye. "Now I'm telling you, Royce, if you or any of your hired hooligans ever comes near my family again, you'll live to regret it! Now . . . get outta here!"

Clutching the money in his fist, the banker spun around red-faced and slipped out a back way. A belated cheer rose from the men in the saloon, above which could be heard the high-pitched cackle of Alkali Jones. As the cheer subsided, there was a barrage of questions thrown in Pa's direction about his newly-revealed family ties.

But before he could answer, even as the doors were still swinging from Royce's exit, they crashed open once more. My brother Zack came racing into the room!

CHAPTER 37

THE CAVE

Zack stormed in, all out of breath and muddy, just like I was.

"Pa . . . Corrie!" he cried. "It caved in! He only got away from me for just a minute, but—"

"Slow down, boy," said Pa, trying to stay calm and laying a steadying hand on Zack's shoulder.

"Oh, Pa, I'm real sorry. I didn't mean to let him go near it—"

"Who—go near what? Tell me what happened!"

"I couldn't get him out—Tad's trapped inside the cave!"

"The mine?" Pa cried, his worst fears suddenly realized.

"He slipped away; I didn't know where he went at first, but I shoulda guessed. You know how he's always wanted to go down there and work with us. Well, first I heard him call to me. I went runnin' after him, but then I heard a rumblin' sound . . . and fallin' rocks . . . and dirt and dust was billowin' out of the mouth of the cave . . . and Tad's coat was laying in front of the opening! After that I shouted and shouted, but Tad never answered back!"

"What then?" asked Uncle Nick.

"As soon as the rocks stopped falling, I ran inside and tried to dig my way through the pile—there was a huge pile of rocks and dirt . . . it looked like a whole section of the roof just gave way—and one of the big timbers was lying there half covered by the rocks, like it'd just broken in two from the weight . . ."

"I wonder if it had a little help," mused Uncle Nick.

Pa flashed a look at him. I knew they were both thinking of Buck Krebbs.

"I was calling out *Tad, Tad*, but I couldn't hear anything, and I knew I'd never dig through it myself . . . so I locked the girls in the cabin and ran off down the road. About a mile out, this man came along and gave me a ride into town on his horse."

For the first time, we all noticed that a man had followed Zack into the saloon. I didn't know him, but Pa seemed to.

Even as Pa said, "I'm much obliged to you, Shaw," the saloon became a flurry of activity. Pa and Mr. Jones and Uncle Nick talked hurriedly together, then broke up and headed for the door. Several other men were grabbing their coats and running outside.

Pa was the first one out the door, and I heard his horse galloping away before the rest of us reached the sidewalk. Other riders weren't far behind him.

Uncle Nick called out to whoever would listen, "Anybody have a cable to move them rocks? We'll need some extra picks and shovels too."

I heard someone reply, "I'll bring rope!" By that time, Mr. Jones had the wagon and team ready, and without even waiting for him to stop, Uncle Nick jumped aboard, took the reins from Mr. Jones, and sent the horses flying down the street, his hat tipped back on his head, and his light hair flying in the wind.

Before I could feel left behind, Zack and I were in Mrs. Parrish's wagon, and she was whipping her two horses into a full gallop. We were bounced along as she shouted to the horses for greater speed. "Hee-yeaah! Hee-yeaah!" she cried, half standing, flipping the reins with her wrists. But I think the horses were already running as fast as they could. Several more men on horseback passed us on the way, but it was certainly the fastest trip I'd ever made between town and the cabin!

The moment we got there, Zack and I ran up to the mine, while Mrs. Parrish went straight to the cabin to make sure Becky and Emily were all right.

The mine shaft was jammed with men—scrambling, shouting, all trying to help at once. Pa and Uncle Nick were right in the middle of them all, frantically heaving away rocks bigger than a man's head as if they were pebbles. Sweat was pouring down Pa's face and his eyes were intense with anxiety. But it was more than fear for a child's life that I saw written there. *Any* child in danger would stir the heart of a decent man to do heroic things. But the look on Pa's face at that moment was the fear of a man for the life of his *own* son!

Some of the rocks were huge, bigger than Tad himself, and took two men exerting themselves to the full, to push them out of the hole. The cave-in left piles of debris and white rock unlike any that I had ever noticed before.

Ten minutes passed in no time . . . then twenty . . . then half an hour. The men were beginning to tire from working so hard and so fast, but they still didn't seem to be getting through. No one said much. The only sounds were the groans and puffing of the men, the crashing of rocks on the pile outside, and every so often a call from Pa: "Tad . . . Tad. . . ! Can you hear us, boy?"

Mrs. Parrish came up the hill now, and stood forty or fifty feet back, her arms around Becky and Emily. From the look on her face, I knew she was praying hard. So was I.

All at once a cry came from Uncle Nick. His voice was muffled from deep inside the cave, "We broke through!" he yelled.

I hurried to the shaft opening, but it was so dark inside all I could see was dust and vague figures of the men moving about.

Apparently Pa was trying to crawl through the small hole that had been made.

"Ye'll never make it, Drum!" I heard Alkali Jones' voice. "It's too blamed small!" There was no high-pitched laugh this time. His voice was more serious than I had ever heard it. "Let Nick try."

A moment of silence followed.

"Tad . . . Tad. . . !" came the muted voice of Uncle Nick through the hole. But still there was no response.

Just as my eyes began adjusting to the dark, I saw the form of Uncle Nick pulling his head back out of the hole. He wiped the grime from his eyes and said, "Still too small . . . I can't make it either."

"We'll have to get more of this outta here!" shouted Pa, who began to tear away at the rocks again.

He was interrupted by the sound of Zack's voice. "I think I can fit in, Pa," he said.

Pa stopped and turned around, gazing at his eldest son for a moment.

"I don't know what's in there, boy," he said. "Could be dangerous. Once there's a cave-in and you've lost your timbers, you never know—"

"I want to try," said Zack. "This is all my fault, and I've got to at least try to get him out!" There was no pleading in his voice, only determination.

"It ain't your fault," answered Pa. "And I'm afraid of the wall comin' down more."

"Then I better move fast," said Zack, edging toward the hole.

Pa stopped him. His eyes, filled with pride, met Zack's. "That's right brave of you, Zack," he said, then paused, still looking Zack over as if seeing him for the first time. "Okay," he said a second later, "get in there . . . and you be careful!"

"Yes, sir!" replied Zack, and a moment later he was wiggling and squirming through the small opening.

First his legs, then his feet disappeared. There was silence for a moment. Then, "It's pitch black in here!" he called back, sounding very far away.

Then we heard him calling Tad's name.

Everyone waited, holding their breath, but we didn't hear anything more. After a minute or so, Pa yelled through the hole after Zack. There was no reply. All remained deathly still while we waited.

My hands were in such tight fists, my knuckles were white. All sorts of terrible thoughts were racing through my brain. What if Tad was badly hurt . . . or dead? It would be my fault, not Zack's! I was the one to blame, the one who had let Ma down. Tad was her baby!

The next minutes seemed like ages. It could not have been more than five minutes, but then I thought I heard something—Zack's voice, more muffled than before. I couldn't tell what he was saying.

Then came the dreaded sound of more rock and debris falling.

I glanced at Pa. His face was white as a sheet.

"C'mon!" he yelled. "Let's clear away more of this rock!"

His hands were already bleeding, but he started to tear away at the pile more frantically than ever. Before anyone could move to help him, Zack's voice came again, clearer this time.

"I got him!"

The next moment, Tad's head thrust through the hole, his face covered with grime and blood from a gash on his forehead. Then his little body wriggled through, and he was free.

A great cheer went up from the men, who immediately fell back to make room. I grabbed Tad in my arms and hurried him outside, where he blinked and squinted from the bright sunlight.

Zack was out of the hole next, and he and Pa emerged from the mine side by side. Before he came to us, Pa turned to Zack and extended his hand. "That was quite a thing you

done in there, son," he said. "No man coulda done better
. . . I'm right proud of you."

Then Pa reached for Tad, scooping him up in his strong
arms like he was a feather.

"You okay, lad?" he asked, his voice shaking a little.

"Yes, Pa."

"You gave us quite a scare, Tad."

"I'm sorry. I made it fall down—but I wanted to help
with the mining. Was it my fault?"

Pa gave a big laugh. "You couldn't have caused that
cave-in, son," he said. "I think it had a little help from the
outside. I'm just glad you're safe."

I'm sure Pa intended to say more, but the words
wouldn't come. He quickly looked away, and when he
turned again, I could see the grime on his face was splotched
with moisture.

"Blasted dust!" he muttered, brushing a hand across his
face. "Can't keep it outta my eyes!"

"Hey, this is some family you got, Drum!" shouted Patrick Shaw, the man who'd given Zack the ride into town.
He had just talked to Mrs. Parrish, and seen the young girls
for the first time.

His statement took Pa by surprise. He looked at him as
if he was thinking over all the implications of Shaw's innocent comment.

"Yeah," he replied slowly. "I guess you're right, Pat. It
sure is."

He paused briefly, then added. "But there's only one
thing you're mistaken about." He looked toward the men
milling around the mine. "Hey!" he called out, "Mr. Shaw's
just brought up a topic that seemed of considerable interest
to all of you back at Lil's. I figure this'd be just about as
good a time as any to make a clean breast of it, once and for
all."

The men gathered 'round with growing interest.

"My name ain't Drum," Pa went on, glancing momentarily in the direction of the sheriff, perhaps having second thoughts about what he was about to say. But he didn't stop.

"Well, that is, it ain't my family name, though it's served me well as a given name all my life. The man you're all gawkin' at is a Hollister by birth—Drummond Hollister, to be exact."

"But why, Drum?" spoke up Alkali Jones, perhaps the most dumfounded of anyone; besides Uncle Nick, he had been Pa's closest friend for several years. "You in trouble with the law or somethin'?"

Pa shot him a quick glance, but then only said, "I had my reasons. What's past is past."

"What about 'ol Nick?" Jones pressed.

"I married Nick's sister. Anything else, he'll have to tell you himself—if he wants to."

Before Mr. Jones had a chance to say anything more, the sheriff walked up to Pa, looking straight at him. I was a little scared, but Pa didn't flinch. He just looked right back at him straight in the eye.

"I gotta tell you," the sheriff finally said, "there've been some folks hereabouts curious about you suddenly turning up with a family out of the past with a different name."

"You got a problem with that, Rafferty?" asked Pa.

The sheriff only had to think for a second or two before he answered. "Nah," he said. "I been in the diggin's long enough to know that half the men here are using assumed names." Then a smile broke out on his face. "Shoot, half of them are lawmen now!"

Several of the men standing within hearing of their conversation chuckled.

"So my havin' a past I'd rather keep quiet about don't bother you none?"

"Far as I can see, you ain't done nothin' to arouse no suspicions, Drum—or whatever I'm supposed to call you! Like I said, half the men who came here looking for gold's got their name on a sheriff's office wall someplace. My job's to keep the law here in Miracle, not go borrowin' trouble by asking too many questions about everyone's past."

He stopped, then flashed a sharp glance at Uncle Nick. "But that brother-in-law of yours is another matter. I'll be lenient for your sake, Drum, but only so far."

"Don't worry about Nick, Rafferty," said Pa. "He'll keep to the straight and narrow—if I got to hog-tie him!" He also shot a glance at poor Uncle Nick.

My uncle squirmed a little, but his sincere smile let us all know he intended to try.

"So the two o' you *is* kin!" exclaimed Alkali Jones, who could keep quiet no longer. "And the young'uns?"

"They belong to my sister and Drum," Uncle Nick said enthusiastically. I think he wanted to tell more, but thought better of it in public. Still no mention had been made of his using the name Matthews, and I figured he wanted to keep it that way.

"Well, blamed if that don't beat all! Hee, hee, hee!" croaked Mr. Jones.

A general murmur of contentment, mingled with nods and smiles and comments like "*I knew there was something. . . .*" spread through the small crowd. There was a good deal of back-slapping and hand-shaking.

Suddenly something jolted my memory. With all the commotion over Tad, its full impact hadn't registered till just this moment. A smile broke out across my face.

"Pa!" I said excitedly, "What was it exactly that you said to Mr. Royce?"

"I don't rightly know, girl," he replied with a puzzled look. "I just told him to keep his scoundrels away from us, that's all."

"No—no—that's not it! What did you say *exactly*?"

"I don't know," he insisted.

"You said that if any of his hooligans ever came near . . ." I paused, trying to get him to remember his exact words.

"Oh, yeah. I told him if his hooligans ever came near my family again, I'd—"

All at once he stopped. The word *family* had brought him up short, and suddenly he got what I'd been driving at.

Gently he knelt down, keeping Tad on his knee. Zack and I were standing beside him. As if understanding what was coming, Mrs. Parrish, with tears brimming in her eyes, nudged Becky and Emily toward us. They stood right in front of Pa. He reached out with his rough, grime and blood-smeared hands and took first Becky's and then Emily's small, white palms in his. Then he glanced around at Zack, then me. He seemed to hold my eyes a moment longer than the rest, then looked back at the little ones.

"This sure has been some day," he said finally. "I don't reckon I've had one quite like it in a coon's age!"

"I guess we been a heap of trouble for you, Pa," blurted Zack.

"Yeah, I suppose you have," he said. Then a slow smile spread across his face. "But I don't guess I been much better."

Timidly, I rested my hand on Pa's shoulder.

"Did you . . ." I began shyly, "—did you really mean what you said to Mr. Royce?" I asked.

"About keepin' his good-for-nothin' rascals away from you all? 'Course I did!"

"No," I said quietly. "I mean—did you mean—you know, what you called us?"

He thought again for a few seconds. "I guess we ain't been much of a family up 'til now, have we?" he finally admitted.

None of us said anything, but by now the younger girls' initial intimidation was gone and they were crowding closer to Pa, and Tad's arm was wrapped around his neck.

"Well," he went on, "maybe we can have a clean beginning—starting today! What do you all think?"

I had never told the kids what went on the night Pa and

I had our talk outside. I did tell them some of the reasons why Pa left us, but I had never told them about his crying and asking to be forgiven. Somehow, it seemed it was meant to be our own private moment. Pa had been a lot different since then, really making an effort to make up to us the lost time.

But right then, with all of us gathered around him, for the very first time I felt all our hearts were open to one another. He and I had gotten a little head start in trying to understand each other. But now I felt it was going to happen with all the kids and Pa—even Zack.

I looked straight into his eyes and smiled. He smiled back, and I think he was remembering our earlier talk.

"We'd all like a clean beginning, Pa," I answered for all of us.

Then Tad stirred in Pa's lap. I guess he'd been still long enough. As he started to stand, I noticed his hand was clutching something. Pa noticed it at the same time.

"What you got there, son?" he asked.

"A pretty rock from the mine," replied Tad innocently. He opened up his hand to show us.

The crowd of men who had been watching silently, slowly gathered around us. Pa was still kneeling next to Tad, the rest of us leaning against Pa. Uncle Nick stood beside me.

The incredulous silence lasted only a moment, finally broken by Alkali Jones' shrill voice.

"Well, blamed if little Tad hasn't discovered ol' Potter's vein after all! Hee, hee!"

"He's right, Nick!" called out another, who was examining the heap of quartz chunks piled outside the mine opening. "That cave-in loosened the lode. This here quartz is full of gold!"

In an instant, all the men were shouting and running back to take a look for themselves. Uncle Nick, not one to be sentimental, was off with the others like a shot. But Pa slowly rose to his feet, not as exuberant as might have been expected. Then a slow, easy smile crept across his face.

Of course, the claim was in Uncle Nick's name—*Matthews* that is. But maybe Pa's composed reaction to the discovery had another cause. Maybe he felt a little like I did—that in reality, we had made an even greater discovery just moments before little Tad had showed us his rock.

We had found each other at last. Perhaps we were ready now to be the family God had wanted us to be from the very first day—when we unexpectedly met our father in Miracle Springs.

CHAPTER 38

THE NEWSPAPER MAN

The town was abuzz for a week.

In the boarding houses, in the mining camps along the streams and rivers, and in every saloon, all folks were talking about was the new vein, and Pa's "new family", and how he and Uncle Nick were kin, and wondering about how we came to be separated. At least that's what Mrs. Parrish and Alkali Jones told us—and who should know better than those two? It wasn't long before the newspaper man, Mr. Singleton, paid us a visit, wanting the whole story.

"I can tell you, Mr. Singleton," Pa said to him, "it ain't that I don't want folks to know that I found my kids after all these years. But there's no way I'm gonna tell more'n that."

"I'll pay you for it, Mr. Hollister—pay you real good."

"But you see, money ain't so much our worry no more," he said with a smile.

"How good?" piped up Uncle Nick. He was still not above turning an easy profit if he could find one to be made.

"Oh, as high as thirty or forty dollars, if you give me exclusive rights to three stories," the newspaperman replied.

"Nick!" said Pa sternly. "What're you thinkin'? Have you forgotten already that there's certain folks we still best stay clear of? We ain't puttin' no news about us in no paper!"

"What about the children?" asked Mr. Singleton. "We

could change their names, tell about their coming west, the wagon train, the hardship of the journey, their Ma dying on the trail, adjusting to this new life. It's a wonderful human interest drama—just the sort women love to read. I have no doubt it would be reprinted in papers all the way back to the East Coast."

"Would we be famous, Pa?" asked Becky.

We all laughed.

Pa shrugged. "I still don't think it's a good idea," he said. "There'd be those who'd put two and two together—"

"Those boys from the gang can't even read!" piped up Uncle Nick.

"That don't mean I'm ready to start bellowing our whereabouts to the whole world! One of the reasons I left home and came out here in the first place was to keep the kids out of danger, and I sure ain't of a mind to start up our troubles all over again."

"What about the gold?" asked Mr. Singleton. "That's a story you could hardly object to."

Pa shrugged again. "Nothing much I could do to stop you even if I wanted to, on that score," he said.

"Why, it's as much as started a second gold rush," went on the editor. "I've never seen such a fever of activity and excitement as in the last week. This'll put Miracle Springs on the map!"

"I'd like to see 'ol Royce get his hands on a single piece of property *now*!" chuckled Uncle Nick.

"My only trouble," said Mr. Singleton, "is that I'm too busy to get the story written in time. I'm still just working to get the paper on its feet, what with advertising and setting up the presses and all. And I've got a big area to try to cover—all the way from Sacramento north. This story about the new gold is already spreading fast. If we don't run it soon, it'll pass us by. Are either of you gentlemen interested in helping me? It was your strike. You could tell it from the 'inside,' as we say."

Pa and Uncle Nick looked at each other, but neither said anything.

I didn't speak either, but the wheels of my mind were turning just the same. Later that same evening, as we sat down to supper, I resolved to say something to Pa about my idea.

We took our seats around the wooden table, then Pa reached out both his hands. Tad on his left took one, Emily on his right took the other, and the rest of us around the table joined hands in turn, including Uncle Nick where he sat between me and Zack. Since the day of the cave-in, Pa had tried once or twice to pray before a meal. I could tell it made everyone happy when he did it. No one would ever replace Ma. But holding hands and praying together like that, even if it wasn't too often, sure did make us feel like we really were a family.

"God, thank you for the good day you've given us," Pa prayed. "And for health and blessings . . . and we ask you to provide what we need—and we thank you for this food— for the hands of the girls that worked to get it ready for us. Watch over us . . . protect us from harm at the hands of evil men . . . uh, amen."

Pa didn't pray fancy. But I could tell he meant every word, and inside my heart I always prayed a little silent prayer of thanksgiving that he was making such an effort to be a good pa to us.

About halfway through the fried potatoes, beans, and cornbread, I got up my courage. "Pa," I said, "what would you think if I talked to Mr. Singleton about writing about the gold in our mine for his paper?"

Everyone was silent, looking first at me, then to Pa.

A thoughtful look came over Pa's face as he sat motionless, his fork halfway to his mouth. Slowly, he turned in my direction.

"*My* daughter, writing a newspaper story?" he said at last.

"I'd like to try."

"What makes you think you could do it?"

"I don't know," I answered. "Maybe I couldn't. But I've been writing a lot in my journal, and working hard to make it sound better."

"Well," he shrugged, finally taking a bite of cornbread and chewing it thoughtfully. "It's okay by me, so long as you don't write nothin' about us. 'Course, it ain't me you gotta convince, it's that newsman Singleton."

"Oh, thank you, Pa!" I exclaimed. "I'll talk to him on our next trip to town!"

CHAPTER 39

A FAMILY TALK

It felt good for all of us to be together after such a memorable day at the mine. But there were still questions and uncertainties to be dealt with.

The next night, when we were all sitting around the fire, the subject came up again. Uncle Nick was tooling a piece of leather; Pa was sharpening an awl. The rest of us were just watching them with nothing much else to do.

Becky finally broke the silence. "Is that bad man, Mr. Krebbs, gonna come back and try to get you, Pa?" she asked.

He glanced over at her, surprised that she even knew the man's name. But we'd all been more curious and paid closer attention to conversations we'd overheard than Pa realized.

"Krebbs, you say?"

"Ain't he the man that's after you?"

"Well, he's one of them, that's for sure," sighed Pa.

"How many more are there?" asked Zack.

"Oh, I don't know how many's left after all this time. How many were there back then, Nick? Six or eight?"

"That'd be about it," Uncle Nick nodded.

"And them's the Catskill Gulch Gang?" Zack inquired, edging his chair closer to Pa.

"How'd you know about them?"

"I heard you and Uncle Nick talking, and Corrie told me some things."

"I thought Zack should know, Pa, so I told him some of what you told me." I hoped Pa wouldn't be riled that I'd done so.

But he just nodded his head thoughtfully. I forgot how much he was changing.

"You done right, Corrie," he said. Then his voice took on a gruff tone. Two months ago, I might have thought he was upset, but now I realized it was just his way of teasing us.

"You know, Nick, I reckon these here young'uns are sharper than I thought. We better watch what we say!"

Uncle Nick got serious. "And ya know, Drum, we ain't out of the woods yet. I reckon these young'uns might just be big enough to know what's happened and what could be coming."

Pa looked at each one of us as if he was sizing us up against Uncle Nick's words.

"Pa," I said slowly, still a little unsure of myself, "if there's still some kind of trouble following you, even with Krebbs gone, well . . . we're all part of the family now. Seems like maybe . . . we could help somehow."

Pa sat back on his stool, let out a long sigh, and was quiet. I could tell he was thinking real hard. For eight years he had been a nameless recluse, a drifter with no ties, no home, living in a wild and reckless land—that had to have rubbed off on him some. Now, all of a sudden, he had a family—five children, at least three of them still very dependent. And all five were counting on him, depending on him to care for their needs, to protect them, to love them. It must have been very difficult for him at times.

At last he spoke, and when he did it was in a tired-sounding voice, with a tinge of resignation, as if he knew that re-living the past eight years and facing the troubles that might lie ahead, even for the sake of his own children, wasn't gonna be easy.

"I ain't proud of anything that happened," he began.

"I'd like nothing better than to never have to tell you kids what kind of man your Pa is—"

"If the kids are to be told," interrupted Uncle Nick sternly, "then at least they deserve to be told the way it really was." Without further delay, he began to tell us the story.

"You kids listen to me, and I'll tell you the *whole* truth about it. It was *me* that rode with the gang, not your pa," he insisted, pointing to himself. "I was just a kid, though that ain't no excuse for what I done. I was hot-headed, and pretty stupid to boot! I knew that gang had a bad reputation, but I just closed my eyes to all the upbringin' your Grandpa Belle gave me. I was a young *fool*, there just ain't no other way o' puttin' it.

"Now your pa, he was as good a family man as you'll ever want to meet, devoted to your ma, and lovin' every one of you kids as you came along—'course you was just babies then, and don't remember. But I seen your pa holdin' you all in his arms—all except for you, Tad, 'cause you weren't born yet. A gentler man with a baby you're never gonna meet, I can vouch for that!

"Well, your pa saw that I was headed into deep trouble, and so he tried to talk some sense into my thick head. I wouldn't listen to him o' 'course, and then next thing I knew he up and joined the gang. I thought it meant he'd started to see things my way, but he done it so's he could keep me in sight and be able to haul me out of trouble when it came! He never intended to become a real part of the gang, but just to stick around long enough to give me a chance to see the light. I finally did, that is, after I seen what kind of evil they was capable of. But by then it was too late. See, they had planned this big bank robbery. Up 'til then, it was just petty stuff—bullyin', raisin' Cain. But then this robbery came up, and afore I knew it I was in on the plans. Your pa wasn't as trusted a member of the gang, so he and a few others didn't find out about it until the night before. I didn't say nothin' 'cause I was afraid of what they'd do to me if I opened my mouth.

"The night before the robbery, they told the rest of the gang the plans. We was all supposed to meet the next day, an hour before the bank closed. Your pa acted like he was going along, but after everyone else went off, he took me aside alone and gave me the biggest tongue-lashing I guess a grown man's ever had. I was nearly ready to listen then— I sure didn't want to end up in prison. But I also knew if I backed out with the knowledge of what they was up to, my life wouldn't be worth buffalo's spit. Fool that I was, I was still thinkin' to go through with it, figurin' to save my neck. But your pa could see it all clearer than me—that I was tryin' to save my neck by stickin' it into a noose!

"The time got closer and closer. I was really scared. Your pa was scared, too—scared I'd really go through with it. Finally, just an hour or so before we all was to meet, your pa laid right into me—slugged me so hard my head spun. You remember that, Drum?"

"How could I forget? It was the only time you and I ever fought," said Pa shaking his head.

"We tussled there in that—livery stable, wasn't it?—'til we could barely stand up on our own feet. But I saw then how much your pa cared for my crazy, foolish hide. I saw that maybe I'd be hurtin' more people than myself if I went through with that robbery."

"I shoulda knocked your block off sooner, Nick," smiled Pa. "In fact, I know just what to do next time you get out of line."

Uncle Nick laughed, rubbing his chin as if remembering the old pain. Then he was serious again. "Your pa saved me from that robbery, but I'd already made too many mistakes to get off so easily, I guess. The gang got off with the loot— leastways I figure they must have, or Krebbs wouldn't still be on our tail. But the law was hot on 'em all, and they scattered all over the place. A couple gang members that I know of were shot, and one lawman was killed. One of the wounded was Jenkins. He'd kinda taken a likin' to me and he knew where I was staying, so he came there to hide out. But he wasn't too careful, 'cause he led the law to my place. I think he mighta told them we weren't involved, but he died before they could get another word outta him.

"So there we were, known members of the gang, caught with one of 'em who'd been shot in the robbery. We'd gone from the deserted livery stable back to my place to get cleaned up, so we had no alibi, no way to prove we was innocent. That's what comes of mixin' with the wrong people.

"My sister never knew half of what happened. You just told her you was going to help me, didn't you, Drum?"

"I figured she'd try to stop me," said Pa, "and I couldn't think of no other way to do it."

"And he didn't want your ma, or my pa, Grandpa Belle, to know what a no-account I'd become," added Uncle Nick. "So we wound up in prison, your pa and I. You tell the kids about the escape, Corrie?"

I nodded, and Uncle Nick went on, "So that's how it was, kids, that's how it really happened."

Zack looked at Pa. I could tell he was trying real hard to understand it all, but it was only natural he'd have questions. "Ma woulda understood, don't you think, Pa?"

"She might have, Zack. She was a good wife," said Pa, "But I guess I was too filled with my own shame to think of that. Before we got married, Aggie told me she couldn't live not knowin' from one day to the next if I'd end up in jail or with a bullet in me. She said she had to believe I'd never go back to that kind of life. Back before I met your ma, I ran with fellers near as bad as that Catskill bunch. Well, I loved your ma and wanted to change, and I promised her I would. She trusted her life and future to my word. And all I could think of was that I'd failed her—and all of you, too. Even if I hadn't been too ashamed to face her, I woulda never have put her through a life of running with me."

He paused and his eyes clouded for a minute as all the

painful memories returned to him. "You see, son, when a man's been in prison, it don't take long for him to start *feelin'* like a criminal, even if he's innocent. You get to feelin' dirty just from what you gotta do to survive. Well, all that together with everythin' else made it so I couldn't make myself go back, no matter how much I wanted to, no matter how much I loved Aggie and you kids. I guess in a way I didn't go back *because* I loved all of you so much. It's the kind of grown-up logic—cockeyed and confused—that's a mite hard for young'uns to understand, I expect."

There was a long silence, just the sound of the crackling fire filling the room. The little ones probably didn't understand all this, but I know they sensed Pa's sincerity, and that would surely make up for whatever confusion there was over the facts.

Before long, a question from Zack brought us back to what had started the conversation in the first place.

"What's gonna happen now, Pa?"

"Well," Pa answered, seeming relieved not to say any-more about the past. "Nick and I suspected all along that the fellers who escaped the law after the robbery musta figured Jenkins told us where the loot was stashed. He musta been carryin' it when they scattered. The rumor we heard before we left New York was that none of them had the money, and they reasoned Jenkins told us where it was. We hoped playin' dead would throw 'em off a mite. Maybe it did; maybe they never bought the story—but it was too much money to give up so easily. So Krebbs and whoever he's got with him just kept followin' us."

"I guess Krebbs has perseverance, if nothin' else!" chuckled Uncle Nick. "I only wish I coulda got a hold of him long enough to tell him he's barking up the wrong tree."

"Probably wouldn't have believed you anyway," said Pa. "I don't know why he didn't make an outright attack in the first place, unless he figured he could make some money out of Royce first, and make us suffer later. We'll have to be careful, I reckon, but now that Krebbs knows we know about him, I think he'll lay low for a while. Like a snake in the grass, he'd sooner attack us when our back is turned." He scratched his whiskers thoughtfully.

"You ain't going to have to go back to jail, are you, Pa?" asked Tad, his voice anxious.

"No, Tad. A few folks know my real name now, and that might be a problem," said Pa, doing his best to sound unconcerned. "But folks here in California don't seem to care much about a man's past. Too many have come here to get away from pasts they'd rather forget. They wanna start clean, and California's far enough away from civilization that it's possible for them to do it. The law back East thinks Uncle Nick and I are dead. Someone'd have to go to a heap of trouble to prove it otherwise to them. New York's a *long* ways from California."

"Maybe we could move away from here," said Zack eagerly. "Go someplace where they ain't heard of you—just in case."

"No, son. That'd be doin' just what I done to you and your ma before. I ain't runnin'. What comes, comes. I suppose that's one reason when I first saw you, I considered not tellin' you who I was. But now that you know—now that I have my family again—I ain't givin' you up, and I ain't gonna hurt you again—not if I can help it."

"Pa," I asked pensively, "couldn't we find a way to clear your name with the law, to prove you didn't have anything to do with that robbery?"

"We might just stir up dust that's best left settled, Corrie. I reckon if trouble ain't lookin' for you, you best not go lookin' for it."

I knew Pa was right, and I was ready to accept him as he was and not worry about what *might* come. Yet I couldn't help thinking that Pa was a mighty fine man, and that it wasn't right that folks should think of him as a robber or any such thing. And I couldn't shake the feeling that Pa would feel better about himself if his name could be cleared. But I didn't say any more right then, though the feelings didn't leave me.

The talk had been so serious, both Uncle Nick and Pa looked almost worn out by it all—especially Uncle Nick, who I'd never seen so serious for so long a spell. But I think as painful as it was for them to talk about it all, it was also a relief for them to get it out. How well I remember, when we kids would have a fight, Ma would always make us "clear the air," as she called it, by apologizing and talking about it. That's what this talk reminded me of. It felt so good to have it all out in the open, and it helped to make us all closer too.

Pa must have sensed this, because after a few moments of quiet, he said, "Kids, I'll never know if I did the right thing, but I'm glad you know everythin' now, even if you may not understand it all. I hope you'll be able to forgive me for the hurt I caused you. I guess all we can do now is forgive and start fresh."

I stood up, put my arms around his broad shoulders, and gave him a hug. It didn't take long for the others to join me, eager to gather around and express their affection to their pa.

Pa looked intently at each one of us, taking time to gaze into our eyes. When he got to Tad, he gave his thick mop of sandy hair a tousle, and Tad smiled broadly.

But it was quiet, softspoken Emily, usually wrapped in her own thoughts, who spoke for us all. As Pa held her eyes for what seemed a long time, she said simply, "I love you, Pa."

He looked at her as though he'd heard something he thought he'd never hear again. Then he took her in his arms and held her tight. After he released her, he stretched his arms wider to embrace all of us.

"It's me who loves you," he said. "Every one of you. You're the best kids any father could hope to have."

CHAPTER 40

SPRING IN THE CALIFORNIA FOOTHILLS

The months passed quickly, and we got on pretty well as a family, considering all we'd been through.

After the full burst of spring in Miracle, along about April, the last group of wagons heading East passed nearby our claim. Needless to say, we Hollisters weren't among the travelers. We rode out to watch the caravan go by. I guess it was sort of a way to symbolize to us that we were here to stay. We watched until the last wagon was clean out of sight—Pa and all us kids; then we headed back to the cabin. There was no doubt after that day that California was our home for good.

I can't say things were perfect after the day of the cave-in at the mine. But they were a heap better than when we'd come here last fall. There was a happy spirit about the claim, and I don't think it was just because of the gold Pa and Uncle Nick and Alkali Jones were pulling out of the mine. I know it had just as much to do with what had happened between us all.

No one saw a trace of Buck Krebbs after that. Pa, Uncle Nick, the sheriff and several other men stayed up all that night after the cave-in waiting for him to show up. But he never did. They figured he somehow got word of what happened and lit out over the hills. Uncle Nick did say a couple of months later that he heard a report of him down near Stockton.

Pa and Uncle Nick got to talking about him every once in a while. They never did find out if he tracked them west alone or if others of the gang were out here, too. And they never knew exactly how he and the banker Mr. Royce got hooked up. Most important, they never knew whether Buck Krebbs ever found out that they didn't have the money. They couldn't help worrying about it some, for our safety more than anything.

But at least I can say that no one out of Pa or Uncle Nick's past bothered us for a long time. I can't say we forgot all about it, but we did quit worrying about it. And by the time we finally ran into Buck Krebbs again, it was . . . but that's part of another story.

Alkali Jones kept coming out most days to help Uncle Nick and Pa at the mine. I don't think he cared a hoot about the money he'd make. He just liked working a claim with some gold in it for a change! They told the story of Mr. Royce's fake geologists every other day, and then they laughed and laughed. Mr. Royce kept trying to buy up land in the area, but folks got wise pretty quick, both about Mr. Royce and about the mining potential of the land. The few purchases he was able to make later on were more fairly priced. And the fires completely stopped after Buck Krebbs' disappearance.

Reverend Rutledge didn't go back to Boston, as he had threatened he might. By the beginning of summer—that was in 1853, he had raised about half the money he needed for his church, and *none* of it came from the bank. On that point at least, he seemed willing to take Uncle Nick's advice to heart. I gradually began to understand more of his sermons. I'm not sure if it was actually because of better understanding on my part, or rather because he stopped making them so complicated and high-sounding—probably a little of both. He still spoke in that preacher voice sometimes, but I think he sincerely tried to be more down-to-earth.

The church quit meeting in the Gold Nugget when the numbers dwindled down to ten or fifteen people, and started gathering in various people's homes, usually at Mrs. Parrish's. Reverend Rutledge and Mrs. Parrish were seen around town together quite a bit, and they both seemed excited about the church's prospects for the future. Pa and Reverend Rutledge were on speaking terms again, but they didn't seem to have a lot to say to each other.

Pa really became a family sort of man. He never drank anymore at all, and always stayed home or took the young ones with him when he went into town. As far as I know, he never played cards again. Uncle Nick was about the same as ever. He was bound to head for town occasionally for an evening, returning home with the smell of whiskey on his breath. But I think he was trying hard, too, to be as good an example to us as he could. Pa got the title on the property changed over to both of their names so Nick couldn't gamble it away like he had once done himself.

I still had fifty dollars of Ma's money. Pa didn't need it, and told me to save it till something came up. The strike Tad discovered turned out to be pretty rich. We didn't become millionaires, but with hard work it brought in twenty or thirty dollars a day. Pa was bound and determined to put the money to good use, "Not squander it like before," he said. But he didn't trust Royce's bank, so he had Mrs. Parrish take it to a bank in Sacramento for him when she went in for supplies.

There were some mighty wonderful changes taking place. Zack grew two inches before summer and was helping at the mine just like the men. In fact, Pa started treating him so much like one of them that Zack quickly shed his sullenness and brightened up. He and pa were together more now, working and talking about what they could do with the mine and the sluices. Pa seemed to like having Zack at his side. And I believe he and Zack gradually became friends.

Emily didn't stop glowing after the day in April when Pa went into town for some lumber. When he came back, there were four horses to his team instead of the usual two. While he was still a hundred yards from the cabin, he called out, "Emily! Come outside and see my new team!"

She went to the door and stood watching for a minute as he came up the road. Then suddenly she recognized the two lead horses.

"It's Snowball . . . and Jinx!" she cried, running out to meet the wagon. Her friends were back, and at least Snowball seemed to remember her.

Pa never mentioned anything about how he'd gotten them back. But I found out from Patrick Shaw that Pa had to pay twice what the horses were worth to get them from the fellow who'd won them in the card game.

Seven-year-old Tad became Uncle Nick's constant shadow, but Nick didn't seem bothered by it. Several times a day I'd see him stoop down to Tad's level and put an arm around his shoulder to explain something they were working on. Tad was also frequently seen perched on Uncle Nick's shoulders, bouncing along on a walk somewhere.

Becky didn't change so noticeably—she remained as ornery and full of energy as ever.

Once in a while, Uncle Nick would read a bedtime story to the children, with Tad or Becky sitting on his lap, and the others snuggled up under his brawny arms. What a sight that was! Of course, he only did that when he could talk Pa out of it. Most nights Pa would read, and all five of us gathered around. Even Zack and I wouldn't miss such a moment with Pa.

Whenever I could, I went into town to visit Mrs. Parrish. She and I had more good talks about living the Christian life. Pa didn't have much to say when I mentioned her, but I think he was interested in what I was learning about the Bible and spiritual things—more than he let on. I kept hoping that maybe someday he and I would be able to talk about such things together.

When my birthday rolled around, my mouth nearly dropped open when Pa walked in the cabin about mid-morning. He was clean-shaven and scrubbed like I'd never seen him before.

"What're you starin' at?" he asked with a grin.

"Pa!" I exclaimed. "I hardly recognized you! Why'd you shave off your beard?"

"Well, I'll tell you," he said. "Your sixteenth birthday seemed like a fittin' occasion to say 'off with the old!' "

"What do you mean?" I asked. "I kinda liked it."

He thought a minute, then said seriously, "I'll tell you, Corrie, the beard was always part of my mask, part of my hidin' who I really was, just like the name and all the rest of it. Well, I don't want to hide no more. I am who I am. My name's Hollister, this here's my home—" he gestured widely with his arms, taking in the claim, "—this is my land, this is my family . . . and this is my face! I'm through with hidin'. Oh, I ain't gonna write to the law back in New York and tell them where to find me, but I sure ain't goin' to go skulkin' around no more, either. We're safe, and I think we can start fresh. This is just my way of showin' it."

He placed his strong hands on my shoulders and looked at me full in the face, and smiled. "So that's my birthday gift to you, Corrie Belle Hollister—just *me*! With my proper name, and the face the good Lord gave me, and a hearty 'Best wishes to you on your birthday!' "

I couldn't help smiling. I put my arms around his waist and leaned my head against his chest. His arms closed gently across my back. It was a wonderful feeling. I don't suppose anyone could understand that feeling better than a daughter who, after a lot of years of doubting, finally knows that her father really loves her.

"That's the best birthday present a girl could ever have, Pa," I said honestly. "I'll never forget it."

Well, I've said how all the others were growing and changing but when I try to reflect on how I changed, it's hard to say. If you are changing yourself, you can't always see it, 'cause its goin' on right *inside*.

It was March when I had my memorable sixteenth birthday, and though Pa said I'd grown, I still felt like a kid, even though I was more content than any time since Ma had died.

I remember how I stumbled at prayer when Ma was sick, and how little I understood how much God could have to do with people's lives, and how much He was really interested in our lives. Now, thanks to Mrs. Parrish, I was beginning to see God as more than just some distant, unapproachable Being. I began to believe that He could really go through life with a person, like Mrs. Parrish said He did with her—helping her, giving her strength as she needed it, making her into a better person—the person He wanted her to be. I hoped someday He'd be that close to me, like He was her.

Oh, and about Mr. Singleton. I did finally have that talk with him. At first he thought I was joking. He looked at me strangely, as if he was thinking, *But you're just a young girl! What could you possibly know about writing an article?*

But when I told him about my journal, he agreed to look at it. And once he'd read some of it, he realized how serious I was. His expression changed considerably, and soon he was saying things like, "Well, young lady—if you can submit a piece that is satisfactory to us, we will see what can be done with it."

Just his calling me a young *lady* instead of a *girl* was a step in the right direction. And he'd consented to let me at least *try* to write something for the paper—and that was all I was asking!

I went home that day very excited, determined to do my best with this chance. I didn't get an article written for his paper immediately. It took a lot of help from him, and some from Mrs. Parrish, before I—

But there I go again, starting to tell the next story before

I'm done with this one! Buck Krebbs, my first article in the *California Gazette*, the building of the church, what happened to Alkali Jones and the trouble Uncle Nick got mixed up in down at Dutch Flat—all that will have to wait.

Now I reckon I've told the story like it was, the best I can remember it as it happened.

I often wonder what Ma would think of all this. I can't help being sad that she couldn't be here to share it all with me. Pa still doesn't talk freely about religious things, but he does say he's sure as anything Ma is up there in heaven looking down on all our goings on, and is pleased.

I think he's right.

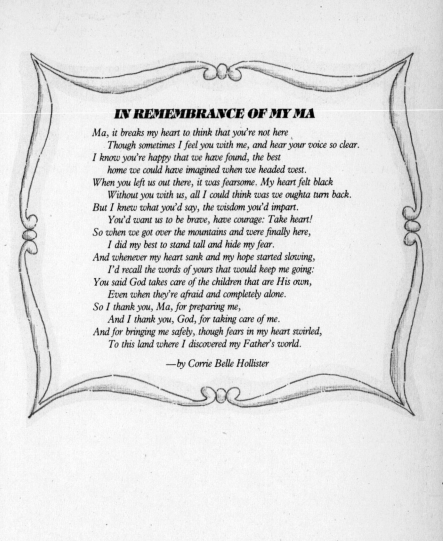

IN REMEMBRANCE OF MY MA

Ma, it breaks my heart to think that you're not here
Though sometimes I feel you with me, and hear your voice so clear.
I know you're happy that we have found, the best
home we could have imagined when we headed west.
When you left us out there, it was fearsome. My heart felt black
Without you with us, all I could think was we oughta turn back.
But I knew what you'd say, the wisdom you'd impart.
You'd want us to be brave, have courage: Take heart!
So when we got over the mountains and were finally here,
I did my best to stand tall and hide my fear.
And whenever my heart sank and my hope started slowing,
I'd recall the words of yours that would keep me going:
You said God takes care of the children that are His own,
Even when they're afraid and completely alone.
So I thank you, Ma, for preparing me,
And I thank you, God, for taking care of me.
And for bringing me safely, though fears in my heart swirled,
To this land where I discovered my Father's world.

—by Corrie Belle Hollister